IN THE WAKE

IN THE WAKE

HELEN TREVORROW

Urbane
PUBLICATIONS

urbanepublications.com

First published in Great Britain in 2018 by Urbane Publications Ltd
Suite 3, Brown Europe House, 33/34 Gleaming Wood Drive, Chatham, Kent ME5 8RZ

Copyright © Helen Trevorrow, 2018

A CIP catalogue record for this book is available from the British Library.

ISBN 978-1-911583-83-7
MOBI 978-1-911583-86-8

Design and Typeset by Julie Martin
Cover by Julie Martin

Printed and bound by 4edge UK

Urbane

PUBLICATIONS

urbanepublications.com

For Vicky

PART I:

SURFACE

PROLOGUE

25th December 2017

Samuel Lane Ward, Eighth Floor, St Mary's Hospital, Paddington, London

An unreliable temporary nurse had not shown up for work, leaving Sister Williams with a staff shortage and a list of other problems. Anyone with any sense knew not to bother Sister Williams without good reason, or face her wrath. She was easy to recognise, always carrying her left arm high, pen in hand as if issuing an instruction.

Her stiff navy uniform whistled as she blasted onto the ward. The yellow woman in bed three had called her over. Her jaundice was caused by a buildup of bilirubin, dead red blood cells seeping back into her system. She was the colour and texture of beeswax. There was a view over Paddington and if you angled your head the right way, a large tree could be seen through the buildings on Paddington Green.

"Yes?" Sister Williams asked, already harassed. Yellow woman had made a right fuss of getting the most senior person on the shift to her bedside. Sister Williams had to cut short her Christmas breakfast bagel with the staff to attend to this rather fussy patient who would, no doubt, be lodging a complaint.

"Thank you, Sister, I know you're busy," the yellow woman said. "I wanted to ask you something; where is Nurse Valérie?" Registering a blank on Sister Williams' face, she added, "the French nurse?" Sister Williams wasn't even sure who this was.

There was an agency nurse, not one of her regular staff, a temp who had been filling in these last few weeks. What was her name? Valérie?

Across the room in the far corner, another patient, partially screened by a curtain shouted, 'Help me! Help!', soon followed by the smell of faeces. She had been brought in by ambulance emaciated and possibly close to death. As the nurses crowded around her, first to clean and then to dress her, she had reared up and cursed them from her state of near unconsciousness. The young French nurse had checked on her every thirty minutes through the night and soothed her with words as soft as silk.

"She's not in today," Sister Williams snapped back, keen to get on with the many hundreds of things she had to do. It was really none of the patients' business who, what or when people were on shift. There were many complexities in keeping a ward running.

"Well, Sister, she was meant to be in today, because we've got her a present and we spoke of it yesterday, didn't we?" the yellow woman said, gesturing to the old Alzheimic lady in the bed next to her as 'we'. The old lady nodded her head, wiping tea from her chin.

"Well, you just keep hold of the present and I'm sure she'll be back soon," said Sister Williams, beginning to walk away ticking the air with her pen.

"Has she phoned in? Is she sick? Because she's from France you know and she was going to be spending her first Christmas alone in London without her family."

Honestly, these young agency nurses telling all and sundry everything about their lives. So unprofessional creating an overly emotional atmosphere with inappropriate intimacy. These were patients, not friends.

"I'll check for you." Sister Williams strode back up the centre of the ward, accosting another nurse by the elbow. "Excuse me nurse, there was an agency nurse here, the French one, Valérie Lagarde?"

"Yes, I was going to speak to you about her Sister; she was on the rota for today, but she hasn't shown up."

"Have you telephoned her?" Sister Williams asked.

"I did and there was no answer, so I left a message," the nurse said.

"These agency nurses. So unreliable. She'll have been out drinking last night. I get this every single year without fail. So we're one down?"

"Yes, and we've another two off sick in ward two."

"Get onto the agency and tell them we don't want Valérie Lagarde back – ever – and get them to send three more nurses."

"Yes Sister, but that's going to be expensive. Are you happy to authorise the budget?" the nurse asked.

"Get two then," Sister Williams said, retracting. "We will just have to cope." A whir of activity started up with a beeper chiming in the adjoining ward. A male doctor wearing a Santa hat ran through asking sternly, 'Help please nurses!' The ward doorbell rang, and the noise of the Salvation Army band playing Christmas carols echoed through the corridor. Sister Williams, focused on other things now, headed for the melee, but wanting to tick the job off, turned about heel and dashed to the side of the yellow woman's bed.

"She went back to France for Christmas – she was very homesick," Sister Williams lied.

"Oh," the yellow woman said, her hands falling open in her lap. "She must have got the Eurostar. It would have been nice to say goodbye."

"Shall I make sure she gets this?" Sister Williams asked, picking up the present, a purple box of Cadbury's Milk Tray bought from the shop downstairs.

"Yes, please do."

Sister Williams smiled and rushed away, throwing the chocolates into the nurses' station where she would eat them later. She was busy with things to do and sick people to look after.

She wouldn't find out for a month or more but Nurse Valérie had not gone home to France.

CHAPTER ONE

The body had been waiting there for Kay Christie. Loosely wrapped in slimy black plastic it had lain flaccid, puddling the dockside before police covered it with a white tent. It was the most exciting event ever to have happened at London's Excel Centre.

It had all started early that morning at what time? Kay supposed five o'clock. She had been lying in bed dreaming about owning a soft black dog. She heard the shrill ring and searched frantically for her phone in the dark, well used to bad news coming either early or late.

Simon Bell, Excel's Marketing Director and Kay's biggest client, had hauled her in to deal with the press while they figured out what was going to happen with the boat show. Kay had sent ahead her deputy and right-hand woman, Jacquie McCoy. She lived closer and would get there quicker. But when Kay arrived at the back stairs of Excel, Jacquie was there with swollen red eyes and black mascara seeping down her cheekbones.

"You're doing great Jacqs, you really are," Kay said while rubbing her back, wanting to encourage and comfort. Kay was like a mother to her team even though Kay and Jacquie were the same age.

"I don't think I am." Jacquie sniffed.

They went up to the press office, S17, which looked out directly over the Royal Albert Dock. Across the river Thames, the Millennium Dome loomed like an albino turtle in traction. Excel's central hall had been eerie. A cleaner's trolley had lain abandoned and a black plastic refuse bag tied to its handle ballooned in an invisible breeze. It smelled of cleaning fluid and delicious ship diesel.

This was where it started to get weird.

The door of S17 crashed open and there stood Simon Bell. He had arrived in his cycling shorts. Couldn't he have just pulled on a pair of jeans? The world didn't have his size; everything he wore was either too big or too tight.

Outside, an ambulance had pulled up on the pontoon and it cast a flickering blue light across the back wall of S17. Simon had got up to look and while he stood at the window, he had bent a knee to rearrange himself using his finger and thumb.

"It's a bit late for that!" he shouted at the ambulance. Then on the way back to his seat, seeing Jacquie's upset, he had inappropriately rubbed her back too. His thumb lingered on Jacquie's neck a second too long.

Being an external agency meant that sometimes you or a member of your team got felt up by a client. A loophole where there was no real comeback. It was eight o'clock by then so Kay had dialled in to the secure crisis conference line as planned and the automated call system requested their names.

"Simon, Kay, Jacquie," Kay said, then there was a long beep followed by a burst of classical music. Kay dreamt away for a moment trying to place it, but she knew nothing about classical music. Common as muck really underneath her business suit. Click. The CEO and the Operations Director had clunked into the call. Kay heard the engine of the ambulance power down outside.

"Your dad wasn't working Kay," the Operations Manager reassured her. Kay had wangled a job for her father on the perimeter security gate checking car passes. He sat there day after day reading the newspaper and listening to sport on a crackling radio.

"Oh, thank God, I was worried and he's not answering his phone," Kay said, but she knew he was probably still drunk. If he wasn't working, he wouldn't get up until lunchtime. As it turned out, it was the new security guard who had found the body on only his third day of employment. He had done a last sweep just after three o'clock and saw a black arc in the water and knew straight away it wasn't right.

"Jesus Christ," Simon said, his lip curling back. Jacquie held her hand up over her mouth, flashing her neat and efficient engagement ring. The level of melodrama was extreme. To be fair they were marketing people and not adept at dealing with dead bodies but still. "He won't be back. I tell you. He'll be claiming psychological disability benefit from us for the next 50 years. I wish I'd bloody found the body!"

There had been discussion about the tide and the weather. As the Operations Director talked about the overnight storm, a gust of wind had lashed the window and they had all pulled away. A banshee-like whistle of wind swooshed its clawed wings around the building.

It was mundane and boring doing the PR for Excel, as you might expect, but such was the size of the site that now and again, things did get washed up or crimes committed. Never anything of this magnitude.

The CEO had charged Simon with telephoning the owners of Excel, the office of Qatari businessman Abdul Bin Harashi, for damage limitation. There was an immediate need to explain, because after all, the body had been found trussed up underneath their luxury boat, The Lusciousness.

Kay had a persistent negative feeling in her gut that using

The Lusciousness as the face of the boat show might have been a bad idea. This was about to be proved right.

A white tent had been put up outside on the southern embankment, and it was here that the ambulance was parked. Kay had assumed that the body must be inside that tent. A floating pontoon had been erected temporarily for the boat show and The Lusciousness was moored to it. Blue and white police tape extended from the tent and cordoned off access to the pontoon.

At least there was a dog. A cute – and only a real dog lover would ever call one cute – Alsatian had been led around sniffing at a pile of rope and ten or so crates which had been piled up. A diver's head had popped up in the blue-black water between The Lusciousness and the pontoon. The water looked like poured ink.

It was dizzying. No wonder Jacquie was crying. It was a million miles away from sending out a press release about The Lusciousness being the World's Most Expensive Boat.

"Christ Jacquie, this is –" Kay had begun to say, but she stopped short. The wind had picked up and rattled the glass again. The side of the tent had been sucked completely inside-out revealing solidly planted feet. It must have been the forensic team examining the body. Kay had watched, eyes glued to the tent like a motorway rubbernecker.

The wind had come again, angrier than before, turning the inky water into white tipped wisps. In an instant, it hoisted up the tent, threw it over, and flung it onto its side where it bounced against the side of the ambulance. White gloved hands had reached out frantically from inside to grab it back. Three police officers had sprinted over to secure it.

But it was too late. Kay had seen the body.

Bloated yes, swollen certainly, but the face with a black curl of hair pressed tightly to the fleshy forehead was clear. A dilute orange froth formed around the mouth, but the face was plain to see. The eyes were fixed open. Kay had gasped.

Her knees had buckled. A high-pitched tone had started up in her ears. She collapsed down into a chair, suddenly burning hot and sweating. Good old Jacquie stood up and ran over.

"Are you alright, Kay?"

Kay shook her head, pulling at the neckline of her shirt and had waved Jacquie away.

"I'm fine, I'm fine."

But Kay was not fine. A vein in her temple was twitching violently.

The dead body in the water.

Kay recognised the face.

She knew him.

CONFIDENTIAL: FOR REACTIVE ISSUE ONLY

Sunday 7th January 2018

Position Statement

A discovery was made this morning at the Royal Albert Dock. We are working closely with the relevant authorities to establish the facts of the situation and provide any assistance required.

Simon Bell, Director, Excel Conference and Exhibition Centre said, "The safety of our guests and exhibitors is extremely important to us. As soon as the discovery came to light, we acted promptly in assisting the relevant authorities. We have currently suspended all activity on site."

For further information please contact Kay Christie or Jacquie McCoy at Christie Dean PR on 0794 400 4000 or email jacquie@christiedeanpr.co.uk

CHAPTER TWO

Still sweating and agitated, Kay was called downstairs to liaise with the police. When the Detective Inspector stood up and shook Kay's hand, she froze. He was a well-groomed, aged public schoolboy. The hair on the back of his head was short enough to light a match, with a longer, Brylcreemed silver sweep from a different age across the forehead.

He gestured for Kay to squeeze into the tiny cavity between the table and the wall. Were they trying to make her feel uncomfortable? There was a second police officer, a woman, DS Harvey, and Kay's foot grazed against her leg when she sat down, sending Kay blushed red in the middle of their conversation.

"Could it have washed in from the river?" the Operations Director asked, pursuing his line of thought about storms and winds and tides.

"Can't comment," the DI said. Stop shaking Kay. Pull yourself together. Then she thought she needed the toilet, and then patted around her hairline, convinced she must be sweating. She would have to wait for the loo, because she couldn't possibly get up and leave now.

"Have you got any idea who it is?" Kay blurted out. The two police swiveled their heads in Kay's direction like a pair of owls. They would both be adept at spotting someone with something to hide and here was Kay sweating and chuntering.

"Our priority is to identify the body and then rule out third party involvement," DS Harvey said.

"Have you got any idea when we can get the halls open again? The Boat Show exhibitors need to get to their stands and set up. The exhibitors are going mad," the Operations Director said.

"Oh, I am sorry to hold them up," the DI said, "please, on behalf of this poor dead bastard, apologise won't you to the boat lot."

"Have you got any idea why he was here?" Kay burst out.

"He? We haven't released information on whether the body is male or female yet," DS Harvey said. Shut up Kay. It's not my fault your lot didn't tie the tent down properly.

"If preliminary findings suggest we do not need further access to the building then yes, you can get it open. We have to rule out third party involvement. Is that understood?" DS Harvey said.

The Operations Director stood up and turned to a diagram of the venue. He drew the cordon on with a squeaky red marker pen. The DI stood up and pointed 'here' and 'here'.

"I don't like PR and I don't like the media," DS Harvey said. Her lips were swollen, bee stung from the cold, and when she wasn't speaking she kneaded her bouncy bottom lip with her teeth. She wore a camel trench coat undone, with a tight black sweater underneath. Far too good a coat for dredging up dead bodies. She started to put on black leather gloves. "Just try not to make things worse."

Kay felt better. It came suddenly as a reaction to DS Harvey's dismissal. Better to be presumed as imbecile than to be implicated. Kay was happy to be patronised and ignored. She had been doing it all her working life.

Kay tried to breathe. It couldn't have been him. She had only caught a glimpse. Her mind was playing tricks. If it was him then he must be much older, but the bloating had regressed him. Somehow.

"I've worked with PR people before and they've got a tendency to overcomplicate things," DS Harvey said. Kay was silent and engrossed in thinking about the face. Perhaps DS Harvey took Kay's silence to mean that she had offended her with her comment and she suddenly softened and tried to explain herself. "I'm not saying you personally, Kay. Can I call you Kay?"

"Yes," she said, coming back to the conversation.

"Don't take it personally, Kay, I'm just saying from my experience. We usually have a PR person who deals with this, but she's in St Lucia."

"Lovely," Kay said. If only she could get another look at the body. She had only ever seen one other dead body in her life. Three months before. Her own mother. But in comparison, this one was like a photographic negative. Kay's mother was hollowed out, not bloated. Kay couldn't believe her mother could get so thin, so concave. Kay had thought that their kin were built differently. Kay guessed every corpse was different.

"Is it lovely? I've never been," DS Harvey asked.

"Absolutely beautiful, very green, nice people," Kay said. She had been there with Julia. She had the idea that police usually holidayed on the Costa del Sol, but not these two – too well dressed. Possibly a pursuit for him, art, Tour de France, rugby in Paris. As for her, Kay wondered, ice hotel? If only Kay could get out onto the dockside, by the pontoon, she could sneak another look. Maybe? Or had the ambulance taken the body? Her journalist friend Belinda Salas might know, if she was working on the news desk today.

"I should go sometime," DS Harvey said. Kay had wondered if the tent was still there. The wind was getting up again.

Kay could hear it screeching through the metal fixings of the building.

An image of DS Harvey in a bikini flashed into Kay's mind, immediately followed by an image of the bloated, distended body. "Did they take the body away yet? In the ambulance? Or is it still on the –?" Kay stopped.

"Say what you like to media about the show, but please leave any details about the investigation to us, and divert to me, personally," DS Harvey said, "and just one more thing."

"Sure."

"Your dad?"

"Yes," Kay answered.

"He works here I understand?" DS Harvey said, and that threw Kay entirely, because that couldn't be another issue. Could it? And he wasn't even working that night so what did he have to do with it at all?

"Yes, he's a security guard out on the perimeter gate. It's very basic, I think. He doesn't have much responsibility. Why?"

"We're exploring all avenues, Kay," she said, "stay in touch. We may need to speak to you again." She didn't shake Kay's hand. She didn't say goodbye.

CHAPTER THREE

Simon Bell stood up in front of the twenty journalists huddling in the cold front on the steps of Excel. The Lusciousness loomed over them. He tried to prolong his time at the lectern but he was only meant to read the latest statement. He was greeted by silence as finished his words and he despondently gave up his position to the DI.

In the distance, the Operations Director was walking the length of the dockside, accompanied by two uniformed police. What was going on?

Something was wrong out there. It was getting busier. The Lusciousness was being examined again more thoroughly it seemed, with white suited agents moving methodically, and four Fire Service divers getting into the water beneath them.

Kay came back inside and went to the press office. Kay tried to call the CEO on his mobile and then in his office, but he did not answer. His secretary defended his privacy telling Kay that he was in a meeting with someone. Kay needed to know what was going on. She already sensed there was something ruinous to wait for.

When the CEO eventually called them in to his office, there were two lawyers. The male lawyer was in his fifties and a younger pale skinned blonde woman sat at the meeting room table alongside the CEO's secretary. Highly irregular but understandable under the circumstances. Kay pulled up a chair alongside them.

"Police have confirmed third party involvement," he said.

"Eh?" Simon had made a loud teenager-style noise. "What does that mean?"

"It means this body didn't float here from the river," the Operations Director said.

"The police will make an announcement at six o'clock and this is under wraps until then. I know nothing more. Sadly, the body may have been there for a week or more. I will finalise our statement myself," the CEO said and Kay was aware that throughout all of this, he never looked at her. He had been looking at poor weepy Jacquie, and brutish Simon and the traumatised Operations Director but never at Kay.

Kay started to obsess over why the CEO was going to do the statement himself. Kay did the statements. That was her job. He was freezing her out.

"Even so, how do they know for sure that it's a murder? There must be evidence? What is it?" Simon asked. "What exactly have they found?"

"The ear was removed." The CEO said.

"Removed?" Jacquie repeated, rather than asked. She was a rabbit in headlights.

"One of the ears has been cut off, and —" the CEO said and then Jacquie fainted. She fell to the floor in slow motion, landing with a dull thwack. Simon fell onto one knee, then he crouched down, holding her head, and she seemed to bounce straight back into consciousness.

"Water," Jacquie mumbled and the CEO scrambled to pour water into a glass. Jacquie drank, blinking. "I'm so sorry," she said, "it's just so shocking."

"Are you okay?" Simon asked Jacquie, boyish and uncharacteristically warm.

"And what?" Kay had asked "You said 'and', as if there's

something else." She could see that the CEO did not want to answer her.

"Well, it's not pleasant, but there was material stuffed into the mouth," said the CEO.

"Oh Jesus," Jacquie slurred.

"Let's get you checked out properly," Simon said, lifting her into his arms and carrying her out of the office. Kay was about to follow.

"Kay, there's one more thing," said the CEO, closing the door behind Simon, shutting Kay inside with him and the lawyers. He guided Kay by the elbow back to the table. "I wanted to tell you this myself, before you hear it elsewhere."

"Gosh, this sounds ominous," said Kay, praying for some minor infraction.

"The police have been looking at our CCTV,"

"Yes," said Kay.

"There's an anomaly," he said. "A large section of recordings are missing."

"You must have a backup or something, don't you have an off-site security system as a backup?" asked Kay, heartbeat hastening.

"It has been manually wiped. Someone altered the settings so that any recordings have been deleting themselves," he said. It had gone dark outside. From this angle, the red glow of London was setting the sky on fire.

"On purpose?" asked Kay.

"Or an accident. Incompetence possibly. Drunk. We don't know yet. We know when it was deleted."

"So you know who was on security at that moment?" asked Kay.

"Yes we do. Over Christmas we just had one guard on duty,

backed up with the off-site provision who would have been triggered if any alarms had sounded, but they didn't." Suddenly something awful occurred to Kay and she realised why he was telling her this.

She felt sick. If she was writing a press release, she would have describe it as bile rising in her stomach, citrus orange reflux.

"Have you spoken to this person?" asked Kay.

"The police are speaking to him now. He's already admitted it, says he was drunk, and that he did it by accident. Says he blacks out from drink sometimes, and when he realised, it was too late – it was already gone."

His description stung. It was like being caught with a steam burn from a boiling kettle, catching you unaware against the soft baby flesh of your inner forearm. The CEO stuttered and looked at his feet. He was talking about her dad.

She looked at the lawyers sitting at the table and realised they were there for her. Not to seek her counsel, but to watch and record every word she said.

CHAPTER FOUR

The tip of the Canary Wharf tower sucked the clouds right out of the sky. Kay asked the driver to stop on the bridge. Barclays Capital and Finlay Holdenbaum grumbled in giant blue neon signage. Kay could just about make out the blinking red light at the very top. She fought the wind to keep the car door open.

She wasn't going home. She was wired and needed a drink. She crossed the road and stepped through a narrow gate that opened onto steep steps that made Kay dizzy. The road surface was scratchy, designed to stop you from slipping. On the ground the wind had disappeared behind concrete windbreakers. It was a microclimate of calm.

Kay hopped onto the pontoon, wine rattling in her handbag. She skipped down the wooden mooring until she saw a little blonde figure emerge from the steering cabinet of a 90ft Dutch Barge, The Klasina. Snowdrops in little white pots lined the route, a row of hanging lanterns lit above. The little figure was wearing a knitted woolly jumper – a real Aran sweater. She looked like a buxom sheep with blonde curls heaped up on top.

"You sent that statement to the Press Association before me Kay? Honest to God, you said you were telling me first," Belinda Salas shouted.

"Jacquie did that. Not me. I'm sorry."

"Well you should sack her." Belinda took Kay's hand to help her into the boat's wheelhouse. Turf hissed out of the chimney. Belinda slammed the door and pulled a lever to seal it tight and they went down the ladder into the living room.

The warmth was comforting as Kay recalled what she had

just seen. Rewinding and replaying it in her mind. The tent went over. It was so quick. She could only see for a matter of seconds and from that distance. What was the fluid? The orange froth? No. It couldn't be him. It just could not be.

The television blared in the foreground. Belinda's things: a laptop; all of Sunday's newspapers; one pink Parker fountain pen; a red and black makeup bag with baby Daschunds' faces; and a battered hair-dryer, were scattered in, on and around the grey corner sofa. A pair of Belinda's knickers were laid out on the floor sunny side up. Belinda opened the wine and passed a large oval glass with only a dribble of liquid to Kay.

"Is that enough for me? I can probably finish that in one gulp," said Kay, downing the wine.

"How are you feeling?" asked Belinda.

"Entirely too sober," said Kay, holding out an empty glass. She couldn't mention what she had seen to Belinda. Who she had seen. Belinda would be compelled to write it up as a story. She couldn't mention her father either. In spite of them being friends, Belinda was still a news reporter. Kay couldn't let her guard down.

Kay's mind was back with the body. She needed another look. She needed longer to go over the features of the face. It could be anybody. How could she see from up there? She remembered the policeman. He was at a similar distance away. She could remember the cleft of a deep wrinkle across his forehead. Could she trust her own eyes?

Belinda turned down the television so Kay could only just hear the satisfying clonk of darts thudding into the board. The boat gave off an insulated hum of electricity. The tap dripped.

"Look, you'll find this out tomorrow anyway. It's a murder," Belinda said.

"Murder?" asked Kay, feigning surprise. The only surprising element was that Belinda had worked it out so quickly. She really was rather capable.

"It's a man," said Belinda. Kay's pulse quickened and her stomach turned over the wine, already too much wine. She felt acid rising into her mouth. Belinda's news desk had been listening to police radio. They knew someone who worked at the mortuary. This person had been paid two hundred pounds to keep them informed. Belinda probably knew more at this point than the police. Kay wondered if she knew about her dad.

"One of the ears has been cut off," said Belinda. "Apparently it is common in gang related murder." All this talk of a severed ear. How had Kay missed such a crucial detail? She had only glimpsed for a few seconds. Was the ear the source of the foam on the face? No. That wasn't at the side. The foam was at the nostrils and mouth. Kay had seen his left side and there was something wrapped around the head. Dark material. Yes. She had seen that. That must have been where the ear had been cut off.

"You're shivering," Belinda said and she opened the stove to heap on another log. "Wasn't carrying a wallet, unfortunately. We'll get ID soon enough, got all my sources working on it. They're pulling dental records now." But Kay had missed what Belinda was saying. She had already got up and rushed to the bathroom.

It felt that Belinda's boat, rather than being moored in Canary Wharf's basin, was moving in a rough sea. Like it was being thrown around. But the storm was inside Kay's head. She made it to the sink and splashed water on her face and looked at her ashen expression in the reflection of a porthole. If Kay was right, if he was who she thought, she knew Belinda would recognise him too. His name repeated in her head: Lance Corporal Benedict Phillips.

CHAPTER FIVE

Walthamstow with its stringy lanes of unruly houses. Uneven brick walls, crevassed pavements with pools of rain water, and evergreen sprouting weeds. Kay had slept on Belinda's sofa. Unable to go back to Excel the following morning, she walked around making calls, worrying, outside the loop. Then rallying, she realised that she needed to start somewhere.

She needed to find her dad.

Kay had walked past the flat she owned herself. It was rented out now, but really it was Kay's home. She had worked hard to pay the mortgage with no help from anyone. Never a penny from a soul. Not even from Julia, although no one believed that. She wished that she could go inside.

Kay couldn't call Ariana, her assistant, to ask her to book her a car. She couldn't call Julia, because Kay didn't know the right thing to say. How could she explain it? How could she make it more digestible, make it sound less serious, when she didn't even know what 'it' was? She couldn't tell anyone. She booked an Uber car from her mobile.

They must have it wrong. She thought her father was harmless. If he wanted to get drunk all the time then so what? She had been surrounded by functioning alcoholics all her life. If he wanted to drink then it was his right – he had just lost his wife. He was getting older and we were all going to die at some point; it was the only unifying thing we all had in common. Life was hard. Keeping it all together was hard. Spinning plates. Kay knew that. Some people messed up. Needed something to help them cope. Needed a drink to get through.

She looked at homeless people on the streets, not the youngsters, not the poor kids put out to pasture by lecherous fathers and blind mothers. No, she meant the old ones, the ones who knew for sure, and couldn't forget, that we are all going to die. It's just the how, and possibly the when. And when you can't stop thinking about that, then how can you go about normal daily business? Paying the mortgage and doing a food shop when all you are going to get in the end is an empty room, and your flesh pared down to the bone like an umbrella blown inside out. No use. No function. Still there, but not quite for months, for years. When you hit double incontinence, that's the time to go. A handful of shit – 'what's this?' – not knowing what a shit is. Better to go then.

So let him drink. Let him have a few. Let him get whatever fucking enjoyment he could get while he still could. What harm could it do? What harm? Oh Christ.

She couldn't call Belinda. She has been watching the story. She would want to write a piece on negligent security. Kay needed quiet. Kay needed to find some time to think, to get her head together. And mumbling, mumbling in the back of her mind, the entire time Kay was asking herself, was it linked? Was her father in some way connected? Was he capable of something like this? Was it linked? How? No. No. Could not possibly be. He was completely incompetent; of that she was sure. He couldn't even buy her a Christmas present.

When she turned up at his house for Boxing Day dinner, he wasn't even there. He had gone to the Golden Lion. When she arrived there, surrounded by all of his old crony pals, and she had given him his present – a carefully sought out and selected Stan Kenton CD – he had just said, 'I didn't get you anything'. It was Kay's first Christmas without her mother and he hadn't even bought her a box of chocolates. She missed her mother's gravy. She washed down her grief with Christmas wine.

"Whiskey please," Kay said. "Large one."

"Straight? Ice?" asked the barman.

"No. No thank you. And not whiskey. Rum, I'll have rum. That one there, Havana club, a double. Just pour it as it comes," Kay said, pointing to the glass bottles.

"Of course, Madam," he said. Kay was thinking that she said 'of course' all the time, that she was just like the bartender at this Ibis hotel, pleasing strangers. Why was it so important to please all of these people all of the time?

"Don't you get annoyed dealing with people all the time?" asked Kay, slamming the empty glass on the hard plastic bar.

"I just started working here," he said, folding a white linen tea towel. She must look mad. Kay felt like she had a mad look in her. Her joints had gone jerky. She was blinking too frequently. Twitching. She was trying hard to keep herself together. To stop from doing anything that looked weird. She routed around in her bag. She hated this bag. Too slim. She could never get anything out.

"Do you take Visa?" asked Kay. He explained that they did take cards but that it was a ten pound minimum, so she ordered another double and then asked for cigarettes before shuddering and telling him that she didn't smoke and she didn't know why she was asking. He just smiled and pointed to a shop across the road.

She downed the second rum. Ariana called her from their PR office in Paddington.

"Are you coming back into the office?" she asked. Kay put her hand around the phone so Ariana couldn't hear the lobby music and the clinking noise of the bar.

"No, I don't think I'll have time. Tied up here. I'll have to go straight to Julia's thing tonight," Kay said.

"Well, I'll speak to you there," Ariana said. From Kay's experience, it was something important. This request often meant notice of resignation (good), or Ariana might be pregnant (not good).

When Ariana first arrived from Kosovo, via Germany, her English was dreadful and Kay had paid for her to do an 'English for Business' course in a college above a phone shop on Oxford Street. If Kay hadn't given her the job then she would have struggled to get anything decent, but Kay did it for her best friend, Dave, to make Dave happy. Why was she always trying to make everyone happy? Now she was stuck with Ariana in a symbiotic relationship. A cow and a duck.

Julia's book launch that evening was a good excuse not to go back to the office, though she didn't need an excuse. She was the boss but Ariana, oblivious to Kay's troubles, screeched excitable words about the launch party.

Kay believed that she could fix everything. She gripped on to the notion of being in control, of being able to change things and make choices. It was slipping, her grip loosening. She pulled up her collar, thanked the barman and left the hotel. The hotel sat on a dual carriageway and her Uber driver had pulled into a drop off area just outside, to wait for her. Cars were whizzing by dangerously, creating bursts of wind. The gusts of air hit her in the face, hot intoxicating diesel.

"Thanks for waiting," she said and got in the back seat. She slammed the door and became insulated, quiet. Lipstick. Get some order going on. She could hear a painful, paranoid noise. Was it laughter? No, she couldn't hear it but they would be laughing at her. Everyone would be laughing at her. She winced. It was painful to sit. Not from any injury, just a pain inside her body. In the driver's mirror she could see that her chest had come out in a red rash stretching up her neck. Her ankles itched, the outline of marks on her skin visible through tights. The rash was starting to creep up her legs towards the knee. Bloody tights; she wanted to rip them off.

Her eye caught the head of a driver in another car. Thick dark hair. She saw the head from behind. Is it him? Benedict? She froze cold. His face was everywhere.

She dialed Jim's number. No answer. She left no message. She had called twelve times. Calm down. She made a groaning noise under her breath. The rum started working and she wondered if she should stop at the shop after all and buy a bottle of some light brown spirit to straighten her. But no. Poor Julia. She thought of Julia on her big day with Kay turning up pissed and embarrassing her. She wasn't even hot enough to be eye candy anymore, not with these patchy red blemishes. Calm down, Kay.

She scrambled to get her notepad out, the small one, an A6 Moleskine; she had them all in different colours. A present from Julia. This one was red. With an enamel fountain pen she wrote some numbers down. Calculations, fee income. She was going to be fired by Excel, her biggest client. She should have diversified, not relied so heavily on them. She knew that. But she was so busy running around for Simon that she had taken her eye off the ball.

She was compromised. Injured from her mum. Trauma or something left over reverberating. Other stuff she should have sorted out before, not just forgotten. She hadn't forgotten, but pocketed, swallowed, hid. It was all clambering out now. Jack in the box. Can of worms. Put it back. Too late. All of it. Oh God.

"You alright love?" asked the driver, a bald, middle-aged man. She was sure that he had driven her before and that they had talked about Ireland.

"Oh," she fidgeted, "not really." She buzzed the window down to let in some thick grey air that she could almost see. She saw a shop front. A bar. A florist. How the fuck did they all make a living? All these crappy businesses, all these overheads, rents, wages, PAYE. How?

"Bad news?" he asked.

"There's no other kind of news these days."

"There's a box of tissues on the back shelf there, help yourself," he said. Kay must have been crying and not realised.

"My mum died." Kay said.

"Oh, I am very sorry. You let it out love," he said, because Kay was now crying her eyes out, big thick droplets bursting out of her eyes from both sides. Her breathing was shallow, red chest pumping. She caught the snot in her nose in a swab of dissolving tissue. She made a noise like a tennis player hitting the ball. "Have you just heard?" asked the driver.

"September the 23rd," Kay said.

"It takes a long time," said the driver. What was that supposed to mean? Of course it takes a bloody long time. She was my mother. Three months is nothing. No time at all. I'll never get over this, never be rid of this pain. Then guilt wrapped its claws around Kay's neck, again.

"She'd been ill for a long time," Kay said.

"Cancer?" asked the driver. People do die in other ways.

"Alzheimer's," Kay said.

"Oh, I'm very sorry," he said and his tone deepened and dropped like lead to a level below sympathy, to pity?

"Seven years," Kay said.

"Awful. Awful. I tell you what, if I had that, well, I'd want to be finished off," he said. Kay winced. She let her eyes stay closed. She wanted to be soothed so badly, but all people think about is themselves. Splice my pain onto yours. It's theft isn't it? But I do it myself all the time. Shut up. Arsehole. Stop talking to him. Go on the phone. Do something.

Kay rummaged in her bag and found a cough sweet. She put it in her mouth. Cherry. There was paper welded to its edges. But she started talking anyway.

"The last year was bad," said Kay.

"She's at peace now."

"I have a stressful job," said Kay, scratching her jaw, under the ear, by the top of the neck.

"Yeah?" asked the driver.

"Not like a surgeon, or police."

"No?"

"I feel like I'm drowning," said Kay.

"You got a husband, or a boyfriend?" he asked. A husband? To sort it all out, to take care of her?

"Yes," said Kay, just agreeing.

"You might need some help. Nothing wrong with that."

"I like this song," said Kay, sitting back, looking out of the window. She closed her eyes again and held her face up to the wind. Piss off. You sound like Julia.

I don't need help.

I am help.

"Shall I turn it up?" he asked, pitying eyes framed in the rear view mirror.

"Yes please," she said and they sped on. The music and the rum finally smoothing Kay's jagged edges.

When they arrived, Kay ran up the path of her father's house.

The taxi waited for her. It was dark and there were no lights on. The Christmas lights and sleigh from next door still flashed in bright neon. The blue side gate was locked. The curtains were half drawn. Where the hell was he? He might still be at the police station. Kay wouldn't have time to go there.

What should she do? Maybe she should forego Julia's launch under the circumstances, but that wasn't an option. The show must go on. Julia would be furious if she failed to show up. Kay let herself in with her key. There was a sudden sound. She jumped sharpish and turned, shoulders up. It was nothing, a car engine two hundred yards away. She was afraid of shadows and the dark. Saw men's hands everywhere. Felt the smothering sensation of being under attack. She was racing on adrenaline. She slammed the front door closed.

"Dad! Dad? Jim?" Kay shouted.

He wasn't here. It was silent. But what was this? The place was clean. It had been recently vacuumed. She walked through the lounge to the kitchen. The white formica countertops were spotless. She looked down the side of the cooker, usually choc-a-block with grease, crumbs, and miscellaneous food waste. It was clear. The ceiling, once beige, was white. Had Jim been cleaning? He was far too tight to pay a cleaner, but he couldn't have done it himself.

Kay opened the fridge and there were four cans of Tyskie lager, a cabbage and a packet of four Lidl pork chops, open to the elements with the thick white rind air-hardening in front of her eyes. But it was clean. From the smell, bleached. Maybe he had had a New Year's resolution. She clicked open a can of Tyskie and drank half down, wiping her mouth on the back of her hand. She belched.

Kay's eyes had taken on an animalistic character, like a cat when a storm is coming. She was nervy and jumpy as she stood looking at old pictures of herself hung in cheap plastic frames on the lounge wall:

Kay's first birthday;

Kay in the newspaper when the new library opened;

Kay graduating from Leeds University;

Kay bungee jumping in New Zealand;

Kay in PR Week.

She went upstairs, into her bedroom. No dog hair, no musty smell. There had been an historic sharp urine odour left over from her mother, but it was gone. She bent under the bed and pulled out a box. It was a shoebox her mum had covered in purple wrapping paper. She had carefully taped it and put inside special, private things. Notes. A memory box.

Kay picked it up. She wanted it now, needed it. It was dangerous to leave something so precious here any longer for that idiot to burn or break. She turned off the light, went down the stairs and did a final sweep through the house, picking up a half drunk bottle of own label Scotch and putting it in her handbag. The neck of the bottle stuck out like a white flag of surrender.

He must be at the pub. The Golden Lion was less than a three-minute drive, down the end of the road and across the dual carriageway. Probably the least golden thing anyone had ever seen in their lives. It was a modern sixties two-storey rectangular building, at the end of an insalubrious row of shops beneath a decrepit block of flats. Kay had once had a paper round from the newsagent but that was now an undertakers. The green grocer was now a Tesco Metro and the hardware store, a bookies.

An old faded sign said PUBLIC BAR and a new grey plastic plaque set out a LIST OF RULES. They stated warnings in relation to drugs and the calling of the police. Rules No.3 to 7 had been painted over with a large crudely drawn cock and balls.

Kay's mother wouldn't have been seen dead in the Golden Lion. But Jim was always here. For Kay, there were memories creeping all through the Golden Lion, propped up in corners, spilt and trodden into the sticky carpet, engrained in dirty grey fingerprints on the nearside wall. The walls looked even grubbier in the light of day and the poor inebriates looked like endangered animals, a rare sight to a workaholic like Kay.

That's how it was here. The people who did well, left. They left behind widowers. They left behind men like Jim, through death or the mover's van. Relics without a cause. A truck pulled up outside and unloaded three workmen in tatty yellow waistcoats. They wanted pints. Jim's red-headed female friend was there. She had been there on Boxing Day; Kay had bought her lots to drink. She took drinking seriously, like it was a job.

"Have a drink, have a drink," she demanded, but Kay waved her off, managing a fake smile. Kay was revolted by her. Was she terrified by the thought of her being Kay's ghost of Christmas future?

The barman was at the cash and carry restocking after the festive period. His wife pretended not to know Kay even though she had seen her at the lock-in on Boxing Day night. At one o'clock in the morning, she had brought out a platter of heavily buttered sandwiches. The bread was soft, white and thick like Kay's mum used to make. Inside was tinned salmon mixed up with lashings of tangy salad cream which dripped down Jim's chin.

It was awkward asking after Jim in front of the builders. One of them with a goatee and Celtic cross neck tattoo was trying to make conversation. She didn't know any of them but she bought a round of drinks anyway. No one had seen Jim since Boxing Day. He hadn't been in.

Kay didn't want to be with the same taxi driver anymore. She wanted to tuck into Jim's cheap Scotch, but she didn't want him to see her. He knew too much already. Nosey bastard. What business of his was it? Where was Jim? When Kay got hold of him... Her temper was starting up. Her heartbeat was racing. Oh. Bloody late now for Julia's thing. Kay asked the taxi driver to drop her at Stratford station and there she hailed a black taxi to take her all the way across London.

CHAPTER SIX

When Kay's taxi pulled up outside the Odessa Gallery on Ledbury Road, she got the merest glimpse of faces that she knew. Happy faces that would be delighted to see her. It made her feel like she wanted to run a mile, to tell the driver to keep going, but she dare not. It was making her tear up again.

The gallery was a glass two-storey building, the second mezzanine floor slightly smaller than the first, giving the impression of children's building blocks. If Kay had organised the launch, she would have done it somewhere in the West End to make it easier to get to, but the publisher wouldn't pay. Julia's friend had let them have the space for free, as long as they did their own catering and cleared up afterwards.

The artwork had been moved to the first floor and bunched together en-masse, in the hope that one of the guests might buy something. Between them, Kay and Julia had got all of the drinks for free from various PR people. Even Veuve Clicquot champagne had donated twenty-four bottles, which proved the point that it was not what you know, but whom.

Downstairs, the artworks had been replaced with quotes from the book and they hung there, giant black words on strong, embossed card:

'Where love has once gone, the trace of love remains–,' Julia Rothman

'The ego does not exist–,' Dalai Lama.

'When friendship fails, efficiency prevails–,' Arthur Rothman.

On the walls were blown up photographs; the young

Rothman family in the early 1990s; Julia as a young girl at Windsor Castle, tanned legs astride, sitting on a cannon in pink shorts and a blue T-shirt; Arthur as a rakish teenager; a wedding photograph of Julia and Arthur, which was made to look as if it had been ripped apart down the middle and then stuck back together again roughly so the original rip remained as a 'symbol'; an enlarged framed decree nisi; a holiday in France, Easter 2013, featuring Arthur, Julia, Henry and Olivia, their children, Kay Christie and Arthur Rothman's girlfriend, a lawyer called Rachael Massey.

Kay would do her duty. She always did her duty. Then she could feel satisfied that she had done everything she could. Jumped through every bloody hoop as usual. She fixed her face, getting the driver to switch on the light and using his distant rear view mirror. She looked OK, not perfect, but passable. It was hard to get her eyes to focus in the mirror.

Belinda Salas had turned up after all, and was making her way toward Kay's taxi. Her head sailed from side to side. As Kay got out carrying her handbag and her mother's box, her legs buckled and she fell. Heads turned in the glass building, but through the wall of parked cars and Belinda's pseudo-happy commentary, no one could see the fracas.

"Who left that there?" said Kay, and she looked up at Belinda. The box was intact, her handbag crumpled. She let the near empty bottle of whiskey roll into the gutter. Kay crouched in the road between two parked cars. One had a sparkling silver exhaust. She had never been that near an exhaust before. It was very posh around here.

"You are drunk," Belinda said, "and you've been crying."

"That's rich coming from you," Kay said.

"It's too late to turn back now. We'll have to get you coffee; how much have you had to drink? Stand up, stand up."

"You look nice," Kay said, admiring Belinda's dress coat.

"You're lucky Julia is so engrossed with her minions. We might have enough time to try and straighten you out," Belinda said.

"A line would sober me up," Kay said.

"No, Kay, don't say that again, not to anyone here, right?" Belinda asked, waiting for a nod. "You'll be alright, just smile." They started to move towards the gallery. "Yes, lots of smiling; you are just deliriously happy because your life is so perfect."

They crossed the footpath to the entrance. An older lady with bleached blonde hair and dangly earrings looked down her nose.

"I'm writing to the council," Belinda shouted so that all could hear her. "There's an uneven paving slab there. Could break your bloody neck."

"My box, my box," Kay said.

"I've got it. I've got it. I'll put it with the coats," Belinda said and they crossed the threshold through the two huge rectangular glass panelled doors. A wave of heat from the fan directly above hit Kay all at once. She propped herself up with one arm against the white wooden bar serving as a temporary cloakroom and felt sick.

Julia Rothman walked into the room, her tight buttocks and sinewy legs encased in black leather trousers. Her arms were spread open to reveal a cream coloured bat-winged satin blouse open to the breast, revealing a flash of bra and a tumbling necklace of silver and pearls. She walked in a jaunty two-step as if the whole world were watching her. Her smile was receptive, demanding conversation, blue eyes twinkling with intent. She could eat the whole world, gobble it up and thrive on its energy.

Kay retched in the small toilet cubicle. It was an empty heave and so, encouraged by Belinda, Kay put her fingers down her throat and up it came, a fiery, fierce smelling liquid. Belinda winced. Pure brown spirit and orange acid. She couldn't remember when she had last eaten. Belinda slapped Kay around the face so hard it stung and it worked, because suddenly Kay was back. Belinda threw her champagne down the sink, refilled her glass with water and gave it to Kay to drink. Kay drank it and then she did it again, over and over.

"It's working," said Kay, as Belinda dabbed cold water behind her ears.

"You need to get to that place where you're incredibly funny but not aggressive," said Belinda.

"Need to go back, do things differently, I've messed up," Kay said.

"That's very dramatic."

"Everything is ruined."

"You are a self-indulgent drunk," Belinda said.

"Is it him?"

"Him?" asked Belinda. "You're so pale."

"Have they ID'd the body yet?"

"Here." Belinda painted on Kay's lipstick. "That's better."

"I just want to know, that's all," said Kay.

"Don't get upset. I'll tell you when they've made an announcement. They've confirmed nothing. It's only been 24 hours. Now, you're going to go out there and you're going to show them you are so much more than Julia's bit of fluff," said Belinda. Kay drew in a deep breath at the mirror.

It wasn't him.

It could not be.

Forget about him.

Forget about it all.

Just as she had before.

Kay pinched at her dress, pulling it away from her breasts and her stomach. She could wear designer. Diane Von Furstenberg, a black and white classic wrap dress that Julia had picked out for her in New York. The dress she had worn all day, in her deepest humiliation and on the longest taxi journey she had ever had.

"Let me smell you," said Belinda, and Kay leaned over while Belinda put her nose close to Kay's mouth as if she was smelling wine, "you smell like a stag party."

"At least I don't smell of piss," said Kay.

"There's still plenty of time for that Kay. Perfume?" asked Belinda, pulled out David Beckham's perfume. "And where's Dave?"

"David Beckham?" Kay asked, confused.

"No, your Dave. Our Dave, you wally," Belinda said and Kay laughed. "Because I can see that blonde slut of his out there and you told me categorically that she wasn't coming."

"Ariana?" Kay asked.

"She looks like a hooker. I can't believe you gave her a job. You are such a mug," said Belinda, smoothing Kay's shoulders and tweaking the collar of her dress.

"I know I am," Kay said nodding, wanting more tears to come.

Any lingering odour of sick had been disguised by the rapid sucking of Kay's cough sweets. She sucked the last of the cherry flavour. Kay was still drunk, very much so, but in control. Functioning, they call it. She went up behind Julia and let one hand slip into the base of her spine. Julia turned slowly as if she had been waiting for it, and gave Kay a small visible kiss on her cheek, their lips brushing, just enough lip to titillate the guests.

"We were just talking about you," said Julia.

"All good I hope," Kay said theatrically. Perhaps she could explain her drunkenness by saying she had won a new client and had been out to celebrate? No good, no. She was an awful liar really, for someone who lied for a living. Julia said that her eyes gave it away. Julia was like the police. She could detect the smallest deviation. Kay would have to think fast, get even more of a grip.

They talked with a woman from Marks and Spencer. Julia thought it would be good for Kay's business. Kay could tell by Julia's open body language, teeing Kay up to speak. The asparagus was delicious. Kay could eat a whole plate. There was a McDonald's at Notting Hill Gate, barely ten minutes away; could she get there and back without Julia noticing?

Of course Julia was right and the woman gave Kay her business card, asking her to get in touch. It was a gift from God that this woman had landed in Kay's lap. Kay would lock on. She would attempt to extract filthy lucre. Kickstart her new business pitch with Marks and Spencer. Get lost Simon Bell. Fuck you Excel conference and exhibition centre.

Kay's own mind attacked her again. Dad. He's let someone get away with murder. That's what he's done. He's destroyed evidence. Jesus. Police. Criminal prosecution. Investigation. Interviews. What else might they find if they bothered to look?

Stop. Thinking. About. It. She would have to phone her supermarket client to make sure they were happy, schedule a lunch, and put some ideas together for another project. She moved away to change her focus, extract herself from the motorway of her mind.

There it was – the book. The Ex-Factor by Julia and Arthur Rothman:

'Make your relationship with your Ex work for you.' It was a self-help guide for the separated and divorced. 'Avoid costly legal fees and create a warm and nurturing environment for children.' It combined Julia's no nonsense, get-up-and-go, mum-about-town attitude with Arthur's psychoanalysis to enable readers to get to grips with subconscious aggression. Its glossy amber cover had been blown up so that Julia and Arthur stood back to back, arms folded, life size in the middle of the gallery.

When they pitched to the publisher, Julia identified the target market as 'Generation BP', as in Generation Blue Peter: all the diminutive girls and boys who watched Julia on Blue Peter from '89 to '94 who were now getting divorced. Julia had done the numbers; she had a graph and a spreadsheet based on viewing figures collated against divorce statistics.

"Just look at Belinda," Julia would say, as a classic example of a divorcee not yet turned forty. Julia had got Belinda to give a quote about how much the book had helped her through her separation. Kay did not point out that Belinda detested her ex, that they were at loggerheads over the houseboat, and that Belinda had slept with his brother in revenge.

A photographer in a multi-pocketed khaki gilet pushed his long lens between the group and began snapping away.

"Press interest has been incredible," exaggerated Julia.

"Excuse me, can I have a photograph with you and Arthur please Julia, and then one with the new partners?" the photographer asked, herding them together. Julia and Arthur recreated the shot from the front cover of the book – in front of the life-size cover of the book. Then the photographer moved them in front of a methuselah of Veuve Clicquot (on loan for the picture only) and asked for Kay and Rachael Massey to move in next to them. A cosy foursome. Kay was the only one without a glass of champagne in her hand. It amused her to think that out of the four of them, she would look like the one who didn't drink. It was so boring to only drink when you were supposed to. Much more exciting to have a drink during the day.

Arthur and Rachael looked like they had just escaped from an architect's only minimalist exhibition – in black. Buttoned down collars, black on black, even black earrings. Rachael looked gothic. Unhuggable. Kay was going on holiday with these two. Somewhere in France. Awful. Just depressing. Kay yearned for a week in Ibiza with Belinda Salas, or even Majorca with Dave. They had a great holiday in Cyprus the three of them years before, such a brilliant laugh, until it all went to hell.

"So, tell me everything, where did you two meet?" asked the book reviewer from Best Magazine. Best, for Christ's sake. She was the Home Economist, which meant she tested all the recipes and reviewed the products that she put in them, and when she wasn't doing that she championed the book review column. She said the column had really taken off after Fifty Shades of Grey. She said that there was a natural synergy between food and sex.

"Everything is about food and sex," Julia said.

"But this book is about divorce," said the book reviewer.

"Oh, but divorce is all about sex, n'est pas?" said Julia, and she flicked her face up, eyes open, prompting Kay to tell the fictionalised account of how they had met. The sanitised version where Julia had already split from Arthur before Kay and Julia had ever set eyes on one another.

Ariana stood alone. Her blonde head hovered above everyone else's. Her physique drew a nasty commentary from other women. It wasn't the way she looked; it was the way that men looked at her. It was as if she ignited their latent lascivious imaginations where they screwed her in their heads, right there in front of their wives.

"We need to have a new business push," said Kay.

"Why?" asked Ariana.

"We just do. Pull this up a bit here, I can see your bra," Kay said, tugging up the front of Ariana's dress. "Tomorrow, if you could pull out the marketing database please."

"There's something wrong?" Ariana said. Kay never talked in depth about the health of her business with Ariana, even though she was her assistant. Kay told her what she needed to know. Ariana did what she was asked in the main, but trapped in the space between being an employee or a friend, Ariana constantly tried to engage Kay in chit-chat. There was detailed private information about Dave. There was the obvious commentary about clients and other people in the team. There was even a paranoid thread about an ex-boyfriend back in town phoning her, bugging her and not leaving her alone.

"No. Maybe. I don't know yet," Kay said.

"I'm so sorry, Kay, I'm so, so sorry. For everything. I'm sorry," Ariana said.

"It's not your fault. We'll be fine; I'll sort it out, and we'll get new clients," Kay said sucking in air, but the words had caught in her throat. She was trembling. Something wasn't firing inside. She wondered if she was a broken thing now. Merchants of doom arrived inside. She was finished.

"Can I ask you something good?" Ariana asked.

"Jesus Christ almighty, yes please, please ask me something good."

"Dave was meant to ask you, but I don't know where he is,

and I just can't wait," said Ariana, bringing her hands together bashfully in front of her long body. Kay had to tilt her head to look up into her eyes. Usually, Kay tried to avoid eye contact with Ariana as much as possible.

"Can I have the day off on Thursday?" asked Ariana. Kay floundered, a fish on the floor of a fisherman's boat. She went to pieces when people asked for a day off. Silly, but there you are.

"What, this Thursday? I don't know, can you? You do the holiday chart. What day is it today? It's quite short notice," Kay said, deliberately obtuse. A scan. Must be a pregnancy scan. She would be taking the piss wanting time off all the time now. It would be awkward trying to get rid of her with a baby on the way. Not just any baby either – Dave's.

"It's Monday today, so it's just in three days' time," Ariana said.

"We'll have to check with this crisis going on," Kay said.

"Kay, I would like to ask you, if you can also have Thursday off? As well as me," Ariana said. To go to a scan? Ridiculous. Might be locked up by Thursday anyway.

"Thursday this week? Me? I doubt that very much. Why?" Kay asked.

"He's here. He's here!" Ariana shouted as Dave stalked through the packed floor, a coal miner in a room of ballerinas. Ariana threw herself up and onto him; the crowd gasped. Men dropped their fantasies into long blue-balled faces. Their jealousy smelled like unripened green bananas.

"I can't stay long; I've got to get off, but," Dave said, "I just picked up your dad from the police station."

"You? Why you?" asked Kay. Why would her own father call him over her?

"He didn't want to disturb you," Dave said.

"Well I am disturbed Dave. Very disturbed," Kay said and she was thirsty again. Itchy again. She looked at the bar. Her head was beginning to throb. There was a shriek of laughter; Julia was being held in the air by two men with naked torsos wearing dickie bows. Julia held up her arms like Marilyn Monroe playing to the crowd and everyone clapped.

"We wanted to ask you something Kay, didn't we Dave?" Ariana said. Dave took a second to compose himself; he ran a hand over his mouth and chin and shifted from one foot to the other.

"We're getting married," he said and kissed Ariana full on the lips, which lingered, then went deeper and became a French kiss. Kay saw Ariana's tongue wrestling into Dave's mouth. Kay tried to look away. Ariana pushed her fingertips into Dave's scalp and as they pulled away she was still biting his lip, holding onto a portion between her teeth. Kay saw Belinda Salas at the other side of room watching through painful eyes. Belinda was not blinking. She was watching Dave and Ariana with a pale ashen face, holding herself upright against the giant 'The Ex-Factor' book cover. Her knuckles were tight and white as if she might snap the precious artefact in half.

"Congratulations!"

"We're not inviting anyone else, well except for Ariana's sister Rhea, who's flying in, but we would like to ask you to be our witnesses — you and Julia," said Dave.

"I'm very touched. I really am. I'd be proud to be your witness and I'm sure Julia will be too, once she gets down off that man's shoulders," said Kay. "Thursday? That's quick." It was a shotgun wedding. Must be. Ariana probably didn't want to say, because Kay was her boss.

Kay watched as Belinda walked out, phone pressed to her

ear. Her stomach knotted again. She knew the call would come any minute. That the police would ID the body.

"Be right back," she said. Ariana and Dave were already kissing again, completely caught up in their love. She manoeuvred between guests and found Belinda outside. She hung up the phone.

"Was that the police?" asked Kay.

"My contact in the morgue," Belinda said. She looked as pale as Kay felt. "They've got an ID." Kay felt sick; she took a shallow breath, tried not to vomit. "We know him, Kay. You know him. It's Benedict Phillips."

CHAPTER SEVEN

It was the middle of the night. Kay woke with a start. All was quiet in the house, just the gentle electric buzz of London humming on a fuzzy indigo frequency. Her throat was barren. It was like sawdust had got inside her windpipe. Her head pulsed; she had a headache. Julia was snoring. A fact she would deny. She was on her back, one arm thrown above her head. Kay regarded her with one open eye and then closed it again, returning to her dark noisy world.

Her head was spinning. She thought about Benedict Phillips. Belinda had promised to update her when she knew more. Kay had managed to hide the fact she already knew. She thought about her dad. Why had he called Dave and not her? Why did she get him a job? You fool, Kay. You meddler. Why? Will you never learn? And then, you think you are so special. Better than everyone else. The sad thing is that you still care what your dad thinks – when he doesn't care about you at all. Then a smaller whimpering voice that pleaded, not for the first time, why can't you just be like everybody else? It was the same voice that used to pray quietly, out loud, in the mirror 'please God, don't let me be a nun or a lesbian.'

Then loudly, you stupid idiot. How many times? How many people must you be responsible for before you are satisfied? He was working at Ford in Dagenham. For years. Got a watch and a 'do' up London for 25 years' service. A working class dandy, the works, hair slicked back, rosy cheeks, fuller then. On nights out his mouth hung slack ready for a joke, for banter. You could smell him getting ready using old style men's grooming things, pomade, something of the war about him, a dapper 1940s feel.

When the factory closed, production moved to a Delhi suburb or a Romanian country town – she couldn't remember, but Jim Christie just ceased. Could pressing a button on a production line day in, day out really provide a source of such bravado? Was it possible this was the sort of job by which he could give himself identity? Dignity? Would the person now pressing his button in a far-away land now feel like Jim once did? Proud?

Kay climbed over herself to get him a new job. She couldn't act quickly enough – identifying the right person, getting a tip off. Setting it up so that he could not fail, a good word here, a wink there. She had just won the account. Simon owed her. Excel was near Jim's house. It was perfect. Why did she have to get involved?

He wasn't meant to be doing anything important. He was meant to be sitting at the gate, reading the paper, looking at the laminated passes thrust in his face, raising and lowering the barrier. That was all. Nothing more.

But someone left. So he moved and did a training course, despite the fact he could hardly turn the telly on. Disaster soared above them like a kite, waiting for the wind to drop to come crashing down. Kay had not wanted to see. But now she saw.

Julia snored. The next whirligig of thoughts meditated furiously on this: had he ever said 'thank you'? You fool! He's never even thanked you and now you are going to lose everything for nothing. No card. No flowers. Not as much as 'Ta.'

He preferred Dave to her. He had always preferred Dave. The listless, dirty faced boy from down the road, with the father who liked to hit him and the frequently missing mother. He soothed

Dave's temper. Sat for hours cleaning boots and mending bicycle tyres. The son he never had.

Oh stop it, Kay. Dave's your friend.

Mum's box. Where was it? Did I bring it home? So reckless with things that could never be replaced. She slid out of the bed. Immediately her toe hit something solid on the floor. Flowery purple paper. It smelled of lilac and even in the dark it called to her, vibrating familiar warmth. Kay reversed back into bed. Beneath the duvet the onslaught began again – never give a job to family or friends. Don't lend them money. Never do it again. And she was stuck now with Ariana as her PA because she was doing Dave a favour. Never ever again. Why did you get him a job? You fool. How was Benedict connected to this? Did Jim know him, too? He couldn't know because she had never told anyone, only Julia. Julia would never betray her confidence. On and on these thoughts raced, like cars on a circular track, vroom, around and around and around.

"Go to sleep," said Julia.

Kay moved onto her side, back facing Julia. She ruffled the sheets and got into a better position, her face finding the cool patch on the pillow. But still she couldn't sleep. She got up, picked up the box. Julia tutted and rolled over, pulling the duvet up over her head. Kay crossed the landing, carefully, turning the doorknobs slowly as they had a tendency to rattle.

She went into the small white-walled spare room and pulled up the covers around herself. She opened the box. She expected it to glow with light, to shine up in her face. There was a silver medal, the sacred heart of Jesus imprinted with Latin. A ring; thin gold band with a large opal. Her mother had bought this for herself, because she liked it. Kay had thought nothing of it before but now it taught her something about her mum that she hadn't known. Her mother's imprint. She had it on until the end, until her face was covered in cloth, and inside the back of the stone, it was dirty. Julia would have it cleaned in a second, but Kay liked the dirt. It had come off her mother, sloughed off her skin. Her DNA still with us. She licked it. She put the ring on her right index finger and it fitted, plenty of room, but OK.

She pulled out the death certificate, which Kay had tucked inside the box after the funeral, wanting to forget. The word 'stroke' written in the doctor's hand. But Kay knew it was not a stroke that had killed her. She ran her finger over the word, then quickly folded it away, fearful, not wanting to look at it ever again.

Work photographs. Her mother stood in a line of secretaries at Ford Dagenham in 1970s clothes. Purple winged collars, beige suits, and long-haired men. She recognised a few from the funeral – older, greyer, sagging versions of themselves. In one picture, her mother had a scratched nose where she had fallen off her bicycle that morning and had been mortified to have a picture taken with a graze. In the later pictures, when she was older, she was sitting next to the big boss. A small acknowledgement of a life well spent.

Under the photographs were old letters. Paper then was tissue thin. Some curled and browned at the edges. The original ticket from the The Innisfallen, the B&I boat that had brought her to England from Cork in 1969. Kay wept softly, as it rose up from underneath her chest. Her eyes brimmed, but tears didn't flow down her face. She could do that now. She could measure her tears.

Then.

A letter in her mother's own swirling handwriting; a love letter. Not to Jim, but to someone called Kenneth Spiers. Kay and her mother had never talked about love. She had never heard the name before. Who the hell was Kenneth Spiers? She added it to the names swirling around her head. Exhausted, she fell asleep.

CHAPTER EIGHT

Mayfair. Number 57 Park Street was a tall Georgian building with a whitewashed façade and a bulging circular bay which kissed the black lacquered railings of the street. This Middle Eastern conglomerate had wished to emulate Charles Dickens with a spine-like narrow staircase. Kay's shoes flashed on the stone entry step like a tap dancer. Atop those steps sat a big Thatcher-like formal black door. The big knocker comprising a fish's mouth, looked like it might actually sneeze at any moment.

Kay had been summoned to a crisis meeting with the Corporate PR Director – a reptilian woman, whom Kay had repeatedly tried to court with no avail. She had requested a report of all of their work for the last five years to be delivered by two o'clock that afternoon. An impossible task. Kay was being set up to fail.

Simon added that he would be dealing with all media from now on, and if Kay could please send him all of her contacts then that would be 'most helpful'. And where was he? Kay was supposed to be meeting him here, but no sign of him so far.

Kay picked up her phone and typed 'Benedict Phillips' into a search engine. She had resisted searching, until now. She had never looked him up in the ten intervening years. Had never wanted to, never even crossed her mind. A list of websites spewed forth. Various mentions for the Berkshire and Wiltshire regiment, army listings. No news. Nothing new. No Facebook or social media. No pictures of his face.

Kay telephoned her father. There was no answer.

Kay telephoned Simon Bell. There was no answer.

On the coffee table lay a copy of the Evening Standard. Kay flicked through page by page, killing time, nerves coagulating. Page seventeen. Hell on earth. A photograph from the party of Kay, Julia, Arthur Rothman and Rachael Massey. Did Kay's left eye look droopy? Kay could tell she looked smashed, but other people might not notice? Text underneath:

Happy EX-tended Families! The Rothmans toast the success at their book launch. With champagne from Veuve Clicquot, the Odessa Gallery on Ledbury Road was aflame last night with excitement over The Ex-Factor, the new relationship breakdown book from ex-Blue Peter presenter Julia and TV psychotherapist Arthur. Rumour has it there's plenty of fact in there, and we're dying to know about when Julia met her now partner, PR gal about town, Kay Christie.

Oh God. Not now. Why now? Kay crumpled up the newspaper and shoved it inside her bag to hide the evidence. Kay's phone buzzed with a tweet and then several messages referencing the photograph. But no message from her father. Where was he? Suddenly sat there in the Dickensian simulacra, waiting to have her arse kicked by someone she hated, her mind spilled over and slipped back into a self-indulgent memory of just how difficult she felt her life had been.

Her mind slipped back to a meeting, years before, when her mother was still alive. She had gone to a big pitch in the company's corporate HQ searing above the drone of cars on the M40 below. She started to relive the telephone call word for word, slowly re-enacting the conversation line by line.

"Your mum has had a fall. I don't want to worry you, but –" said Jean, a wispy lady from the day centre.

"Is she OK?" asked Kay, stomach dropped to wait for impending doom.

"Yes she is fine now. This is just to let you know," said Jean.

"Thank you," said Kay, hiding her eyes from the assembled group of senior executives chatting amongst themselves, filling their cups with corporate coffee from silver-plated jugs.

"She fell in the street when she was coming out to the bus when we went to collect her this morning," said Jean, pausing. Kay could hear noises of the day centre, teaspoon on china cup, an adult voice shrieking something incomprehensible, and then Jean said, "I know it is slippery out there, but your dad went down too."

"My dad?" asked Kay.

"He was trying to support her and they both fell together," said Jean. Had a fall. That's what they usually called it. But him too? "Your mother is OK. She's got a little bit of a bruise and she has been crying, but we've given her a cup of tea, which she seems to have kept down. She's just sitting here in front of me now and she seems much more content."

"Oh my God."

"It is a little shock but as I say, nothing to worry about now; she's quite happy and I just wanted to let you know the situation," said Jean.

"Thank you for looking after her," said Kay.

"The bus driver said that your father seemed agitated," said Jean, moving onto the pressing business at hand.

"Agitated?" asked Kay. Not an adjective Kay would ever use to describe her father.

"Yes," said Jean.

"How do you mean agitated?" asked Kay.

"The bus driver thought that he might have smelled alcohol," said Jean.

"Alcohol?" asked Kay.

"We pick your mum up at seven o'clock so it could've been from last night, if he'd had a lot–"

"Right," said Kay.

"So, as you know we are finishing early today at two o'clock so I wondered just what the situation might be when she is dropped off at home?" asked Jean.

"Yes. I'll be there, at Mum's at two o'clock this afternoon," said Kay, understanding that everyone was waiting for her.

The woman behind the reception, all red glossed lips and nonchalant eyebrow, raised her face from her computer screen. She announced that the Corporate PR Director would be another ten minutes. A door banged. Someone was coming down those narrow stairs. First the toe of a black boot and then the thick sewn hem of a grey coat, and last the gliding swoop of her dark grey Fedora. Her coat swung open to reveal a soft low V-neck sweater. It was DS Harvey.

"What are you doing here?" she asked. Kay stood up.

"I think I'm going to get sacked," said Kay, "what about you?"

"The owners of the boat–" DS Harvey flicked her eyes towards the receptionist to warn Kay that they were being listened to.

"The Lusciousness?" said Kay.

"Yes, they own The Lusciousness, and the venue of course. Have you got time for that coffee?" asked DS Harvey.

"Miss Christie?" interrupted the receptionist. "She'll see you now."

"And I'll meet you afterwards," Kay said, heading for the stairs.

The Corporate PR Director had a jaw that protruded over the top of her teeth and when she spoke, her mouth moved very little and her eyes were hooded with aged, steely pupils. Each time she spoke, she coughed to clear her throat and the cough came out upwards through the protruding bottom teeth.

"I haven't got a lot of time," she said, straightening the lapel of her suit jacket.

"Thank you for making this time to see me as I know you are very busy," said Kay.

"Well I am busy now, dealing with all of this," she said.

"If there is anything at all that I can do to help ease your workload, then please do not hesitate to ask," said Kay.

"I think you've done enough," she said, "thank you." Kay started to think fight or flight. Whatever she said or did, she was doomed. The Corporate PR Director cleared her throat again. "You've been called in today because there are a number of things that we are finding very concerning over at Excel. Now then," she coughed twice, "as part of a thorough review of many elements of the operations going on over there, I have been charged with reviewing PR to make some recommendations about what we need to do going forward."

"We have produced outstanding work over the last five years," Kay lifted her branded 'Christie Dean' recycled bag onto the table and pulled out a three inch thick bound book of reports and cuttings, "this is just a snapshot of some of the brilliant work that we have done."

The Corporate PR Director rolled her eyes towards the book but didn't touch it. Kay manoeuvred her arm to turn the pages for her. Then Kay saw the newspaper on the desk. She hadn't clocked it before. The Corporate PR Director, seeing Kay notice it, said:

"Nice picture. I didn't know Julia Rothman was a..." she raised an eyebrow and licked her bottom lip which was taut against her teeth. Kay shifted in her seat. This wasn't fair. This wasn't bloody fair. Fuming. Bitch. Scratchy throat and burning sting in Kay's eyelids.

"I have prepared a short presentation of highlights," said Kay, but the Corporate PR Director had closed her notebook and was putting the lid on her pen.

"I'm afraid the police kept me later than I had intended and I've run out of time. I'll look through these documents myself and get in touch with you in the next few days," she said.

"I really believe that you could not have got a harder working team, totally committed 24/7; we represent great value," said Kay, scrambling to recover, but not wanting to recover. Not wanting to do the right thing, wanting to leap across the table and scratch out her fucking eyes. This is my life. And then angry – what a wasted, thankless life, surging loss, get away.

Out on the cold hard pavement, the fringes of Kay's faux fur blew in the wind. She was lighter for the loss of the report book. It was her biggest account. It represented around 70% of Christie Dean's entire business income. She would have to sack people, make them redundant. Then she would need a new business push. She would have to call in some favours, reach out to people who knew her, beg, borrow, steal to get better clients. She had done it before. She could do it again.

Kay thought about her phone and wondered if it had been a mistake to Google Benedict Phillips. Could the police trace that? She gripped it tight in her pocket. Too late now.

CHAPTER NINE

Shaftesbury Avenue was dark and chilly. Her father was still not answering his phone, so she decided to pluck him from her mind. Be gone. For now he ceased to exist. Her fingers started to jam up in the cold as they sought out messages on her phone.

An excited message from Julia said that she wouldn't be back tonight. BBC Radio London had called and her agent had set up a meeting to table a discussion about a radio show. Her own radio show. Based on their book, the show would be called 'The Ex Factor' and would fill a vacant late night Friday slot to begin immediately. Julia was ecstatic. It all hinged on the chemistry meeting that night. It was everything that she ever wanted.

The French House was on a side street linking Old Compton Street and Shaftesbury Avenue. The tiny gridlike roads rejected conformity; it was as if when entering the heart of Soho you left behind the rigid conformities of life. You didn't have to be grey.

Someone had abandoned a skeletal tree in the street, dying from the season's excesses. Kay installed herself in the front of the bar, behind the glazed window. The bar was old-fashioned and wood throughout, basic, not too comfortable, made for the more serious drinker. There was no music playing, only the sheer scrape of hard chairs. Two media men stood talking at the bar, long black trench coats, glasses, checked shirts with the top button done up, sipping glasses of red wine. Her dad would think them twats.

Three copies of the Evening Standard littered the wooden sideboard behind the front glass. Kay crushed them together, roughly folded, and tried to shove them into her bag. There were no bloody bins in London anymore. Then in she walked. DS Harvey.

"Hello PR gal about town," she said.

"Hi," said Kay, trying to zip up her bag and then surrendering.

"It must be nice to be called a 'gal' at your age," said DS Harvey.

"I'm almost forty," said Kay, shuddering and then pausing to consider how she should greet a member of the police service. It didn't feel quite right to double kiss under the circumstances. She decided not to.

"She's very attractive," said DS Harvey, and Kay paused, locating the comment and just who she was talking about. "She's a bit old for you isn't she, Julia?" Desperate to take control, to dominate, both women jostled passively with strong forced smiles while Kay folded the newspapers and put them underneath her arm.

"Shall we have a glass of red then?" Kay said.

"You are over eighteen aren't you?" asked DS Harvey, and as she took off her coat amidst the jumble of wooden chairs, she dropped her phone out of her pocket. She sprang down, the curve of her bottom filling her very tight blue jeans. Kay couldn't take her eyes away. Then she was up again, catching Kay looking.

"It's Polly, by the way," she said, "my name. No need for formalities."

"Polly," repeated Kay, turning robotically to the bar, depositing the newspapers with the barman and coming back with two glasses of red wine in short stumpy glasses.

"I wasn't going to drink during January, but I'm not doing very well with that," said Kay, thinking that actually Polly didn't need to know about Kay's drinking habits. In fact, much better not to know.

"I don't really drink."

"No me neither," lied Kay, heavily medicated and still dehydrated from the previous day's consumption. Then, silly, girl-like, suddenly full of energy, Kay said, "there's a brilliant restaurant upstairs; it's a tiny Italian place –"

"I can't talk about the case, if that's why you're here Kay," said Polly, deadpan. Her hair was chestnut, properly rich brown chocolate fondue.

"Well, of course, and that's not why I'm here," said Kay, not knowing why she was there. Why am I here?

"I met your dad. He likes a drink doesn't he?" asked Polly. Kay could see Polly's lips pressed against the glass, juicy, red wine flowing. She licked her mouth.

"I haven't spoken to him yet," said Kay, "he's not answering his phone. I've all but been sacked." Briefly, Polly reached out and touched Kay's hand. It took Kay aback. She wasn't expecting that.

The night was dark and dark early, so the only way to mark the passing of time was the way that people shook and shuddered when they came in through the door. Trailing breaths of thick white steam and a shrug of shoulder, lifted as if to throw off the cold. Night was drawing in, frosty and black.

They drank more wine and Kay was telling Polly how she used to watch Jill Gascoine in the Gentle Touch – how much she loved it, with Jill's perm and her Ford Escort. Was it an Escort? Maybe a Vauxhall? Then Polly was saying that she didn't think Kay's dad was a bad person, that perhaps it was just grief, and Kay didn't protest. What was the point in explaining?

Kay had forgotten why she was there, leaning in chatting

with Polly, laughing, having her hand touched so sweetly. Until, until that is, Polly said his name, dropping it, shattering it across the pub floor.

"We ID'd the body," said Polly. "Benedict Phillips. Have you heard that name before?"

"No," Kay said as simple as that. Drunk enough to say anything. Don't look away. Don't look away because, Kay thought, she is trained to spot liars, so front it up. You don't know him. Haven't seen or heard of him for years. Kay shook her head. What would I ask if didn't know him? Who is he? Yes, who is he? "Who is he?" asked Kay, glass lifted to her lips, eyes wide, blinking over the rim.

"He worked in close protection. Do you know what that is?"

"No," said Kay, knowing.

"Personal security." Mistaking Kay's nonchalance for not understanding, Polly said, "for rich people. He's got links to Abdul Bin Harashi's office —"

"Really?" asked Kay, "to the owners?"

"This is confidential," said Polly, leaning in so close her face just inches away from Kay. They must have looked like lovers. Kay noticed Polly's bottom lip was fuller, plumper than the top lip. "So you don't recognise the name from your work with Excel?" asked Polly. Twice she's asked. Twice. Kay picked up her drink, again, and stared at Polly's mouth and sure enough, as people do when you stare at their nose, or at their ear for long enough, Polly touched her mouth, like a question.

"Are you interviewing me?" asked Kay. Why was she with Kay in the pub? What should she do? She didn't have to lie. She had nothing to lie about. It was nothing to do with Kay. Kay could just say that she knew Benedict, once, years ago. But that would sound strange surely, with her father involved.

"You work for them, like you were in there today. I was just wondering, in your dealings with them, if you had ever heard his name? If you'd ever come across him? I'm not interviewing you. I just wondered," said Polly.

"Well, in my dealings with Excel, I have never come across that name, no. I'm sorry," said Kay, technically not lying.

"Has Simon Bell ever mentioned a Benedict Phillips?" asked Polly.

"You mean Simon my client?" Kay said. "Not that I know of." The complete total incompetent arsehole.

"Yes," said Polly.

"No. But in relation to what?" asked Kay.

"You're close, you and Simon?" asked Polly.

"Well he's about to sack me, but yes, we've worked together for years. A work husband. We rarely talk about anything other than work. It's all professional, all deadly boring. That's not a good description."

"The deceased is his brother-in-law," said Polly.

"It's his who?" asked Kay, baffled.

"Simon's sister was married to the deceased, Benedict Phillips."

"Simon's sister?" asked Kay, mouth wide. His sister, yes, lived near the Excel. Simon had been around there once after a meeting; he said he had to leave early. There had been trouble, he said, with his sister's husband. "Shall we get another drink?" asked Kay, suddenly perking up, anxiety slipping into excitement.

"I'll get these – it's my round," said Polly, standing up swaying. "Just thought that it might be a bit like you getting a job for your dad? Nepotism. Friends in the right places? Who you know?"

"No, no idea Polly, totally out of my remit –"

"Might be better to get a bottle?" asked Polly.

"Sure," said Kay; another bottle was just another bottle. One time, with Simon, he had said that his sister was a 'right one'. Pregnant at eighteen. Two bad marriages behind her. Simon had complained that he would be saddled looking after her and her kids. Simon? Kay didn't think he had it in him.

They decided to go home, but then there they were in another bar. It was dark and chrome and the stools were so high that you had to stretch to climb onto them. Loud music and long drinks now, fizzy in clear highball glasses. Kay should really have gone home ages ago, but it seemed Polly liked to talk. A relationship just ended. Stress of work. She thought Kay was frivolous and a bit shallow at first and wouldn't believe her Mulberry handbag was a fake; "a woman like you wouldn't have a fake handbag."

Then Kay was back onto her own mother. Seemed ironic to be talking to the police about her mother, somehow dangerous, reckless.

"Actually, detective, I don't know what to make of this. On Monday night I found a letter amongst her things. A love letter," shouted Kay over the top of the music. Polly came in close to look at the piece of tissue thin blue paper that Kay had brought out of her bag.

"To your mother?" Polly asked.

"No. Written by my mother, but it seems like it was never sent," said Kay, handing the note over to Polly, her empty fingers tapping out the beat of the song on the table.

"Is it to your dad?" asked Polly, turning it over in her fingers.

"No. It's to someone called Kenneth Spiers," Kay said, pointing out the name and address at the top.

"Oh, yeah," Polly said.

"Some detective," Kay said, trying to take it back.

"Careful, careful," Polly said, "this is precious evidence."

"Evidence of what?"

"Well that remains to be seen. Do you want me to look him up?" asked Polly.

The bar was somewhere on Old Compton Street. Kay should have known it, but it was familiar from an old, much younger life. Perhaps it had changed hands? A black taxi was easy to come by on this cold January night. Frost blistered beneath their feet. Polly put her arm through Kay's and they strolled, determined. They would drop Polly off first and then on to Hampstead. It wasn't really on the way but hey. They squeezed in side by side on the back seat.

Kay felt Polly's hands lightly on her neck, in Kay's hair line at the back. Polly started tracing a finger down and to the front of Kay's neck. Shiver. It felt good and Kay lengthened her neck. It wasn't a conscious movement. Then Polly moved towards Kay and she kissed her neck. Kay turned to her and said, "stop it." Kay could see the top of the driver's balding head. He must have been short.

The taxi shook along and Polly kissed her again. For a second time Kay said, "stop it," but something about the lack of severity in the command was not getting through. Kay looked forward. A green Christmas tree shaped air freshener was jiggling up and down.

Polly reached across and cupped Kay's left breast and kneaded and rubbed it. She pushed Kay's blouse apart and pushed her hand inside her bra. Polly kissed Kay's neck and moved forward onto her jawbone and as Kay turned to tell her to stop again, she put her mouth around Kay's lips, pushed them apart with her tongue, and was inside Kay's mouth.

Something dropped inside Kay, wanting, aching. Just as quickly as that. It surprised Kay how fast that feeling took over. Kay kissed her back. It was like Kay's mind was saying no, but her whole body was aching, cheering her on to go for it. 'Yes,' Kay's tits said. 'Yes,' Kay's lips said. Full on drunken snogging on the back seat of the taxi. Before Kay knew it, she looked down and her own hand was working away between Polly's legs. Kay pulled away.

"God, I'm sorry," Kay said. "We've got to stop."

"No," Polly said, "don't stop." She held Kay's hand and guided her to rub between her legs. Kay could see Polly grinding down onto her hand. They were both watching Kay rubbing Polly's pussy through her jeans, watching her getting hotter and hotter. Polly was stern when she said "you've got to come back to my flat," and Kay kissed her again. The taxi took a corner and they both fell to the right, nearly off the seat. No one laughed.

Eventually, Kay's senses took control and guilt over Julia resumed. Kay pulled away to the other side of the seat. Polly sat there breathing and said, "please we need to go somewhere." Then she pulled at the low V of her sweater and pulled it down to expose her right breast and she sat there, breathy and solemn, goading Kay to do something. So hot.

Oh sweet Jesus. The wanting. Kay hadn't had this feeling for years. Was she so neglected? By Julia? Polly's lips were so rich and juicy and she wanted Kay. Right there. Kay dropped to her knees in the taxi and took Polly's breast in her mouth and sucked. She licked it and moved her hands around Polly's arse and pulled her in towards herself.

"Rivington Street," said the taxi driver, not fussed. Kay sprang away.

"Thank you," said Polly to the taxi driver, and then to Kay, "are you coming in?"

"No. I'm going home," said Kay and suddenly Polly was gone and Kay stared out of the window into the black of night.

25th November 1994

My dearest Ken,
To see you again made me feel like a girl. I had forgotten that my heart could feel like that. Now I am sitting here smiling ,remembering the way you touched my hand. I've been thinking about the future.

I cannot walk away. No prison can keep me away, no mistake, no rules, no false promises can keep the love inside me from coming out.

All my love
x

CHAPTER TEN

5th November 1994

"A car is like a loaded gun," Kay's mother said, sitting in the passenger seat in the car park of the Galtymore in Cricklewood. She had the window rolled right down. She took a cigarette from the packet, held it between her teeth, and then lit it with a yellow plastic lighter.

She was scary when she was like this. Kay didn't know what she might do next. They had gone to get a McDonald's up the road and now here they were miles away. The green neon sign fibrillated. Her dad would go mad. They were in the new Ford Fiesta. Paid for on hire purchase and with a seventeen percent staff discount.

The air outside was smoky with fireworks. A group of lads had run through the car park and one of them was holding a rocket. It must have burnt. A boy that looked like Dave slid by the car deceptively slowly before jumping at Kay and banging on the bonnet.

"I said a car is like a loaded gun, Kay. It could go off at any time. Do you understand? You could kill people," Kay's mother said.

Kay pushed down her little foot to release the clutch and put the car into first gear. She looked in the mirror and released the handbrake. With a huge cough, the car lurched three feet forward in one single motion before making a screeching noise and stalling.

"Jesus, Mary and Joseph," Kay's mother said, throwing her

cigarette out onto the tarmac and rolling up the window. The tarmac in the car park was perfectly laid like the inky black keys of a grand piano. "Go again."

"I can't, Mum."

"You will, Kay. Now start the car. Be careful." Kay's fingers trembled as she turned the key in the ignition. Nothing at first, and then the engine pounced into life; her mother's cigarettes sitting on the dashboard rattled.

If a car was a loaded gun then surely she was too young to drive? Especially through central London at night? Kay left her hot and sticky fingerprints embedded on the wheel. Her bottom was hot from sitting on a lilac cushion out of the boot to give her height. Her mother smelled of gin. Kay could smell her own nervous sweaty palms, bubble gum and farts.

'This is the BBC news at 11pm. A fire has broken out at a fireworks display on Clapham Common. Twenty firefighters have been involved in fighting the blaze which began when a firework misfired into a hot dog van –"

"Bloody fools," Kay's mother said.

'Ronald Reagan has confirmed that he is suffering from Alzheimer's disease. The former President of the United States of America wrote an open letter to the people of America confirming his battle with the disease –"

"Shoot me. Jesus. If I get that then don't waste a moment's thought; just put a pillow over my face. Christ, if I ever get sick, don't leave me with that man and his out of date food."

"You always say that. Don't say that Mum, please."

"A pillow over my face – that's all I ask of you Kay."

"I'll use this cushion I'm sitting on, shall I? Save it for when I have to suffocate my own mother."

Kay gave the engine a rev. The lights flickered low to high

and back again against the shabby brick wall of the Galtymore. A man shot out through the fire escape. He was wearing a suit and tie, hard to make out in the dark but a camel coloured jacket that blew open and a dark brown tie.

He moved right in front of the beam of the headlights, disturbing the quiet of the crates of empty bottles stacked one atop the other. He brought the sound of the band with him – high treble, organ, tinny drums, sheer shrill of a cymbal.

The man ran a hand through his hair then set it to rest in his trouser pocket, one side of the jacket tucked loosely behind his arm. Behind him someone closed the fire escape shut, locking the man out.

Kay's mother wedged herself up, braced between the headrest and ceiling like Spiderman hiding in a corner.

"Let's go now," Kay's mother shouted.

"Now?"

"Yes. Now!" she said, and Kay tensed, concentrating on letting the clutch out and balancing the accelerator. Her mum reached across and pulled the steering wheel hard to the left and the car moved off like a jelly sliding off a plate. The man took a step closer and he put up a hand to stop them. Maybe he knew Kay didn't even have a provisional licence, never mind insurance.

"Never mind him," Kay's mother said, slapping the dashboard so hard that the magnetic crucifix fell into the footwell. Kay roared out of the car park in a hard left turn and the man banged on the roof of the car as she narrowly missed his body.

"Am I okay, Mum?" asked Kay, but her mum was busy looking in the mirror, leaning forward extending her neck left and right. Then she turned herself completely around to look back and rose up in the seat, almost to be seen.

"You can do anything, Kay. You're brilliant." Kay's mother was still looking behind. She turned back around and picked up the crucifix and reattached it to its perch on the dashboard. "There now," she said, smoothing her skirt with her hands.

PART II:

SUBMERGE

CHAPTER ELEVEN

On Hampstead Heath Kay looked up through streaming eyes. She fell forward and rested on one elbow. A thick tear of sweat ran down her back into the crease of her buttocks. Her nose was spouting mucus. Her heart was flipping and there was a bowling ball in her stomach.

She wiped her nose on the back on her hand, looked at the snail's trail of snot and collapsed onto her back. The trees above her were barren. An inside-out X-ray of the lungs, white cloudy sky populated by the interlocking black tributaries of empty branches.

"Get up," Dave shouted, and she rolled onto her front. She could see her breath in long white lines in front of her face, appearing and instantly gone, over and over again. The air felt like fire, slashing the inside of her throat, an inferno in her lungs.

"Water," said Kay.

"You've just had water. I don't want you to be sick again," said Dave. "Wait, I'll stretch you while you're down there." He lifted up her right leg, shook it, and held her foot at a right angle, more than right angle, more acute than that, in fact like it had never been stretched before. "God you've got tight calves," he said and he kept hold of her foot but crouched down, bending her knee up towards her ear creating an intense stretch in the hamstring.

"Christ, Dave," Kay said.

"Is that too much?" he asked.

"You're nearly inside me Dave," Kay said, and he laughed and swayed recklessly, almost losing his balance to fall.

When he laughed, his head lolled back into his neck. "Do you do this with everyone? Don't you find it a bit 'interpersonal'?"

"Shut up you helmet," Dave said.

"Helmet? I haven't heard that for twenty years. Seriously, my leg's going to snap," said Kay.

"—and the other leg," said Dave. Kay grunted a noise like 'oomph' as all the air left her lungs.

"You'll feel great later," Dave reassured her.

Her head fell back. There were hundreds of spiky spheres hanging from the branches of the tree like decorations. She didn't know what they were. It was too late for conkers. She was supine, in the mud, exhausted. Not for the first time. But safe, here with Dave.

"You know that bloke you were in the army with? That you shared a room with," said Kay.

"Which one?" asked Dave.

"In Cyprus," said Kay, "Benedict Phillips."

"What about him?"

"When did you last see him?" asked Kay.

"I haven't seen him for years," said Dave, running a hand over his balding head. For more than twenty years he had shaved his head and now it was really starting to go, he had begun to wear it longer. We always want the things that we cannot have. When Dave liked Jim Morrison and The Doors and he smoked loads of pot, he had hair past his shoulders. But then he went and joined the army and they shaved off all his curls, and his body went hard from the training, and he went from a soft lad to a strong man overnight.

"Why are you asking?"

"I don't know; he just came into my mind," said Kay. Should she tell Dave what she knew? Trust him? But Kay didn't know what she knew; that was the problem. So she didn't say anything about Belinda, Simon, the body, and certainly not DS Harvey, or Kay's mouth around her breast, the taxi throwing them to and fro. Kay wanting to pull away but locked onto her like glue. Thinking of DS Harvey made her hot, flustered. She was able to replay the entire taxi journey over and over in her head blow by blow, regardless of who or what was happening around her. She was back there now, Polly taking her hand and saying, 'no, don't stop.'

"I haven't seen him in years," said Dave, bringing Kay back to earth, "I don't know where, maybe at a funeral a few years ago."

"How many? Two years? Three?"

"Nah, more like five," said Dave, sweaty and angry, his normal 'go to' look.

"What was he doing?" asked Kay.

"I don't know,"

"For work," said Kay.

"For fuck's sake, I don't know," he sat back and upright. "I think he left the army and was looking after rich people. Bodyguard, driver. He'll have been going all over the world doing that sort of job. Making a lot of money."

Kay's mind flew back to DS Harvey. When Kay had woken up, it was as though she was still in the taxi. Her heart was racing. She could still taste her. She waited for Julia to leave the bedroom so that she could touch herself thinking about Polly.

"Turn over," said Dave. Kay rolled onto her front and he grabbed her legs again. She wasn't really sure what he was doing to her, but he had both legs bent at the knee held up to her buttocks, then he got her arms and pulled them behind so she was almost being crucified.

"I'm not thinking about that lot, and the army and working security and all that. I like what I do now. I don't want any hassle. It's all falling into place here with Ariana," Dave said.

"And tomorrow you'll be married," Kay said.

"Christ. Tomorrow. Who would have thought I'd be getting married?" asked Dave.

"'Course." said Kay, but her heart was racing again. It bumped and lurched and a sensation of vomit burned up her windpipe.

"You alright? What's the matter?" asked Dave. Kay spat out bile or mucus, a slimy white nothing. "It's the beginning of January, Kay. Most people are on a detox and you? You're hungover on a Wednesday morning. Watch yourself, you don't want to end up like your old man." The cheek. Suppose he had a point.

"I'm having a bad start to the year," Kay said.

"Oh, I know you had a bloody terrible year losing your mum. God bless her. Even so, you're going to have to snap out of it," Dave said, moving to the park bench and taking some long rubber band in his arms. He snapped it off the railings of the bench a few times.

"I can't. It won't let me," Kay said getting up, her feet squishing in rich wet mud.

"What won't let you? Hold the band. Both hands. Now pull, like this. Keep your elbows high," Dave said.

"It won't calm down. It's relentless. It's just one thing after another. The body they found, and then my dad screwing everything up and now I'm getting sacked. I've got a meeting this afternoon where I'm sure they are going to sack me and now it looks like –" Kay stopped short. She was going to say that now it looks like the body was Benedict, but she didn't. It would be in the newspapers soon enough, later today or tomorrow, once all of his family had been notified.

"And now what?" asked Dave.

"You know my client Simon Bell?"

"The arsehole?"

"Yes. Him. He's related to the dead person. Brother-in-law or something. They think he might be linked to what happened," Kay said.

"Really?" Dave asked, his face lighting up and bursting out laughing. "Higher, thirty of those."

"It's not funny Dave. I don't want to be involved in any of this," Kay said, dropping the band. "Don't tell anyone either. I'm not meant to know. It's confidential."

"Higher. How do you know?" Dave asked.

"I shouldn't say —" Kay said.

"Belinda obviously?"

"No," Kay said.

"Who then?" Dave asked, leaning back, quizzed.

"The police," said Kay. Dave put his arm out to stop Kay moving, then placed two small weights into her hands.

"Step up please," Dave made Kay step up and down onto the bench, "why are you talking to the police?" asked Dave. Kay ran hot again thinking about her. Don't think of kissing her, Polly's mouth, her tongue.

"I was..." Kay could hardly speak from exhaustion and lust and hangover.

"Now, start in the middle then run to each of the four trees, then into the middle to box me. Go!" Dave said, pointing out the four trees. Kay picked up her feet, trainers caked in mud, hot muscles tired but elongated, a post coital sensation running through her body. She slipped on mud and corrected herself from falling. If she went down now then she might never get up again. Stop thinking about DS Harvey. But I can't. I can't stop.

"What were you doing with the police?" shouted Dave, as Kay ran from tree to tree.

"Writing the statement for Excel."

"And he tipped you off about Simon?"

"She," said Kay. "She."

"She? Does she think Simon's done him in? Come back over here," said Dave.

"Well yeah, that's what they think at the moment, they don't know."

"Fucking hell, that's a turn out!" Dave was delighted. He pulled each of Kay's hands into a cherry boxing glove, tugging and pushing and smacking them with the heel of his hand to make sure they were firmly tied in place.

"What's she called?" Dave asked, pulling Kay's hands into him hard like he might pull them off. Her wrist and shoulder joints wretched. It gave a sense of urgency, as if she was being sent in to fight.

"DS Harvey," said Kay, "don't tell anyone."

"I won't. Poor old Simon."

"He's going to sack me whether or not he's involved with this."

"I should think you're the least of his worries. Now come on! Fucking hit me!" Dave shouted. Punch, punch and then a kick and then ten kicks in a row as hard as she could with her right leg into an oval pad Dave held above his hip. She kicked and that small oval became Jim Christie, and Simon Bell, and the Corporate PR Director, and all the other ungrateful bastards she worked so hard to please who were not worthy of her loyalty.

CHAPTER TWELVE

Outside Julia's Hampstead house was an unchained bicycle. The red and black of the Santander logo had been roughly painted over with matt black paint. It had been stolen from the municipal cycle scheme. A crime. Jim had 12 bicycles in the last six years and he was not buying another one. He had acquired this one from someone in the Golden Lion, who had stolen it from a tourist. Jim had never driven a car. Not legally with a licence.

Kay could smell cigarettes. Julia and Jim were sat at the island in the kitchen. They were both smoking. Jim had one lit in his skinny decrepit hands. His fingers were enlarged, round at the joints. The index finger of the right hand was stained yellow. The skin was taut and wrinkled like the skin of a fossilised mammoth discovered after a millennia. Jim was cured meat. Smoked and pickled.

Julia was bending her cigarette over backwards in the ashtray, like she used to do when they had first met. Bringing its white lower body back and over to meet its brown tip in ashtanga.

The ashtray was a relic too, just like Jim, but classy. Stolen from The Bluebird on the Kings Road in the mid-1990s when it was still cool to smoke. Julia pushed her fingers off from its solid round base. All the cool people stole them; it was thing to do – de rigueur. No one had smoked inside this kitchen since 1999, not to Kay's knowledge anyway, but she was beginning to doubt that she knew anything about anything. Two mugs of tea sat empty, drained of life; circles of aged tannic residue stained the insides. Behind Julia the kettle boiled again for a second cup.

Kay put her keys on the granite countertop. Jim heaved his head up off his hands using the giant weight of the counter as ballast from which to lever his freshly combed head.

"Tell me you didn't cycle here?" Kay said.

"My mate the taxi man was coming over this way. He dropped me at Archway and I cycled from there," Jim said.

"Your dad was just telling me what's been going on," Julia said.

"Has he? Has he told you why he's not contacted me since?" Kay asked.

"I'm here now, Kay," Jim said.

"Why haven't you told me what's going on?" asked Julia, and she stepped back away from the counter, gesturing for Kay to come out into the hallway with her. Kay followed and Julia lowered her voice into a tornado whisper. "Your dad turns up here and I know nothing. Nothing. About any of this. What the hell is going on?"

"I haven't had a chance to tell you yet," Kay said.

"Tell me yet? You should have told me the moment you knew," Julia shouted.

Mirasol, the housekeeper, burst in the back door carrying two huge shopping bags over her shoulder. In the other hand she held some clothes hangers in swishy plastic cases from the dry cleaners.

"Hello Jim, Happy New Year," Mirasol said, blowing kisses into the air at Jim.

"Mirasol, how are you?" Jim asked, picking something out of his tooth.

"Have you been alright since Mrs Jim passed?" Mirasol

asked, missing out the word died but settling gravely in front of Jim.

"Pah, you know. Terrible really," Jim said, expert in efficient chit-chat while relaying no real information.

"You had any luck backing the horses?" Mirasol asked. Julia tried to close the hallway door.

"You should've told me as soon as you heard," Julia shouted at Kay. Julia didn't mind having a row in front of Mirasol, or in front of Jim.

"Not now, Julia. I need to speak to him," Kay said, pulling the door back open.

"Speak to him? You need to speak to me," Julia shouted.

"You are not here Julia. You are off with Arthur in fantasy land," said Kay.

"I am working my arse off for this family," said Julia. Mirasol mounted the stairs with the dry cleaning trying to be invisible. She had left the shopping bags on the countertop. A plastic wrapped head of broccoli rolled across the counter.

"Now, girls, please, come on now, don't argue," Jim said, and Julia looked as though she might murder him.

"What a mess. He could be arrested, he could be in jail next Friday, and he's certainly lost his job," said Julia.

"I don't need a shitty self-help book to tell me my business is ruined and my reputation is trashed and it's because of him," Kay said.

"I told you that you needed to diversify. I can't remember how many times I said you needed to mitigate your reliance on one big account," said Julia. "I can't believe you didn't tell me, I really can't believe it."

"Come on Dad," said Kay.

"Where are you going?" asked Julia.

"Out of here," Kay said.

"No. You are not going anywhere," Julia said.

"I am. Come on Dad. Right now," Kay said.

"Run away, run away. What little plans you make, Kay."

Kay was engulfed by an uncontrollable temper; she wanted to lash out and scream. Kay scanned the countertop. Riedel wine glasses. No, too expensive. Too dangerous. Spanish style decorative fruit bowl. No. One of the last things Kay's mum had ever bought her. Magimix. Too heavy. Then she saw it. A siren red pepper. She threw it as hard as she could against the wall. It shattered unexpectedly; thousands of circular seeds scattered across the floor. It was in one explosive second, violently beautiful.

A bedraggled Jim stood on the drive. He pointed at the slammed shut door.

"I left my cigarettes," said Jim, patting down the pocket of his trousers.

"You can shove your cigarettes," Kay shouted and they walked down the street towards the shops, pushing Jim's stolen customised bicycle alongside them.

"Why couldn't you just phone me and arrange to meet like a normal person?" asked Kay.

"I thought it would be better to meet face to face," said Jim.

"Well it wasn't. We're not getting on very well. I don't need you messing it up for me even more. You've caused enough trouble."

"I didn't want to put you out," said Jim.

"Well I am put out Jim, you could not put me out more if you took me up to space, up to the international space station, opened the door, and pushed me out without an air supply, into the abyss. I wouldn't be any more put out than I already am," said Kay, as Jim gasped and then shrugged his shoulders.

Kay went into the newsagent's on the corner and bought twenty Silk Cut, noting the price. Ten pounds. Thank God she didn't smoke anymore. They crossed the road and into the actual garden of the Garden Gate pub; equipped for outdoor smoking all year round. There were wooden tables and an enclosed smoking area that ran the length of the pub. She sent Jim in to buy two pints, they had to wait for ten minutes until 11 o'clock for the bar to open. Not an unusual occurrence for Jim. She couldn't stay long, because she was meeting Simon for a meeting at lunchtime which she was dreading.

While she waited for him to return, she watched a bird sit in the arms of a spindly tree and then fly away alone. She watched person after person walk by the gate; none but her and Jim came in. She was chilling cold where her sweat had dried. A police car went by. She wondered where Polly Harvey was today.

"It's £4.90 a pint," Jim said.

"You're in no position to go off about the price of beer," Kay said.

"£2.75 in the Golden Lion."

"For piss water. This is Camden Brewery. Proper good stuff. Artisan. Quality. And it's Hampstead. Anyway, who cares? What do you want?" asked Kay. It was actually Staropramen, good imported Czech lager.

"You've got mud on your face," said Jim, as he licked his finger and reached out to Kay who shrieked and pulled away. He pulled instead a dirty hanky from his trouser pocket and made to dab at her with it.

"I'm fine. It's clean mud. I'm going to have a shower. What do you want?" asked Kay, as Jim took a long drink from his pint and licked his lips. He burped. Short like the first pip of the BBC news.

"Pardon me," he said and his face dropped to the floor. He lit a cigarette. His mouth seemed to chew, his lips parting and closing as if there was something in there, a hair, some irritant; he flicked it away with his tannic fingers. "I'm a useless idiot, Kay. I didn't think any harm would come of it. It was Christmas. It was dead," Kay screwed up her face at his choice of words, "dead quiet. I didn't think and you know, someone should have been watching me. You can't leave someone like me with all that responsibility. They're putting it on me. I did wrong but they're making me an escape goat. I'd never ever do anything to upset you. I didn't mean to do it. I had no idea. The police. Everything that has happened, I had no idea. I'm so sorry."

Escape goat? What manner of beast was that? But it was all he needed to say. The word sorry. They were silent for long enough to allow the anger in Kay to dissipate. It was easy to let go of any hatred for him.

"It'll be alright Dad," said Kay, and found herself pacifying him.

"Not me. You. I'm sorry for you, to you," said Jim.

"We'll get you a lawyer. It's not a crime. You'll be sacked without pay. It's gross negligence," Kay said, as Jim hung his head and chipped away at the peeling paint on the table top. Flaking, crumbling green, revealing beneath it something more stark and unforgiving – an old coat of scarlet red, lain hidden for years.

"Dave's getting married," Kay said.

"To your one? Blondie?" asked Jim.

"Yes. Ariana," Kay said.

"Better looking than the last one," Jim said, nodding in

approval. Then he appeared to well up with tears which he swallowed back down with beer.

"She's a lovely girl," Jim said.

"What do you mean?" asked Kay.

"You know, was a bit unusual wasn't it? What with her..." Jim looked for the right word, "job."

"What job?" asked Kay.

"I've said too much, and I don't know anything anyway. I'm just a silly old fool."

"It's a scapegoat by the way," Kay spelled it S-C-A-P-E. Jim didn't know what she was going on about. Jim shuffled in his seat as if he wanted to confess something else.

"Well, it's more serious than anything I know about, Kay. This whole business is rotten and you're better off out of it," Jim said, pushing out his chest. Kay finished her drink and stood up.

"I've got to go now Dad. I'm going to be late for my meeting with Simon."

Jim pulled back the pedal on his bicycle and got ready to mount it. He looked up at Kay, his face gone ashen.

"There's a missing girl."

"A girl missing? What are you talking about?" asked Kay, astonished. Was he that drunk, that maudlin, already at this time of the day?

"The fella that died. He had a girlfriend. A young French girl. Apparently she was a nurse at St. Mary's in Paddington. Anyway, she's gone missing," he said.

"And how would you know?" Kay asked. He threw one bicycle-clipped leg over the crossbar of his bike.

"The police told me. Asked me if I knew anything about her," Jim said. But it couldn't be true because wouldn't Polly have said? And wouldn't it be all over the news? And who would trust Jim with such information? No, he must be trying to get himself off the hook, look innocent so that Kay would feel sorry for him.

"But why would they ask you?"

"They're asking everyone. But only on the quiet. She's missing. A missing nurse." His eye must have caught a bird or a car, because he started looking out into the distance of the street.

"Do they think she's dead? Do they think it's to do with what's happened?" Kay asked.

"If she's not dead already, she soon will be." He mounted his bike and pushed off. He cycled down the road, slowly gathering speed, morphing into something small and insignificant.

CHAPTER THIRTEEN

They sat in a private nook at The Boisdale restaurant in Belgravia, underneath the ornate glass and mirror bar that protruded on the right hand side as if it had time travelled from 1920s New Orleans. It was as if she was seeing Simon for the very first time. Kay sat there and instead of Simon, her client of many years, she saw only Benedict Phillips's brother-in-law.

"You choose the wine Kay; I'll bend to your superior knowledge," said Simon. Kay searched his face for any echo of guilt, for the whiff of fear, for any fleck of anxiety. He was a basic man who couldn't feel; well that's what Kay had always thought. A wolf in sheep's clothing perhaps? But if Simon was involved at all, this would be better for her dad. It would look as if the entire company was incompetent and corrupt. Her dad would become insignificant as a result.

"Kay, choose the wine will you? You're miles away," Simon said. The waitress was at the table. Kay chose a bottle of Pouilly Fume; it would complement the acrid smell of cigars coming from the smoking terrace. The waitress had to pull the table out to allow for Simon's girth; this flustered him and he started to sweat even though it was cold outside. Was it guilt?

Kay believed that she already knew what he had to tell her so urgently. She didn't want to get sacked, but she didn't want any other nasty surprises either.

"What do you fancy, Kay? This one's on me. Have whatever you like," Simon said, and as soon as he had offered to pay, he had confirmed Kay's worst suspicions. He had never so much as bought Kay a coffee. She always paid for everything. He was covering something up. Kay couldn't hear clearly. Her mind was doing risk analysis.

"Kay," said Simon.

"Yes, Simon," she answered, coiled. She should stay in an open built up place like this. Don't go anywhere, and make sure that he doesn't follow her to the toilet. In fact, don't go to the toilet. Kay looked at her watch. Don't drink too much. If she didn't drink at all, he would know that she was onto him.

There had been no naming on TV yet. No announcement. The police were saying that they needed to inform family first, but they had known since Monday night and it was already Wednesday afternoon now.

Simon hadn't mentioned Benedict. To think, it was his brother-in-law lying out there in the cold, while Simon blustered around organising. He was a fucking cold, calculating bastard. And what of this girl? This girl Kay's dad seemed to think was missing? Could Simon have hurt a girl as well, enough to make her disappear?

"What would you like as a starter?" asked Simon. Kay had no appetite, but she ordered, playing along. Simon ordered something with snails and meat. He ordered a gin and tonic to quench his thirst and then he complained about his wife. Simon asked about Julia's book and kept winking as Kay gave a brief outline of the focus. He always winked when he talked about Julia. Kay imagined that when Simon was in prison, his wife might screw the milkman, the postman and the gas man. What other utility personnel could Simon's wife have sex with? TV repairman? Painter, builder, decorator obviously.

The waitress brought the carpaccio of beef. Simon dropped his shoulders, creating a rounded, ball-like shape, from head over neck and into back; he leaned over the tenderly plated meat like a bully over an easily felled child. The tiny silver cutlery was in his hands and he tore at the meat, a piece hung from his lips for a second, before he scoffed it back in, blinking, making a sound with the back of his throat. Kay thought about Simon on top of her. No. On top of his wife. He surely would look something like this when he was fucking her. Or, even worse, pulling at his own meat.

"This is delicious Simon, really delicious – would you like to try some?" asked Kay.

"Oh go on then. Bloody hell, I'm never going to get on this diet with you around," Simon said.

An hour passed.

"Simon, what did you want to speak to me about?"

"Kay, you know I respect you very much. I love working with you. That's why I wanted to speak to you in person, face to face as it were," said Simon, rambling on as if he was frightened to get to the point. Simon's face began to move in slow motion. Globules of perspiration sat on his top lip. His cheeks marooned. He loosened his tie. He belched.

"Excuse me," he said, and Kay became still. She was so bored by him that she became peaceful in anticipation, for the first time in days, perhaps for the first time in a year or more.

"So, I'm afraid that's it," Simon said. Kay missed it. Too many words; she had missed the ones that really mattered, lost in a sea of bullshit as so often the most important things were.

"Sorry Simon, could you say that again?" Kay asked.

"Kay, it's not my choice, but it's not working, and I can see that they have a point. This is official verbal notification that we will be ceasing our contract with you as of today," Simon said. Kay's eyes spiced. She knocked over the salt as her wrist seizured.

"For crisis PR?" Kay asked.

"Everything. All projects to cease."

"Consumer?" Kay asked.

"Yes."

"Trade? What about sponsorship?" asked Kay, now frantic; she didn't care in that instant who he might have killed or not.

"Yes, that too. It's a bloody murder inquiry Kay. This bloke had links to Abdul Bin Harashi," and to you thought Kay, "who knows who he was working for? This is as serious as it gets. Be glad to be out of there, Kay. It's a dangerous place," Simon said. Kay considered that he was setting her up. If he was involved then it would have been possible for him to get rid of the CCTV and link both her and her father by implication. He could get them both sacked to heap suspicion on them in the face of no real evidence.

"I've done so much for you, Simon," said Kay.

"Move on, Kay. Look, it was great work. A1 at the time, and now we need to move on and the business is changing and we are looking for different kinds of agencies to work with. As I say, the only thing constant in life is change," Simon said.

"I've had to sit here for an hour and a half listening to you go on and on," said Kay, finding her mettle. "Bin Harashi isn't the only one he's got links to, Simon. Oh yes, I know. They'll announce it any minute now; he was your brother-in-law. Benedict Phillips. Good luck dealing with the fallout from that on your own. A PR disaster. A right cock-up. Doubt the CEO will be happy when he finds out, and you're sitting here stuffing your face with me."

She wanted to lunge at him. Simon. Jim Christie. Benedict.

I'll kill you, Simon. She was surrounded by men laughing. Her whole life was spent listening to men laughing. A few feet away, a rotund head lolled backward, rolls of flesh giving way to sparse wispy hair and mottled scalp. Evacuate. Get out of here. Kay got up and left. Simon tried to stand and banged into the table. She ran out into the bitter winter sunshine. She put her hand up at the sight of a dirty orange taxi light.

Kay spread herself along the back seat of the taxi. She had a vision of herself with DS Harvey. What must they have looked like? There was a camera. Shit. Of course, they all had cameras on their back seats these days. She could almost feel Polly's mouth on her neck again.

Kay telephoned Belinda. She would give her enough information to hang that ungrateful bastard with.

"They think Simon Bell's got something to do with it," Kay said, hanging onto the handrail as the taxi swept around the corner.

"No way," said Belinda, abruptly stopping tapping on her keyboard. "Who's they?"

"It's true," said Kay. "I'm in shock. Can you believe it?"

"How do you know?" Belinda asked, her voice shrewd and inquisitive.

"I can't say how I know, but I can say that the police are onto him," said Kay, "they are collating evidence, probably to make an arrest." Kay didn't know if that was the correct terminology but if you said it slow enough, she found that people tended to listen.

"So the police must have told you?" asked Belinda. "You wouldn't have phrased it like that otherwise." Bingo.

"Yes alright, whatever, please do not quote my source. The main thing is," said Kay, "and this you'll be able to verify

yourself, is that Simon's sister Karen was married to Benedict
Phillips. That he is the father of her children. And she had a
restraining order against Benedict."

"That's a good tip off Kay; I'll be bunging you some cash for
that if it follows through."

"Just a favour, is all I want," said Kay. "Can you look and see
if there's a missing person? A nurse? She's French apparently and
worked at St Mary's in Paddington. I don't know her name."

CHAPTER FOURTEEN

6th November 1994

Kay got ready in her dressing room mirror. It was dark wood.
Plastic. Wonky hinges. A hand-me-down from her cousins,
where three of them shared a room. Imagine. It was pushed up
to the window so it took light out of the room and cast its
macho brown shadow across Kay's flowery wallpaper.

She pushed her face closer into the mirror to inspect for spots
and if she found any, eliminate them. On the shelf, there were
short green jars from the Body Shop and a paper tub of Japanese
washing grains. She had make up – not a lot compared with the
other girls but enough to make it look like she was bothered.

She had an electric shaver in a blue leatherette pouch. It was
beautiful and looked like something from the 1950s. Once there
had been an electric light in the secret alcove that housed the
mirror. It was like a confession box, dark, hidden. A place that
no one could overhear and while she was getting ready she often
talked to herself, counselled herself, and made decisions. She
leant forward, onto her knees, threading her fingers together
to pray.

Just a quick prayer this one, because she had seen Dave
circling outside on his bike. He had packed in his BMX and
was riding an adult man's bike now. He turned his knee out,
slowed down with open stance and went round in a long circle.
He never knocked at the door. If Kay didn't come out within
ten minutes, he would just go away.

Jim didn't mind Dave. He liked him. He knew his dad

who worked at Ford's, and occasionally drank down the pub. Kay was an only child and Dave was like a brother or a cousin, except that they rarely shared a bad word, such was the way they rubbed along – the same but different. Dave hated that other boy who had been circling. Tom Slack. What a name. Kay had seen him at the shops by the Golden Lion and he had followed her home. She had never seen him before, but apparently he had lived around there for ages.

Dave knew Tom Slack from football. It was an embarrassing mistake. Kay had sat out late talking to him, out the front, when it was mid-summer, boiling; they must have been out until nearly ten. Jim looked annoyed when he went out to the club at eight o'clock as normal and instructed Kay and 'the boy' to call it a night, but they just stayed out there chatting.

Tom Slack wasn't too bright and the next time they had gone to the park together, he had got her up against the wall at the back of the playground. He was thrusting and rubbing his region against her and she couldn't ignore it, because all of his focus and attention was willing her to notice. She wished she had said that she had to go home.

But Kay didn't. She didn't want to let him down. She didn't quite know why. More like she didn't want the embarrassment or the confrontation, better to just do it and get it over with. Better to get some experience under her belt. Apparently Dave had already had sex with an older girl in the lower sixth. He was very quiet about it. He hadn't told Kay, which was nice she supposed. Every other boy his age would be shouting about it from the rooftops.

So out it came, pulled out from the top of his grey tracksuit bottoms, this thing with a bright red helmet. Kay was shocked. Literally, was it supposed to be that colour? And nothing over the top, no foreskin or whatever it's called. God knows. All she could was do was sort of rub it up and down as she had been shown how to do on pornos and told by Dave and all the various other people at school who talked about wanking all the time. She didn't really think about his pleasure but he seemed to be enjoying himself with his meaty long tongue stuck into her mouth. He tasted of salt and vinegar crisps and beef burger, as his tongue stabbed back and forth.

Several times her front teeth banged his. He made some measly gesture to push her down, but really fuck that; she wasn't having any of that. And afterwards, she thought there was a funny smell on her hands so she wiped it on a grassy patch and rode away quick, the flag on her bike blowing in the wind.

Dave was appalled that she had wanked off Tom Slack. Spitefully, he said that she would get known as a slag and that she needed to watch herself. But Kay knew that was the least of her worries. She had wanked Tom Slack like a robot on the production line at the Ford Car Factory. A wanking machine. It was nothing. She had taken no joy in it. If this was sex then she was finished.

And then it dawned on her one night during The Gentle Touch, watching Jill Gascoine with her mum. Just a feeling, an excitement, something she didn't know. Gascoine's perm, her waist, her mouth. She was so beautiful and strong. So Kay had taken to prayer, and on her knees on the pink shag pile carpet inside the balsa wood confessional, she joined her hands together in prayer.

"Father, Son and Holy Spirit,
Dear Jesus,
I haven't much time.
Dave's waiting out front.

Please, please, please don't let me be a nun,
And please don't let me be a lesbian.
Amen.
And I appeal to the Blessed Virgin Mary on this too.
Amen."

Kay opened a clear plastic bottle in the shape of the Virgin Mary that her auntie had brought back from Lourdes in 1982. The lid was a blue crown. She drank from it. It would never poison you, would never go bad.

Kay wrote the prayer on a piece of pale blue note paper from a Basildon Bond pad, wafer thin for Airmail. She tucked it into the plastic wallet with a picture of Padre Pio, and a piece of his sandal. A genuine and holy relic. It would get heard sooner. Padre Pio would work to ensure she turned out normal. They were all praying hard for the beatification of Padre Pio.

Occasionally Kay and her mum would pull out a kitchen chair and kneel either side, eyes closed, glassy blue rosary beads clasped in Kay's hand. Her mother's rosary was black and old, her own grandmother's, and there on the laminate floor they would hold their own Holy Novena.

Later that afternoon, Dave and Kay were in Dave's garage. Well Dave's dad's garage. It was a scary private lock-up underneath the flats where Dave's dad lived. There was a ramp down and then a tunnel of garages, lit only by fluorescent tube lights which made a humming noise. It was subterranean, like being in the bowels of a ship. A small Italian man waved at them and said something Kay didn't understand while holding up a terracotta pot he was varnishing. Dave slammed shut the doors of the lock-up.

There was a loud sound. It was such an archetypal fart that

Kay couldn't tell whether it was an actual fart or an impression of a fart Dave had made with his mouth.

"Dave," Kay said.

"Sorry," whispered Dave.

He held the joint in his mouth, the burning end much wider and smouldering orange. He cupped Kay's face with his hands and she lifted her mouth up to his and he pushed the end in and she cupped her hands too. His hands were long and thin. He was more than six feet tall at age fourteen, his head a mass of curls.

He blew into her mouth and Kay inhaled smoothly at first and then coughed because it was hot. An inferno in her mouth as she took down the hot, ashen smoke. Dave pulled away and like a surgeon, extracted it from his own mouth; on his haunches he turned over the joint on the ground side to side to get rid of any ash.

A blotch of matt black oil the shape of France had soaked slowly into the cement. You could still smell its sticky sweet tar. Dave was sat on a decaying wooden garden chair and Kay on a yard of green swirly carpet leftover from someone's front room. Dave had decked the garage out as a place to sit around smoking and drinking cider. He let lots of kids use it. A dim greenish light came in through two windows in the side. The window rattled in the wind where the putty had perished and fallen away.

"I'd better sit down," said Kay, wobbling.

"Bit strong that," Dave said, raising his eyebrows and looking into the burning ember of the joint's end.

Brandy barked and then ran to the door and pressed his snout to the tiny gap that ran along the bottom. Dave was up at the door, bending to push Brandy away from his legs so that he could get out of the door fast like a shot. There was a noise outside and then Dave came back in holding a boy by the scruff of the neck. Kay knew the boy. He was off the estate, just a snotty little kid probably trying to get friendly with Dave. He winced in pain. Dave had hold of his ear and was almost bending it in two.

"Caught him spying, Kay. What are you doing spying on us you little fucker?" asked Dave, and as he spoke he twisted his wrist so that the boy's ear spiralled around tight and he squealed.

"You left your keys in the door," the boy said, opening his hand to give Dave his keys.

"Dave, stop it. You're hurting him!" Kay said. Dave gave one last twist and flick of the boy's ear before setting him free. The boy's hands went up to grab the side of his face, eyes prickling with tears, the entire side of his face blood red. Dave kicked him out of the door, a proper kick.

"Now fuck off!" Dave said, returning to his haunches.

"Your temper," Kay said.

"I know and I'm stoned. Mr Mac says I'll have to go in the army."

"Best place for a lunatic like you," Kay said, soothing Brandy who was sat in front of them whining, his head cocked to one side, concerned eyes trained on Kay's face, wanting to go to the park. Kay held out her hands.

"It's alright boy," said Kay, and Brandy stood up and went into Kay's side, nuzzling in. Kay lifted her head as Brandy licked all over her neck and face. Kay dug her fingernails into Brandy's blonde fur to scratch and the dog's head went back in ecstasy. "I feel so guilty doing that in front of Brandy."

"Smoking?"

"Yes, smoking weed. I feel guilty doing it in front of Brandy."

"Pity you didn't have Brandy in the park with you when you wanked off Tom Slack," said Dave, and Kay laughed. Smoke evacuated Dave's nostrils the way water leaves a whale's blow-hole. He bent down onto his haunches; his tracksuit made a sound like a tent being taken out of its bag. He had taken to wearing a cyclist's cap, like the ones they wear on the Tour de France, bright yellow, with the peak turn up with a tuft of curl coming out under the front. Kay's hair stuck to the carpet as she lay back and laughed. Brandy hopped about barking, nudging her with his nose to stroke him, but her hands were grabbing her own aching sides.

CHAPTER FIFTEEN

At Kay's Paddington office the team had all left on time. The first week after Christmas they would be attempting to maintain a new work life balance. New gym membership. No booze. Cauliflower rice and decaffeinated tea. Kay looked around the desks. No one had turned their computer off. She could tap her foot to the buzzing hum. She spat her cough sweet into the bin. Frank had a packet of cigarettes in his desk drawer for emergencies and she took one, lit it, and waltzed back to her office.

Should she phone Polly? Tell her that they should never see each other again? Remembering her mouth and a kind of rollercoaster kiss where Kay went over the top as Polly kissed her. She phoned Polly from an office phone. No answer. Of course she wouldn't answer. Kay had been rehearsing scenarios of what she would say; we should never meet again; I am married; we could go to a hotel.

"Hi Polly, it's Kay Christie. Remind me never to go out drinking with you again. I feel dreadful. Just ringing to see if you are OK," said Kay, leaving a message on her answerphone. She turned on the TV. Kay liked to watch Sky News. Kay's mobile rang immediately.

"Hi Kay, I just missed you," Polly said.

"That's alright, I was just ringing to see how you were," Kay said, choked with awkwardness.

"Well, physically and emotionally I'm still a bit fragile," said Polly. She was somewhere with the noise of lots of people and telephones ringing. She was probably still at work at the police station investigating Simon.

"Me too," Kay said.

"It just seemed to escalate very quickly," Polly said.

"Well don't give it another thought; it's just something private that happened, that I think we should put behind us," Kay said, willing Polly to say again, 'no, don't stop.'

"Yes, sure, yes," Polly said. But what about the intense sexual connection they had? Kay couldn't have imagined that? Regardless of how much they had drunk.

"We'll probably laugh about it sometime in the future," Kay said, knowing that she would never ever laugh about it. Do the right thing. Kay was running out of right things to do. "Look, I wanted to call you about my mother's letter. I really need to get that back off you," said Kay. "I don't even know why I gave it to you."

"Yes, I've got it here. It's safe, don't worry."

"Don't post it, I don't want it getting lost," Kay said, trying to create another opportunity to see Polly.

"I won't. I've got to go in a second – there's a lot happening here this evening," Polly said. Kay agreed it was about time they named him and it was all out in the open with Simon. Kay wondered if they might refer to this girl that her father had talked about.

"Look, I am interested in the letter, which is why I called. But if I'm honest, I really just wanted to talk to you," Kay said, lighting up another cigarette and wincing with embarrassment.

"Hang on," said Polly, moving. The pitch changed; she was now somewhere quiet and echoing, as if she had gone into the bathroom for privacy. "Carry on talking."

"I don't know really. I'm just going to say it. I mean, I just can't stop thinking about what happened," Kay said.

"Right," Polly said.

"I don't want anything from you. I don't want you to say anything and I don't want anything to happen, but I just can't stop thinking about it, and about, I suppose, you," Kay said.

"Look, I've put it down to the drink," Polly said, puncturing Kay's hopes and offering relief and sanity at the same time.

"Oh, OK."

"It wasn't there before. So it was the drink. Like it wouldn't have happened if we hadn't drunk so much."

"That's true. You're right." Kay was dying for a drink.

"You need to be strict on yourself. Your mind can just go wild with these things," Polly said. She was very strong-willed and powerful.

"I've never done this before," Kay said.

"You can get carried away, thinking too much, going over it," Polly said, but Kay was already remembering herself kneeling down in front of her and Polly begging her not to stop, asking Kay repeatedly to come into her flat with her.

"Yes, you are right, but –" said Kay.

"But what?" asked Polly.

"But it was so hot," Kay said.

"I'm embarrassed," Polly said.

"You've got nothing to be embarrassed –"

"So it's lust?"

"Yes," Kay said.

"Look, you're married. It's not good for anyone."

"Sure."

"You should block it out of your mind. It's just not worth

it. With my work and your partner, and your family and everything," Polly said.

"OK. Let's forget about it," Kay said, and heard a kerfuffle at Polly's end. A man was calling her back and there was the sound of a door opening and muffled conversation.

"I have to go. There's going to be a big announcement. We'll speak again sometime," Polly said, as Kay, bereft, stared into the TV.

Main story. Six o'clock news. Images of the world spinning and a grey suited sombre announcer.

"The body of a man discovered in London's Docklands has been formally identified by police."

Kay dropped the cigarette in a mug of lukewarm coffee.

"Former British soldier Benedict Phillips, age thiry-seven, was discovered in deep water at the Excel Conference and Exhibition Centre on Sunday morning. Police have announced the launch of a formal murder investigation."

The DI appeared, his eyes squinting against the glare of lights. Kay couldn't see Polly in the camera's viewfinder.

"We are appealing for information about Mr Phillips's movements prior to his death. Mr Phillips was a decorated member of Britain's armed services. We are keen to hear from any friends, colleagues or associates of Mr Phillips who may be able to help us paint a picture of his lifestyle as we continue to investigate circumstances leading up to his death," the DI said, and the pictures switched back to the studio and the solemn presenter.

"Mr Phillips served with the Royal Gloucestershire, Berkshire and Wiltshire Regiment in Kosovo as a UN peacekeeper, and had undertaken three tours in Afghanistan. He leaves behind two young children."

There was no mention of a missing girl. Kay's father was a stupid drunk; he must have got it wrong. Kay scrambled back to her computer and opened the file that Belinda Salas had sent her. Kay had pleaded for it and Belinda didn't want to share, because she shouldn't have had it in the first place. Someone in the mortuary had been paid only £200 to hand the information over. Kay swore it was for her eyes only and it truly was. A photograph of the body. Head clearly visible, close up. Chest hair sprouting over the top of the white sheet that covered his body.

The side of his head where an ear had been hacked off was sheared. There was just a flap of skin where the ear should be. The entire area was surprisingly lacking in blood, which had been washed away.

Froth tinged with red had come out of the nose like a melted fizzy sherbet ice lolly. Kay didn't know how that could still be there, but Belinda had told her it comes out once they've taken the body out of the water.

The face looked wet, like it was sweaty but ill sweaty, not sports, more like a fever or druggie dancing on ecstasy. Wet curls were stamped to the side of his head. His hair had receded completely on top after all. Mouth closed. Kind of fat, swollen cheeks, neck, even forehead rounded. She avoided looking at the eyes because they were open and strained, white red yellow. Kay didn't want to look there. Made her bilious and chilled to the bone.

It was clear it was him. The hair alone. The swarthy wet look and frothing spittle she had seen before. She dropped her head into her hands and sobbed. Bringing her head back, she felt that there were no tears, only a prickling in the outer corners of the eyes. She realised that this water forms when you laugh. It was the kind of glistening prickly tear that Olympic medal winners get when they cross the line, the kind that mothers have when they push their baby out, the glorious tear that a rescued sailor has when he thanks his hero.

Kay was thrilled sick. She turned up dance music through her computer speakers. She got up and danced. She ran around the room pumping her fists.

"Yes," Kay shouted. "Yes. Yes. YES!"

Whatever happened next, Kay knew that the world would be easier to live in with him not in it. For that private precious moment there was euphoria for Kay. Sweet ecstasy.

CHAPTER SIXTEEN

7th November 1994

Kay cycled up the street against the tide of queuing traffic. The wind pierced her thin navy jumper. Her legs were red raw at the knee where her socks had fallen down. Her keys were painful in her shoe, but it was the safest place to keep them. Tracey Grubb was outside the comprehensive. She was a foot taller than every other girl her age with boxer's hands. If she caught you, she would tax you by taking all your money and possibly even your bike. At weekends her cousin came from Ladbroke Grove and if you got caught, they would take everything, even your trainers.

"Your mate's a nutter," Tracey Grubb shouted, flagging Kay down. She would have to stop. Otherwise she would catch up with her another time. "Your mate. What's he called? Dave? A nutter."

"Why?" Kay asked, surprised by an unusual camaraderie, nay respect, emitting from Tracey.

"He's broken Tom Slack's nose. Went mental. Properly beat him up," Tracey said, impressed.

"No," Kay said, shocked.

"Fucking temper on him. A right wrong 'un. Are you going out with him?" Tracey asked.

"Tom Slack? No, well, I just —" Kay began to go back over the sordid details.

"No. Dave. Are you going out with Dave?" Tracey asked.

"God no. He's my best friend. We grew up together."

"Do me a favour? What's your name again?" Tracey asked.

"Kay Christie."

"Kay, do me a favour yeah? Put in a good word for me. Tell Dave I want to deal with him," Tracey said, patting Kay on the shoulder. In Tracey Grubb's vernacular, 'deal with him' meant 'kiss', and probably a lot more.

As the shock of Tom's beating subsided, Kay picked up speed again and thought about the prayer. Why on earth would she write that down? What had possessed her to write something so incriminating? She prided herself on being savvy and she had written that down in her own hand. She had to go home now and get it. That morning at school Sister Mary Joseph had been doing an introduction to the law in Humanities. She had explained different kinds of evidence and that something written in your own hand was a confession.

Kay had a terrible feeling. Fear and panic. She shared that Padre Pio piece of sandal with her mother, more or less, whenever she needed it. Her mum propped it up against the telly when the football was on. It backfired badly when Ireland played Italy in the World Cup, for obvious reasons. It wasn't safe. She needed to get that holy relic back with its dirty secret. Take out that prayer and burn it and not write anything down again. She needed to return home and get it.

Normally she could go a back road but she didn't have time; she needed to be back before the end of lunch and no one would miss her. She had asked Claire Notting to tell Mrs Cohen that she had a heavy period and had gone to sit quietly in the chapel. That should buy her the hour she needed. Claire was solid. Shin pads, double thickness hockey stick bag. On the hockey field she was a bamboo cane that flexed under duress and sprang back leaner, hungrier, and harder. Kay thought about her a lot.

Kay took the corner of the street like a racing car driver.

Outside her house tubs bubbled over with flowers. They dripped, dipping flowery heads, from one pot onto another. A pastel ceramic boy peed into the lawn smiling. They were starting to give off a viscous vegetal odour of decay.

The lawn looked like it had just walked away from the barbers, short back and sides. No one would be at home. She pushed her finger down the side of her shoe and lifted her heel. She panted like Brandy after a walk. She let her body lollop as she took in air to replenish her aching lungs.

She put the key up to the lock and froze. Kay froze. Someone was home.

She stalled herself at the door. Burglar? Jim? Mum? Auntie? She removed the key like she was pick-pocketing the lock and flattened herself. Her back was against the wall next to the window. There was music. Sounded like Irish music, same jaunty air. But not, more…she didn't know, sad? Kay recognised the music:

'Please release me, let me go. For I don't love you anymore.' It was by Engelbert Humperdinck. Kay's mother treasured this record.

She peered one eye around the blue wooden window frame. She pressed her face against the buff white brick. It was hard, dry compacted, and left a line of pure gold grit on her cheek. She could clearly see inside. The lights were on; a halcyon warm pink light floated. As if on a carousel, her mother rotated slowly.

Rotated. Slowly around. In the middle of the room she was dancing. Old-fashioned dancing. But close. Not the slackened outstretched arms of the waltz. They were pressed together. Her eyes were closed. Was she crying? He was tall. He held her in both arms like he might squash her, but tenderly. How? Tender how? He looked down at her hair. Pushed his mouth, chin, cheeks into her hair. One hand came up and stroked her neck. Then further up, a finger wiped away a tear from her cheek.

Kay recognised the gait, the confident stance, hair swept back. It was the man from the car park of the Galtymore.

Release me and let me love again.

CHAPTER SEVENTEEN

The Marylebone room at Mayfair library. The Old Marylebone Town Hall was closed for refurbishment, not that it mattered with no other guests. Kay stood poised at one side of the room and then crossed six paces to the other. The sun had come out after all. She would have to stand with her back to the light; she was not a professional but she knew that much. Julia sat in one of the four chairs lined up in front of the desk. She folded her legs, one over the other, cabaret, lips pursed, a shoulder raised, she winked at Kay, and flared her nostrils as wide as the channel tunnel.

"Beautiful," Kay said from behind her camera lens. Julia used to be really funny. She used to laugh a lot. When your worth is measured in what you look like, then it's harder when you age. Trapped, trying to regress, going desperately against nature.

The newspapers had all followed Belinda's story that Excel Marketing Director Simon Bell was the brother-in-law of the deceased, now identified as Benedict Phillips. Simon had given the first announcement to the media on Sunday. More coverage popped up all over the internet. Tales of domestic violence. Simon threatening Benedict in the street retold by a neighbour on ITV News. It didn't look good for Simon. Which was better for Jim. For everyone. Kay caught a glimpse of his fat arse hightailing it out of the Mayfair office. In all likelihood, he would be getting the sack too. If not today, then another day when the HR department sanctioned it.

Then at lunchtime, Belinda called. The police had made an

arrest. Simon was in custody. That's all they were saying. Kay was stunned. It was all over. It had been Simon all along.

As a thank you, Belinda told her that she had found a record of the missing nurse. She was from Normandy. A town called Deauville with a promenade and race track and probably a casino. Kay had wanted to go there for years. There was a family waiting for her. Her name was Valérie Lagarde and she had not been seen or heard from since Christmas Eve.

Behind Julia were twenty rows of empty seats, covered in white linen with bows at the back. Kay imagined her own wedding to Julia. Jesus. An inebriated Jim passed out at the front; Kay's mother in a wheelchair, defecating; Henry and Olivia with the rings; and half of Hampstead's media elite amused on the other side. Forget it. That's why they had never done it. Now she didn't have to worry about her mum, but there was still the question of Jim and another question festering at the edges of Kay's imagination: Would she want to marry Julia after all? Was Julia asking herself the same question about Kay?

"Couldn't they have got a smaller room?" asked Julia. Kay shrugged, bent onto one knee, difficult in a dress and heels; there was no one to see her knickers so she squatted slightly on her haunches, pleased with her own flexibility. Holding it with both hands she angled the camera up towards the vase of lilac flowers and clicked away. Please don't say anything about us getting married, please, please. Kay's phone beeped.

"Turn that off," said Julia.

"I can't. It's got the music on it," Kay said. Maybe she could get tablets to relax? It was too late for yoga. She needed to be medicated. She would call the doctor. She had been offered counselling when her mum was dying, but she had laughed it off. Now she knew that she needed strong medication and therapy.

"Remind me to make an appointment with the doctor, will you?" asked Kay.

"Turn that bloody thing off will you for two minutes," said Julia. Kay held the telephone up in the air.

"It's got the fucking music on it. Cher, for when they come in," Kay said.

"Cher?" Julia laughed.

"Yes, Cher," Kay said. Heels tapped across the marble floor. Big wooden doors slammed shut. Kerfuffling noises gathered pace. A large blonde woman in black entered the room.

"The registrar is with Ariana and Dave. I'm Natalie – I'm the assistant registrar."

"Julia Rothman. Pleased to meet you," said Julia, and held out her hand. Her nail polish was muted grey, to match her dress, which had long sleeves and elegant ruching pulling the fabric of the dress to one side. Simple. Stunning. "And this is Kay Christie," Julia said.

"Are you the only guests?" asked the assistant registrar.

"Guests, witnesses, friends, employers," said Julia.

"Can I ask you to turn your phones off please?" asked the assistant registrar.

"I will, once I've played the entrance music," said Kay. "It's Cher."

"They bought the cheapest package, I'm afraid. No music," said the assistant registrar.

"They wanted a quiet wedding, but not a silent one," said Julia.

"I'll let you play it off your phone, OK? But you need to turn the phone off once they've come in," said the assistant registrar.

"Thank you," said Kay. "It just wouldn't feel right without Cher."

Lighter footsteps approached. The registrar entered first, a small woman dressed in black carrying an important looking book.

"Hello, I'll just get settled and then I believe one of you is going to play some music, is that right?" she asked. Julia took the phone and readied it in her hand as Kay moved in front of the entrance.

Dave was in a grey three piece suit with a striped tie of the Royal Gloucestershire, Berkshire and Wiltshire Regiment, beige, navy and a tiny line of red. Ariana wore an extravagant Spanish lace vintage wedding dress. Julia struggled to catch her breath, but eventually she closed her mouth.

"Beautiful. Wonderful," said Julia, her words merged into Cher's 'I've Found Someone'.

Kay knew Ariana's sister straight away. She looked like a squashed version of Ariana. The same sad brown eyes but etched with something. Kay didn't know what. Kay couldn't tell whether she was older or younger. She had mousy coloured hair instead of the peroxide blonde that was Ariana.

Despite the empty chairs and the vicious assistant registrar, Kay become infected by Dave and Ariana's happiness. Dave whispered something in Ariana's ear. She giggled. They didn't look behind. They didn't acknowledge the empty seats.

Kay did an impression of photographers she had seen working. She followed the action, interrupted.

"Look this way," said Kay. Everyone was happy.

"Sign here please," said the registrar, "and now the two witnesses will sign here." Kay and Julia went around the desk. Beautiful fountain pen.

"Let me take one of you signing, Kay; Julia you stand behind," said Dave. They left by the far entrance and as they came out under a marble archway Julia threw confetti up into the air and Kay snapped away. Vans on the Marylebone Road honked their horns. Two African tourists stopped to take pictures. The next wedding party congregated under a plume of smoke.

Kay drove them from Marylebone to the Oxo Tower and on the way Dave and Ariana sang to Katy Perry, Ariana's favourite. They raised their glasses, said cheers and ran inside. Only one photograph out there on the windy balcony.

Their table was turning an orange-pink with the first hint of sunset winking from the west, sun slung low. Julia had arranged a delicate plate to share, with cold meats, Cornish crab and whitebait, adorned with purple and yellow micro flowers. It was beautiful. Dave ordered ribeye steak. Ariana, Rhea and Julia had seared tuna, samphire and seaweed salad (the lowest calorie option on the menu) and Kay had a large gin and tonic. Two glasses of champagne. She ordered a bottle of Albarino for the girls and a good glass of Aussie Shiraz for Dave to wash down his steak.

"On behalf of my wife and I," said Dave, Julia and Kay clapped, "I would just like to say that there is no one else we would have wanted to share our special day." Julia lowered her eyes and clasped her hands together in delight. "Thank you so much for all you've done for us. Not just today. Always, but especially today," said Dave. A lump collected in Kay's throat.

Kay supposed that she must be lucky to have these lovely people, family, surrounding her. But she didn't feel lucky. What was her problem for God's sake? She would stop complaining, worrying and enjoy her life. She should get a dog. If she couldn't have a child then she would get herself a dog. She would stop caring about work. It was just a job. Just. A. Job. Kay went out onto the balcony for air. Rhea, Ariana's sister, followed her out to smoke.

Kay stood on the balcony of the Oxo Tower. She wondered about throwing her phone from up here, how far it would travel into the Thames.

"It's a beautiful view," said Rhea, blowing out a jet of smoke. Her eyes seemed to bore into Kay. "Do you come here a lot?"

"Sometimes for work," said Kay.

"Exactly what business are you in?" asked Rhea.

"PR," said Kay. "Public Relations. Marketing, we're a marketing agency."

"Yes, Ariana told me. She's done well for herself," said Rhea, inhaling long from her cigarette, "but why would you employ Ariana?" she asked, puzzled.

"Ariana? She's my assistant, like a secretary I suppose," said Kay, and Rhea shook her head, eyebrows raised. Her mouth was a cheery smile and her head was pulled back almost in shock.

"Well that is good news," she said, "she looked lovely today. That's our grandmother's necklace, and the earrings. We don't have much from our past, but we do have those."

"She looked beautiful," said Kay.

"Is he a good man?" asked Rhea, "Dave?"

"Well, yes, of course," said Kay, and he was in his own way. What was his best characteristic? "He's very loyal."

"He must be loyal. He was a client of Ariana's in Pristina, so you worry what kind of man does that," said Rhea. What on earth did she mean? Kay didn't want to ask, with them sitting there and in love. What was her sister trying to say? She didn't get a chance to ask, as Rhea made her excuses and left.

"Come inside," said Julia, holding open the balcony door.

The heat hit Kay. Her chest flushed with blood, opened up like a rose into a sea of red discoloration. The waiter pulled back her chair. She sat on her serviette; she pulled at it with one flexed hand, ready to punch, slash and lash. She waited for them to ask. Ignored their concerned faces.

"Why didn't you wear your uniform?" asked Kay. She knew that he had worn it recently, that he liked to don it for special occasions. Dave put his arm around Ariana.

They had had enough of uniforms apparently. Kay picked up her glass, swinging it with intent, wanting to ask them why. Julia held up her glass and toasted the new couple.

"Dave. Ariana. Congratulations," Julia said, and she turned to Kay. "I love you, Kay, I really do." Maybe she did really love her. Maybe she did.

"Ah. Such a wonderful couple. How many years?" asked Ariana. Kay put her elbow on the table and rested her head on her hand. Was she bored? Bored of telling this story? Bored of never being the most important thing in Julia's life.

"Too many," Kay said.

"Ten," Julia said, and she shifted in her seat, her body facing Kay, ready to recount the story of their meeting in the way that people who have been together for a long time like to do.

"Wow," Ariana said.

"We have an official and an unofficial," said Kay.

"Dave did say there was a sort of on and off period to start with," said Ariana.

"They were work colleagues and then yoga buddies weren't you? Always going away on yoga retreats together. Didn't you even go to an ashram in India one time? When Julia was still married?" asked Dave, and he snorted into his wine.

"We were secret lovers," Kay said.

"It's not common knowledge," Julia said. "We tell people that we met after Arthur and I divorced. Better for the kids."

"She had me trussed up in a flat off Ladbroke Grove," Kay said.

"Kay. It was a hard, scary time but tremendously exciting," Julia said, running a slow finger around the rim of her glass. She looked out over London and then turned to focus on Kay. Kay was starting to get tiny wrinkles around her eyes, "a decade."

"A decade of my life spent with you," said Kay and she saw a memory of Julia on top of her in her old flat in Ladbroke Grove. Julia's hair tickling Kay but unraveling everything she had ever expected her life to be like. The skin on her shoulders, the smell of Julia, just intoxicating and classy.

"You haven't put that in the Ex-Factor?" Ariana asked.

"Certainly not. No one needs to know, not Arthur. Not the kids," Julia said.

"How did you two meet?" Julia asked, unprompted but typically and perfectly timed. Kay couldn't have done better herself. Kay sat up to listen. Dave and Ariana were silent, as if waiting for the other to answer. Not speaking for each other. Dave put out a flat palm to encourage Ariana to speak but when she opened her mouth, he started speaking himself.

"On the internet. Didn't we babe? We talked for a long time. We were emailing each other. We clicked, I couldn't stop thinking about her, and eventually we fell in love. And I said to you, you've got to move here, and then you moved here didn't you darling?" said Dave.

"Yes I did, I moved here," said Ariana.

"Amazing. And you were in Albania at the time Ariana?" asked Julia.

"Kosova. I was in Pristina when we met," said Ariana,

looking intently at Dave. Serious. Not smiling. The intensity was growing. Kay grew fearful that they wanted to consummate the marriage there and then.

"Excuse my ignorance Ariana, but Kosovo, is it a 'vo' or a 'va'?" asked Kay, trying to break down the forces of their passion. A suitably controversial question which was sure to induce a more potent reaction. On they went discussing Kosova and the occupation but all that Kay could hear, ringing in her ears like wedding bells, were the words that Ariana's sister, Rhea, had said outside;

'He was a client of Ariana's.

In Pristina.

You worry what kind of man does that.'

And what kind of woman does that?

The desserts were displayed on fine white china. No wedding cake. Shavings of white chocolate and gold leaf. Julia poked at the ice cream and heaved up a big spoonful but instead of eating it herself, buoyed by love and romance, good food and wine, she slipped it into Kay's mouth.

At first, in shock, Kay's jaw didn't open and it hit her teeth. Kay did not reject the advance. She opened her mouth readily. Jumped at it. Their chairs had grown closer together, the way shoes move under the bed in the night. Julia's arm came to rest on Kay's leg.

The sun dipped before it turned night's corner. The glow caught Julia across her upper torso and neck as she was smiling. Julia split her sides laughing at something Dave had said. Kay missed the joke, but she laughed, body vibrating because she wanted to be part of it too. Julia slid and knocked a fork and Kay jumped to pick up and set it down.

"Don't worry," Kay said, and they resumed their positions

with Julia's arm on Kay's leg, Julia chattering away about Arsenal football club.

"You may be wondering," said Julia, patting a huge box next to the table, which was wrapped in elegant green paper with turquoise birds of paradise and was as high as your knee, "what is this large box? Congratulations. Ariana, do you want to come around here and open the paper?"

Ariana got up, tucking her lace train under her arm, back around to her right, curving like a thin white cat turning to lick its back. She stepped sideways behind the chairs, bent at the waist like an American oil well drill, her hips the hinge, dropping to plant a kiss on Julia and a large cuddle from her long arms, which Kay always found unexpected in very tall thin people. She could feel their linear frames through their clothing, like wobbling on the boney crossbar of Jim's bike as a kid. Julia was muscular. Sinewy. Lithe. If Julia was an animal, she would be a cheetah, a gazelle, a lioness.

Ariana peeled away the paper. It ripped a steely line across the white box beneath.

"Oh!" she said and she breathed in. "Oh, beautiful." She breathed again, a theatrical heave of her chest.

"I hope you like it," Julia said.

"Oh it's beautiful," said Ariana.

"It's Vera Wang. The designer. She's done a range for Wedgewood. It's a limited edition, the whole set, I just thought, or rather we just thought it would be lovely for you have a proper dinner service," Julia said.

"Magnificent," Ariana said; it was a word that she had learned at her English classes, paid for by Kay. Kay wasn't sure Ariana would know who Vera Wang was. Kay wasn't sure herself. Kay did know that there weren't enough Veras in the world. When she got her dog, she might call her Vera.

"Julia thank you. This is so nice," Ariana said, and her eyebrows spiked and stretched, two arched wooden bows overextended above her round doll-like eyes. Sheer joy. To Kay's knowledge, Ariana had no mother, no father and only this one sister Rhea who hardly spoke to her. Kay recalled that Ariana had said once that her sister was judgmental, and now Kay knew that to be true. But what was her sister being judgmental about?

She lifted up a plate. White glistening china. Beveled edging in a gunmetal grey, silvery in appearance. A row of tiny delicate dots. Julia had impeccable taste. Even Dave was smiling because he knew that he now had finer plates than he ever thought he would have in his life. Kay imagined Dave lapping up his Sunday dinner from one of those plates, perhaps even dipping white buttered bread into the gravy.

Kay imagined Ariana serving Dave his gravy. In full makeup of course. An apron perhaps, and in the comfort of their own home, nothing else. Quickly, Kay imagined them having sex. Dave and Ariana. Obviously Dave on top, hard army thrusting with an angry face. Kay had heard him shagging Belinda a few times before and it had sounded like that. Belinda squealing in delight and words, talking, instructions.

Then she imagined Ariana on top riding Dave like the whore of Babylon, massive smile, posing for the cameras. Perhaps calling his cock 'magnificent'. Kay had never seen Ariana without makeup. Not ever. They had shared a room in Dublin for a meeting and right before bed, when Kay was contact lens-less and tucked up, Ariana had replaced the make-up with layers of cream, eye mask and a net over her hair. It seemed far-fetched that someone would make so much effort.

CHAPTER EIGHTEEN

Later that same evening, Kay leaned against the wall of the lift.

"I like your hair like that," said Kay, as Julia fixed her hair in the mirror. Julia pouted. She was drunk and giggly. Julia took Kay's hand and kissed it. Kissed inside the fleshy enclave of her thumb, down the exposed inner wrist. Slip away. All anger. Forget. Work. Please just go with it Kay, try and get back to normal. Kay put her lips on Julia's; they parted slowly. Soft mouth. Familiar. But it had been so long that she could be a stranger in a lift. Then they were palm to palm, and breast to breast, with elongated breath. Could you still get breathless for someone you had been with for so long? Theirs had been a full on erotic whirlwind. Hotels. Cars. Parks. Everywhere and at all hours. Danger. Excitement. Giving way to social acceptance and a shared home in Hampstead. All that they had ever wanted.

"I want you now," said Julia.

The lift bobbled on landing and the metal doors fired open. They had stayed late after Dave and Ariana had left. On his own wedding night Dave had left at 6pm. He had pulled Ariana by the hand and said, 'we have to go now', looking deadly serious and she obeyed like a mindful wife. They had gone and a different night had been spliced onto the day. It was raining heavily. The way London rain is more colourful than anywhere else on earth. It seemed to trap the fluorescent bubble of the city and red bus braking lights in the length of its droplets.

The entrance to the Oxo Tower was a dreary, trying-to-be-arty lobby, open square, old warehouse cum gallery but down here at this end of the Southbank, with its mixture of council houses, offices and galleries – a wasteland of sorts and not a taxi in sight.

Julia wrapped her arms around Kay. Kay held the umbrella. The taxi company was busy. Busy. It was only a Thursday for goodness sake. They would be 40 minutes and could not even guarantee that. Kay would have tried an Uber but Julia was against them for ethical reasons and Kay didn't want to spoil the moment.

A hotel? No, they needed to get home. Everything depended on it. Julia held Kay's face, pulled it, kissed it. This public display was alien to Kay, but she embraced it, kissed back, one eye looking out for a taxi. They were just two glamorous but arguably middle-aged women snogging each other on a dark street in the rain. Kay loved London. Love. Love. Love. Must get home. Julia's hands unbound. Then she was laughing. Pulling away and then back again into Kay's neck.

She saw it before she thought of it. Long, silver, sporty, old, and not flash but cool. It was her car. She had planned on leaving it there and picking it up the next day. It was a naughty thought, but desperate times call for desperate measures.

"I don't feel that drunk, Julia," said Kay.

"Huh?" asked Julia.

"The car's just there," said Kay pointing, acting out as if the idea was just occurring at that second. As if it was the logical next step.

"Kay. No," Julia said.

"Honestly, I'll be really careful, you're getting soaked," said Kay. "Let's just get in it for a moment to get out of the rain."

It was freezing. Kay put the key in the ignition and the radio purred. The voice of Grace Jones punctuated the drill of rain on roof. Seemed to fire it up, remix the scene. Julia tilted her head back and bit her lip.

"Love this song," Julia purred, and she started dancing in her seat. Shoulders lilting one way and the other. The window steamed up. Windows so scarred with droplets, she couldn't see out. Julia bit her tongue between lip and teeth.

"I wish I had a cigarette," Julia said, still dancing. One foot raised, her heel on the dashboard. If Kay put her foot on Julia's dashboard she would have been killed. But it was not the time to split hairs. It was sexy. It really was. "And cocaine. Years since I've done that, I'd love to have a line of coke," said Julia.

Kay needed to decide. They could meander to Soho in search of cocaine and dancing. It breeds itself. Fun. The more you have, the more you have. And vice versa. But Kay was wearing high heels.

The other option was to have sex. To get home quickly while the aroma of possibility hung in the air. To get Julia upstairs, the door locked, to get her naked on the bed. Or partially clothed; actually that would be more urgent. Kay believed that somehow it would press a kind of reset button in their relationship. That afterwards they would be back to normal. Better than normal. Free of stress. Moving forward again. It was a moment that needed to happen.

No Soho. Home. Now. The music went off. Kay started the engine. The music blasted back to life again as Kay put the car in gear.

"Well bloody be careful," said Julia, but it was fake, flat. It was the no that meant 'yes'. Kay needed to get them home and she would be really careful. She would drive so slowly that she wouldn't be able to smash a drop of rain never mind anything else. It wasn't far. She would go over Blackfriars Bridge. Then straight up. Towards Farringdon. Then Kings Cross and then you are more or less up into Hampstead, just go through Kentish Town and then they would be there. Dump the car. Don't tell Dave. Holier than thou Dave. Don't tell him for God's sake. Old paleo work-out-army-discipline-follow-the-rules Dave. Julia heaved up in her seat and put her hands around Kay's torso, feeling her tits and she started kissing lower down Kay's chest and then up to her mouth.

"That's decided then," said Kay.

The car was floaty. No bumps in the road. Not much traffic. They meant to keep the music quiet but Julia was wired in. She was dancing alone for the benefit of Kay. It started quiet, it did, but it got louder and louder, incrementally, bar by bar. Kay looked at her speed. 24mph. She would have to drive a bit faster, because this was too obvious. She stood out like a sore thumb. Just put her foot down. Just ever so slightly. Julia wound her window down over Blackfriars Bridge, her face pushed out into the rain; splashed and smeared with water Julia screamed, "yeah." She turned up the music even more. Kay turned it down from a control in her steering wheel. They passed a petrol station and Kay was going to go in for cigarettes but thought better of it; if they smelled her and witnessed Julia salivating in the passenger seat... Kay would forego the cigarettes.

"What about the coke?" asked Julia, slurring as she turned the radio up.

"They don't sell it at petrol stations," shouted Kay, laughing.

"Always working, must call my client back, teacher's pet. Goody fucking two shoes. I couldn't believe you'd do what you did, couldn't look at you again after I knew what you did."

"I didn't do anything," said Kay. There was a new blot on

Kay's copybook. A new misdemeanour that Julia knew nothing about.

"Who cares now, anyway," said Julia, pulling up the hem of Kay's dress and putting her hand up in between Kay's legs. Forceful. Kay swerved the car, just a foot or so, enough to pull it over the right.

"Julia! I'm driving," Kay said and Julia threw her head back and laughed. She could have caused a crash. Kay had nearly rammed the car up the curb and into a lamp post. The swerve had made Kay sway into the oncoming lane. So stupid when she was trying to be careful. Maybe they should have gone to Soho? The way Julia looked she might be too drunk for sex anyway by the time they got home.

Kay looked back to the road ahead and saw him. A policeman. In fact not just one policeman, but several. A pack of policemen. She didn't know the correct terminology but she knew she was fucked.

CHAPTER NINETEEN

It was the early hours of the morning when they rode home, finally, in a black cab. Over and over, like a mantra, all Julia kept saying was; 'my radio show. My radio show.' The policeman was a child. He looked like one of Henry's friends. The way Kay saw it, the problem was Julia. She kept saying as much.

"It's your fucking fault because…No. Shut up. Hear me out. I was driving fine. But if you hadn't put your hand up my skirt."

"Dress," said Julia, "it's a dress."

"Dress then. Then I wouldn't have swerved and that's why. It was nine o'clock on a Thursday night for Christ's sake. We are two white women. Middle-aged white women," said Kay.

"I am not middle-aged," said Julia, "thank you very much."

"Yes we are. I'm nearly forty years old, and you are, well, we're not really sure are we? But you are well over fifty," said Kay.

"I am forty-seven," said Julia. She was not. "My radio show. All I ever wanted. My career was back. Back where I wanted it to be." She started to cry, no sobbing; she just held her face up to the sky in the direction the morning sun was coming up.

"We should have just booked an Uber, but oh no we couldn't do that, could we? The police were looking for people with no tax, no insurance. They weren't even looking for me, only I swerved," said Kay.

"You shouldn't have done it Kay. You shouldn't have been driving. No matter what," said Julia.

"All I had to do was drive in a fucking straight line. That's all I had to do. Oh God. Oh God. Oh God. I'm sorry. Will I go to prison?" asked Kay.

A car is like a loaded gun.

CHAPTER TWENTY

7th July 2006

Dave had made his way from barracks on the other side of Cyprus. He just pushed open the door of the apartment, because Kay had left it on the latch. She turned, frightened, then screamed in delight.

"You are so thin," Kay shouted. He was still able to lift her up with one arm. In the other he was carrying a large black canvas holdall, it's thick strap garrotting his left shoulder. He had clearly been working out. His face had muscular contours around the jaws. Kay could see tendons in his temples like she was looking inside him at his inner workings. His head was shaved bald; a microcosm of stubble was sprouting, rebelling against the tedious rule of its enforcing masters.

He smacked through the door on both sides. He could have taken the wooden skirting with him, left a rugged imprint in his own shape where the door once was. There was sweat under his arms and down the centre of his back. He fell backwards into the chair and splayed his arms and legs like a giant cross.

"I should've got a taxi," said Dave.

"How far have you walked?" asked Kay.

"I didn't think it was this big, Paphos. Three miles I'd say."

"In this heat?" Kay asked.

"The bus station is in the old town," Dave said.

"Anyway you're here now," Kay said, and she ran over to the kitchenette and opened the fridge. "Beer?"

"Beer? Yes please," he said. She crossed back over with two

golden cans. Dave grabbed his. It instantly became small in his hands. It frothed up. He put his mouth around it to stop it spilling all over the floor.

"Your mum is going to be so jealous I've seen you," Kay said.

"I've been so excited," Dave said.

"You are lucky I was back up here. I only came back to get my book," Kay said.

"Where's Belinda?" Dave asked.

"By the pool. I'll shout her now," Kay said, going back through the kitchenette and over to a glass door. She stepped out onto the tiled balcony and shouted, "Belinda. Belinda!"

Belinda turned around to see who was calling her. Her breasts rolled over, pertly pointing to the balcony where Kay stood. Her brown little body hissed in the sun like a Christmas turkey basted and ready for eating. Her nipples were pink, her skin puckered caramel, her tattoo a dark murky green, her thong illuminating her crack in vibrant scarlet. In the children's pool, a mother covered her small son's eyes.

"Is he here?" Belinda shouted back.

"Yes," Kay said.

"He's here. He's a day early. Oh my god, oh my god, oh my god," she sang to the football tune of 'here we go here we go here we go'. She jumped up and pulled on her bikini top, placing her feet into dainty jewelled flip flops; she rummaged in her bag for something, a mirror, lipstick, looking panicked as she mopped the sweat from her perspiring face.

Kay brought beers, and then Dave got out a bottle of vodka that he had carried with him in his bag. He had been saving it from Duty Free. Kay went and got two large bottles of cola from the bar across the street. They were cold and sweet and the glass frosted with wet ice. They moved onto the balcony, squashed together, toasting like winter chestnuts on a street vendor's grill. Kay could smell their skin browning.

There were only two chairs. Kay took one, stuck to the seat. Belinda sat like a starfish on Dave's knee. She held up a copy of the newspaper to the sky. The sun beamed through so that you could see the type from both sides at the same time, making it illegible.

"What about you then, Kay, are you still gay?" asked Dave.

"Not just gay – she's into geriatrics," Belinda said.

"What's this then?" Dave asked.

"Older woman," Belinda said, writhing on Dave's lap.

"Belinda!" Kay shouted. "Stop it!"

The sun lengthened its stride and the shadows spread out. Kay's skin had started to become crisp. They were interrupted by a knock at the door.

Dave held his hands up.

"Don't look at me, I'm pinned down," he said. He tickled Belinda and she giggled. Kay huffed and got up. Standing outside was a man, short, dark hair, young, but you could see the rounded peak where his hair had started to prematurely recede. A black rucksack on his back. He asked for Dave. His face was fleshy. There were two lines from his nose to the ends of his mouth. He was simian with hairy arms.

"He hasn't told you I'm coming, has he?" the man asked.

"No," Kay said.

"I'm Lance Corporal Benedict Phillips."

Dave couldn't place the conversation where he had agreed that Benedict was coming. They went back and forth and eventually Dave relented and said something welcoming like, 'you're here now mate.'

Benedict had brought a crate of beers and though things

were a little awkward, they soon settled down, once they had a few drinks under their belts. Dave put his arm around Belinda. It seemed to Kay as though he wanted to give off a sign to Benedict that he was with Belinda. Belinda was focused on Dave, focused on their forthcoming consummation. So, where did this guy think he was going to sleep?

Belinda begged Kay to take Benedict into the bedroom so she and Dave could be alone together in the living room. Kay didn't want to stop their fun; she liked the idea of her two best friends being together. They had crafted the setup to suit that scenario, but they had rules. Kay could not share her bed with a strange soldier friend of Dave's. No way. Belinda became moody. She slept with only a tiny thong, on the outside of the sheets, buttocks floating in the warm stream of air from the open window.

Kay preferred it just the three of them. When you know people very well, it's easy to be on holiday with them. Benedict sat with his legs open. Insisted on being called by his full name. He chewed gum incessantly. Dave and Belinda threw a ball to one another in the pool. Kay burrowed into the book; she could smell Julia on every page. She wanted to call her. What if the husband answered the phone? Or the kids. No. Better not. The book had been, most probably, in Julia Rothman's bedroom. Oh. She could call her and say it was something to do with work. No. Don't.

"What are you reading?" Benedict asked.

"Cloud Atlas by David Mitchell," Kay said, clutching the silvery raspberry cover. Julia had brought the book around the night before her holiday. She had said that she thought Kay would enjoy it and then later while on the bed told her it was just an excuse to see Kay. Julia had said that she was married and a mum and this was impossible. Kay had replied that she was free and it was up to Julia. Kay knew, they both did.

"What's it about?" Benedict asked.

"I don't know really, it's quite complicated," Kay said honestly.

"Well you must know what it's about, you are reading it," Benedict said.

"It's like several stories, all linked but —" Kay said slowly, because she was thinking about how to best explain it while she spoke.

"Or, do you think I won't understand it because you think I'm thick?" Benedict asked.

"No," said Kay, "not at all."

"Has it got lesbians in it?" Benedict asked.

"Pardon?" Kay asked.

"It's just that Dave said you're a lesbian and you're really into that book so I thought there must be lesbians in it," Benedict said.

Kay got up, closed her book and went up to the room on the proviso of going to the toilet. Benedict leant back in his red plastic chair. The two front legs came up off the ground. He adjusted his sunglasses and drank one of his beers. Brush it off. It wasn't that offensive.

Kay squirmed in her seat at being left alone again with Benedict. He spread himself in his chair opposite and scratched his head where it receded in a widow's peak. Odd for someone so young. Funny little monkey man. He wanted to ask Kay a question. Asked if he could ask, which was ridiculous because how could Kay say no without seeming defensive?

"Are you definitely sure you're gay?" he asked.

"What's it got to do with you?" Kay said.

"Hey. Come on. There's no need to be like that. I'm just asking." His face was beaming from side to side. "Have you got a girlfriend?"

If Kay disengaged it would seem rude; it might cause a row and ruin the night, better to put up with him.

"Yes I'm seeing someone," Kay said.

"Bet she's nice looking isn't she?" Benedict asked. It was such an odd feeling to talk about Julia with this person. He was enjoying thinking and talking about this. She wanted it to stop.

"Yes, I suppose she is," Kay said.

"And it's not a phase, no?" Benedict asked.

"No," Kay said.

"You don't miss cock? No?" Benedict asked.

"What? No," Kay said.

"When's the last time you had dick?" asked Benedict. Kay thought of leaving then. She just wanted to really get up and go, but she was rooted to the spot.

"Don't know, can't remember," Kay said.

"Couldn't have been a big one then. Did you use to like it?" asked Benedict.

Kay was stuck like glue to his questions. To slap him down or leave would be rude? No? She wanted him to go away. Why couldn't she swat him aside. Something too direct about him. No shame. No empathy.

"Would you have a threesome?" Benedict asked.

"You are disgusting," said Kay.

"Me? I'm just asking. That's all, don't take offence. We're just having a conversation," Benedict said.

"I'm going now," Kay said, finally getting up.

"Kay, Kay, come on, I'm only having you on, banter, come on, I'll get you another beer."

Walking down the strip, Kay thought about how much she wanted to get home. He had ruined her holiday. Why did Dave invite him? But of course he hadn't – he had just shown up. She told herself to concentrate on getting a good tan. Sunbathe all day long. She wanted to look good and as soon as she got back to London she was going to invite Julia around. There were only a few days left.

The next morning Belinda had been in the shower. Huddled, it was a tight squeeze. A tiny square box. She told Kay later she had been washing her hair. Soaked. Suds up. She opened her eyes and Benedict was in the doorway in his shorts. One hand on the door where he had pushed it open. The other hand over his cock. He was doing nothing. He was just standing there watching Belinda in the shower. They discussed it and decided not to tell Dave, because they didn't want it to get nasty.

It was a stupid idea.

For sport, the plan was to pretend that Kay had changed her mind and did fancy Benedict after all. A U-turn. As it turned out, he was very easy to fool. It only took Belinda to mention it and he was clapping his hands together saying, 'I knew it, I knew it.'

It was after midnight. They had all had a lot to drink. He smelt like spiced aftershave and meat. Kay lay back on the bed and beckoned him over. He took a step towards her.

"Wait, wait," Kay said, "I want to look at you." He shuffled from one foot to the other. The apartment was silent, the bedroom dark. "Take it off," Kay said, "all of it." He stood there and undid his trousers. Pulled his shirt over the top of his head. And the boxers too. He pulled them down to his ankles. Red candy striped boxer shorts. His penis was erect and flayed over to the left hand side with a strange bend. It had reared up. Was pulsing. All those weeks stuck in the steaming hot Alexandra barracks in Dekahila. Hair gathered in a matt between his belly button and dick. Thick. Dark.

It was hard to see at first, but when Belinda stood up and threw on the lights you could see it all, the hair, banana dick, his startled face. It took him a moment. Enough time for Belinda to click away with her camera. He was kind of coughing, eyes sprung open, blinking, then teeth gritted. Kay couldn't tell whether he was disappointed that he wasn't going to have sex or whether he was embarrassed about his body.

He stumbled pulling his boxer shorts up. He was really drunk. His feet wouldn't work fast enough. Belinda collapsed onto the bed with Kay and they laughed together. She sat up and took more photographs. Bum. His balls seen through the gap in his legs. Anus. How they laughed. Because really they both hated him, and they understood clearly his view that they were holes to service him. And they laughed because their plan had worked so beautifully. They were best friends, the best of best, on holiday, high jinks, Benedict deserved it.

"I'm going to wet myself!" Belinda shrieked, cackling away, crossing her legs. They didn't see him picking up his clothes, but they heard him calling them bitches over and over again. It made them laugh more. Dave had come into the room. He had known what they were planning and let them get on with their joke, kept out of it, played dumb.

They had wanted to teach Benedict a lesson. He might stop or leave and they could enjoy the rest of their holiday. They were still laughing when he came back in pointing, cursing and calling them slags.

"You think you're funny? You think you're funny do you?" Benedict shouted, still slurring despite the shock. Dave called him out, put one bulky hand on his shoulder and one around his waist.

"Come on mate, they're just having a laugh," Dave said.

"Fucking bitches," Benedict said with one long string of spittle gushing out of his mouth. His feet came back up off the floor as Dave carried him out.

"We're on holiday. Come on mate. They're good girls. Leave it," Dave said.

The next morning Benedict was gone. There was no note. Dave hadn't heard him leave, which wasn't surprising, because he slept like a log. Belinda had stayed in the room with Kay thinking Benedict was still there. His backpack was gone. There was no trace of him.

In the café across the street, over a full English breakfast, with tea and white toast and strange amber margarine, Dave worried that they might have upset him. He said that he should never have let them do it. That Benedict was known for being a bit touchy.

Chippy.

Narky.

That Benedict Phillips could not take a joke.

CHAPTER TWENTY-ONE

Hyde Park. Polly's dog was black and tan. His name was Reggie. He was old. His eyes were like those in a child's toy, black round pools with a thin splash of bright white all the way around. He held Kay's gaze until she shyly looked away. Kay rubbed his chest.

Polly was feeding him organic food so that he would last longer. She was worried about his hips. She was giving him cod liver oil. One spoonful a day. At first she was mixing it in with his food, but he loved the taste and he had started taking it right off the spoon.

The geese surfed to a stop right in front of them. Miniature waves splashed up under their seats. Though it was cold, they sat outside the hexagonal shaped café, right over the water, because they couldn't take Reggie inside. Kay didn't have the right coat. She had spent most of the night in a cell, and then on release had a day of tears and accusations from Julia before collapsing with exhaustion at nine o'clock. She couldn't sleep properly anymore, and saw that isolated image of Benedict with fizzy red liquid coming out of his nose. She woke obsessed that Polly would know Kay had been nicked. But so far, Polly hadn't mentioned it.

Polly wore a trendy insulated blue coat that matched her eyes. Kay could tell it was expensive. She came out of the café and put down two white cups, a thick funnel of steam emitting from the tiny drinking slit.

"Don't burn yourself," Polly said. She wore fingerless gloves.

Kay hadn't seen them since 1992. Polly took them off and gave them to Kay to try on. "Are you cold?"

On the way, Kay had created a list of questions in her mind that she was going to ask about Benedict Phillips. She was going to ask Polly about the investigation, and about Simon. She was chewing it over in her head about telling Polly that she knew Benedict and also telling her that she had been done for drink driving. Is it excusable to drink drive? Especially after their last meeting, Polly would think her an alcoholic, and maybe she was right. Kay couldn't sustain lying to anyone else, or keeping any more secrets.

Kay supposed that she could say that she had known him as Ben Phillips, friend of Dave's, and that she hadn't put the two together. Polly pulled her chair next to Kay, so that they sat seamlessly side by side. Polly unzipped her coat; Kay sighed, lustfully remembering the last time they had been together.

"Kenneth Spiers," Polly said. "Here. He still lives in the same house in Queen's Park."

Relief.

"Really?" asked Kay, amazed. She had forgotten about her mother's letter. "Does he have a criminal record?" Kay didn't say 'like me?', but she should be more fearful of police. This could get out of hand. She shouldn't let Polly delve into her life in this way.

"Nothing serious. He was arrested at a picket line in 1979 at the Ford car plant in Dagenham. A fracas. Charges later dropped. Only a caution," Polly said.

"That's where they worked, my mum and dad," Kay said.

"So it is definitely the same man. He was involved in local council so that's where I got the pictures. You could have found all this on the internet yourself to be honest."

Kay took out a large black and white photograph. It was years since she had seen the face, but seen it she had. At the Galtymore for one. She couldn't be sure, but his outline, his shape, matched. She had seen him through the window dancing with her mother. This same man. And now she saw him, she realised that she had seen him other times too. She just couldn't remember when.

"Do you recognise him?"

"I know his face, but I can't place him."

"Shall we pay him a visit?" Polly asked.

"No. I mean how? What would we say?"

"We won't actually speak to him. When you see him in the flesh, you'll know what to do. We'd just sit outside."

"You and me?" Kay asked.

"Yes, surveillance," Polly said. They arranged it for the following Sunday morning – a time when an elderly man is bound to be at home. Polly wanted to spend her Sunday morning with Kay? Kay could hardly hold back a breathy, screaming 'yes'. Julia didn't want to share the same universe. Every time Kay tried to go near her she shrieked away.

"Thank you," said Kay.

"That's settled then," said Polly. Polly would have to drive, obviously, with Kay now pending a ban. Not a good idea to get behind the wheel again for a while or be in a stake-out with a policewoman. Thank God for London transport.

"How is your work, Polly?" asked Kay.

"Awful," said Polly.

"But you've got him. Simon. You arrested him," said Kay.

"Didn't you see the news? We've had to let him go." The news made Kay dizzy. They would let Simon go free. He mustn't have done anything. Then someone else did it.

"Why?" asked Kay.

"It's a fuck up. The press got onto the Simon Bell connection too quickly," Polly said, looking pained.

"Yes, I saw it on the news," said Kay, wide-eyed; she had told Belinda in a fit of anger at Simon.

"Well you know what happens, and the hierarchy called in the DI and put on massive pressure and there was circumstantial evidence and a previous history of violence between the two." Violence? Simon was an idiot, but violence? Should she feel guilty? No. He sacked her. He deserved it.

"Simon couldn't account for three key periods of time in the week between Christmas and New Year," said Polly.

"So that's when it happened?" asked Kay.

"In the days over Christmas we think, when they had reduced the security team, as you know."

"So where was he?" asked Kay.

"You've got to keep this to yourself," said Polly.

"Of course I will. I didn't say anything about Simon to the press if that's what you're thinking?" asked Kay. There was a smothering sensation around her neck; thankfully she was too covered up for Polly to see the red rash of shame swelling up her throat.

"No? I only told you, Kay," Polly said, laughing. "Of course I'm joking, I don't know where it leaked but these things happen."

"Huh," Kay said, in a half laugh, her insides rotating.

"But you're not going to like where he was." Oh fucking hell, why? What next?

"He was with Jacquie McCoy."

"My Jacquie? Working?"

"Did she work over Christmas?" Polly asked.

"I don't know," Kay said. "I just let her get on with it, I don't keep tabs, I'm not that sort of boss," said Kay, meaning that she didn't really care and that she was too wrapped up in her own desperate veil of woe to give a shit about Jacquie's Christmas.

"They were having an affair."

"But she's engaged, she's getting married – I've seen the dress hundreds of bloody times and I've had to look at the venue on the internet," Kay said. She couldn't get the idea of Newland Hall, the venue for Jacquie's wedding, out of her mind, and all the fuss and farce that Jacquie was making and all this time... All this time, in meetings, yes, Kay had seen the odd lingering hand, chair pulled out. Kay couldn't even sort out one comprehensible thought from the other. How could she? And with our biggest client?

"She's confirmed it," said Polly, "started last February when they went on a conference in Dusseldorf together."

"I was meant to go, I had to pull out because my mum was ill," said Kay. Polly's telephone rang. It was her sister and she made excuses to get her off the line. Kay had always wanted a sister. Polly finished her coffee and patted the dog.

"Benedict Phillips had a girlfriend that he'd only just met on Tinder. She's only 24 years old and we can't find her anywhere. Her name is Valérie Lagarde," Polly said. So it was true and it was linked and somehow this Valérie was important. The hospital hadn't bothered to raise an alarm because she was just a temporary nurse. She had slipped through the cracks.

Polly had a record of all of the correspondence between them, lifted from the dating app Tinder. Benedict and Valérie had only known each other for a month and she hadn't been seen for over two weeks.

"We're flying the family over to make an appeal. It's not

Simon Bell. We're sure of that. He's out of the picture, but then there's this," she said. Polly opened a black and white image on her phone. It was so tiny and grainy that Kay could hardly see. It showed a figure on the footbridge which ran south of the Royal Albert Dock. The figure was grainy, sepia, very hard to make anything out, but he was wearing a dark baseball cap, a hoodie and a rucksack.

"The nearest working CCTV footage, a footbridge four hundred yards away, after your dad deleted everything else on his bender," said Polly. "This is taken just before midnight on Christmas Eve. This person is walking towards Excel. In my mind, he or she is obviously concealing their identity. We think this is either Benedict or his killer," said Polly. Taken on Christmas Eve, this figure did not look like Simon at all. It could have been Benedict himself with that posture. But the more she looked at it, the more it looked like...

Kay's phone pinged. She had been keeping it close and the notification made her jump. Most of the emails she got were spam, or news notifications, but this one stood out. The subject line was too intriguing, too topical to discard, like a horse running at Ascot with your mother's name. Kay had to back it.

The subject line read: 'You're not the only one who knew him.'

There was no text, only an empty message with a video attachment. Polly looked over, and asked if Kay was alright.

"Work," Kay said. "New business, I need to deal with this, sorry." She walked out of the cafe and into Hyde Park and opened the attachment.

The video started to play.

It was light, as in daytime, inside a room where the sun was hitting a wall and there was a shadow cast by a metal hanging light. The phone – Kay presumed this was filmed on someone's phone – angled up towards the ceiling. In the wall there was a partial sighting of a round metal window. A porthole?

There were noises.

A man was sighing, grunting, breathless, like the running noises athletes make in the latter stages of a race. There was the sound of furniture under duress, the creak of straining wood and the rub of material. And beneath that something wet, something squelching. A woman was panting.

"Fuck me harder," the female voice said.

The perspective of the screen changed. Someone had picked up the phone. It went dark. The noises persisted and then Kay saw a close up on dark skin, hair and follicles; it took Kay a moment to adjust and understand. The view pulled back and his cock went inside her.

Kay pushed the phone away, dropped it face down onto the floor, disgusted but with the faint sense of arousal at watching sex that she couldn't control.

It played on.

"Don't film me," said the woman, the camera panned up to her face, over her breasts bouncing up, bang, bang, bang. He was fucking her harder now and she couldn't catch her breath, couldn't close her mouth.

Kay knew the voice. Kay knew the woman's face. It was Belinda. Kay recognised the hanging light fixture, the sofa and porthole because it was Belinda's boat.

The perspective changed again. He propped up the phone on its side, offering a longer profile of Belinda. He bore down on her using both hands as leverage. His face moved around in side profile and then he looked full on at the camera with his own gurning face ringed with perspiration. It was Benedict Phillips.

CHAPTER TWENTY-TWO

Belinda worked in a gargantuan office. Three receptions, two revolving doors, heaps of security guards, and many people with passes rushing through flashing plastic on tiny scanners. Belinda worked for a corporate monolith. All of the senior executives wore suits; even the staffers and junior reporters looked as though they worked in a bank.

Kay needed to see Belinda. Belinda was a liar. She had out and out lied. Kay was trying to think back to exactly what she had said when they first discussed it. So much had happened, but Kay was sure Belinda said she had not seen him for years. She certainly hadn't said that she had sex with him on her boat. It was recent. Kay could tell by the paint, by Belinda's face, by Benedict's face, that curl.

Kay's ears were drawn to the orchestral pip of news. She responded to the swirly jingle of the news programmes' opening theme as if they were a fire alarm. There was a flat, iridescent television screen blaring out the latest stories, and as if by magic, there was Valérie, her beautiful face, her precious smile. She was tall and slim and her blonde hair had a touch of red. The broadcast said:

Fears grow for the missing French nurse, Valérie Lagarde, who has not been seen since Christmas Eve. The twenty-four year old had been working at St Mary's hospital. It is alleged that Lagarde was in a relationship with Benedict Phillips, the former soldier whose body was found in the Royal Albert Dock. Police urge anybody who may have seen Lagarde or is aware of her whereabouts to contact them.

It wasn't Belinda that had got punished. She had got away scot free. They had both humiliated Benedict and Belinda had got away with it. Betrayal. Sleep with whoever you like Belinda, but not him.

And then suddenly there she was, Belinda. Little blonde curls, oversized coat. They call that trend 'boyfriend' ironically. Belinda's face was ashen. Kay had never seen her look so serious. They went out of the building and across the road through a thread of slow traffic, careful of motorcycles, down a side street and into a large square of gardens contained by wrought iron railings. It was cold and empty apart from a flock of hungry pigeons and a man vigorously exercising.

"Kay, I was still married when it happened. If it got into the hands of Roberto's lawyers then I would be finished. He would have me on adultery and I'd lose my home and I'd have no claim against him. That's why I couldn't tell you," Belinda said. God she was good. So plausible and off the cuff. As if it was an excuse that she had prepared in advance, or, it was the truth.

"I had to conceal it, Kay," she said, pleading, "I have to keep the boat. Secrets like that will get out in this sort of investigation. I'm afraid and if anyone finds out I will lose the boat certainly, that's for sure. I'll have no pay out, there are no kids to support, I'll be ruined, financially, I won't have anywhere to live."

"I want to know why?" asked Kay.

"I was low in myself," said Belinda.

"He was disgusting. He was a sex offender," Kay said.

Belinda did up the buttons of her coat. Kay was boiling, fire brimming over in her head. Disgust swirling in her stomach. Kay held her phone in her hand, ready to press play; if she did, she knew their friendship would be over.

"Don't watch it, Kay. Please, I'm not proud of it." Kay shut off her phone and shoved it into her pocket. "And I've already seen it. Someone sent it to me too, yesterday, in an email attachment," Belinda said, and Kay was stumped. Who sent it because it couldn't be Benedict and why send it to both of us? Why show it at all?

"You don't care about anyone but yourself, Belinda," Kay said.

"He wasn't like that with me and I don't know what he's meant to have done, Kay, because you never trusted me enough to tell me."

"He gave me this, Belinda," Kay said, touching the scar on her lip.

"But you cut that drunk in Cyprus."

"No. Benedict came back. Yes, I had been drinking. I left you in the bar and he waited for me."

"I'm sorry," she said.

"I've had to live with that," said Kay. Belinda bent over the park bench and vomited a string of yellow bile. They sat quietly and Kay rubbed her back.

"I'm all alone Kay," Belinda said slowly. "There's no husband, there's no babies, there's this job which is lonely and brutal, but it fills the time."

Belinda pleaded with Kay to forgive her. She talked about Kay having Julia and never being on her own. Little did she know. She was hiccupping and crying. Kay wanted to know all the details.

"I was on the rocks with Roberto; he had been in Brazil for a month with work. He came back and I knew he was up to something. He didn't want to touch me. I knew he had someone else. I was lonely and upset. I called Dave. I thought I could do something with him to make me feel better. He didn't want to meet so I booked a personal training session."

"Did you come on to him?" Kay asked.

"Yes I suppose so, but he was smitten with Ariana. I thought he might be a bit bored with her, have got bored of the accent and all the make-up and the terrible clothes, but he just went on and on about how much he loved her," Belinda said.

"What has this got to do with the video, Belinda?" Kay asked, getting angry again.

"Dave told me that Benedict's wife and kids had moved to Leystonstone, around the corner, just by coincidence. They had split up, she had left him, but Benedict was around there all the time to see the kids. Dave said that he was pestering Ariana, that he had knocked on the door, that he had some kind of thing for her. It sounded like they both knew Ariana from their army days."

"Benedict had a thing for Ariana? He knew Ariana?" Kay said, disbelieving.

"Yes. He knew her. I suppose I called Benedict because I was on a rebound from Roberto and Dave. I don't bloody know, Kay. It's all a horrible mistake," Belinda said.

What bullshit. Kay didn't want to believe her. She had lied to her. Belinda must be making it up to get herself out of trouble. She always did that. She always tried to drag other people into it to cover up her own mistakes.

"Where did you meet Benedict then?" asked Kay.

"Smollensky's."

"Smollensky's? That's where we go," Kay said.

"And then when it was clear we were both up for it, we went back to the boat."

"When?"

"Last June," said Belinda. "I was vulnerable and I needed to get one over on Ariana by doing something stupid."

"He's dangerous."

"He was dangerous," Belinda said. "He's dead now."

"What's going on, Belinda?" asked Kay, exasperated.

"It was a one-off, and the only time I ever saw him," said Belinda, and she took Kay's hand and held it in both of hers; she was freezing. "What is more worrying Kay, is not what I did, but I think you need to ask yourself who sent that video to both of us? And more importantly, why?"

CHAPTER TWENTY-THREE

10th July 2006

Benedict Phillips was right there. He had been waiting. Must have. Kay was seeing things blurred. The lights of the strip were behind her. They cast a long shadow so that she could see herself in front on the pavement. She turned around; it was ten steps back to the strip. Not far. Or was it?

She looked back and he wasn't there. Then she felt his hand on her shoulder. Then his hand was on her mouth – perhaps it was his other hand. The skin was rough; she could feel dry lines sticking out on her soft lips. His hand was huge, smothering.

He swung her round, at least it felt like swinging around, but what had actually happened was that he had pulled her backwards. Kay's feet couldn't keep up with the backwards motion and dragged. She lost a sandal trying to back step, side step; it came off. An alarm sounded inside her head. It was petrifying.

This is not right.

This is not a joke.

At first the concrete scraped the back of her heel and as she struggled to get on her feet, she caught her little toe and it seemed to rip just slightly; as she processed that sensation of pain, it was as if something ran through her to sober her. Her eyes saw clearly.

He pulled her round the corner of a shuttered closed down shop, into a covered walkway and then onto a patch of wasteland, a tufty mass of wild dry grass and baked earth. Some large industrial bins overflowed with rubbish. A cat shrieked and ran; Kay saw its eyes, bright, wide, take her in and dash into the street.

The strip was gone and he was in front of her and he pushed his mouth onto hers. He smelled of aftershave. Dark violet, floral, light for a man's fragrance. But still that meaty undertone of butcher's shop liver and sweetbreads. His jaw was smooth, as if freshly shaven and it was damp and sticky with sweat. She bit and spat and she heaved her head forward as if to head butt, anything, push him away. He rammed his fingers inside her.

"There, that's what you like," said Benedict. She couldn't get her hands near her groin to push him away. She flexed her wrists, opened her palms searching for anything to grab, but her arms were wedged to her sides. He pulled his head back and spat in her face. It dangled on her chin and she wanted to wipe it away, but she couldn't. She pulled up her knee to try and make contact in his groin. They tussled on the uneven earth, his face temporarily lit by the moon or a street light; the beam hit him and she saw his eyes were wide and excitedly bright. Then his eyes narrowed viciously.

There was a huge thud. It was sharp. He hit her in her face. She felt her stomach lurch. She wanted to urinate, defecate, and open her bowels to expel. She was frightened. Her body was bubbling, heart racing, limbs fitting as though acid was running through her veins.

His sovereign ring had caught the top of her lip and slashed it there; blood ran into her mouth. On her tongue it tasted hot for a second, then the texture went like cold tasteless tomato soup, salty and overly tangy. He hit her again. In the same place. Her nose opened and blood oozed down her face.

He stood up as if to look at her; he shifted from foot to

foot, looking around him in the darkness. She could still hear the music from the strip. A group of people laughing in the distance. This enraged him and he swore, muffled, under his breath. She looked at the ground, her head on the floor facing to the right side. She could see his reflection in the dark glass of the closed down shop. He undid his belt. He unzipped his trousers. Her hand searched out a tennis ball sized rock. He kicked it away hard, her hand still around it; her arm bounced with the force and Kay cried out as a pain went up through her elbow and into her shoulder.

Somewhere across the road, in a block of apartments in the distance, a light went on and it caused him to turn to look at it over his shoulder. As he did, and quite by chance, a car drove by on the road and the two things together seemed to shake his confidence. He crouched down, licked his bottom lip, brought his hand up to his face and pinched his nose, wiped his mouth. He was thinking. Thinking fast, weighing things up.

He stood up again and took out his cock. He leaned his weight forward and pissed. It landed on Kay's face and chest, a stream of warm droplets, bad beer. A searing sting cut through the cut on Kay's mouth.

"You know what?" he asked. "I wouldn't touch you with a barge pole. And do you know why? Fucking answer me!"

"Why?" Kay managed to say.

"Because you're riddled with AIDS. You fucking dyke." He shook his dick to finish. Did up his trousers. He laughed, giddy, excitable and ran away, like hopscotch, jumping up and away.

Was that it?

Was it over?

He hadn't raped her. Thank God. Her clothes were on her. Her small bag still tied across her body. She scrambled up. She

was fast. Onto her side first and she lingered a second just to
see what hurt. Her arm. Her face. Her foot. Her tongue went
to where the cut was but all at once she was repulsed by the
stench of piss all around her and on her, and in her mouth. She
spat. The scorched earth was damp with it, and it had run off
in a trickle.

She put down a hand, singeing with pain, got up to one foot,
then the other and ran. For a moment she couldn't remember
which way he had gone. She made towards the strip, but veered
left away from the main throng. A group of Cypriot men
drinking coffee looked out.

"Hey, girl," they shouted, but she kept running. One sandal,
then none. As the road turned there was a small opening to a
rocky scrag of beach and she ran onto it and went into the sea
fully clothed. Naked feet on sand, then sharp stone; she tripped,
and went forward, down into the water, letting it come into her
face and fill her mouth and cover every hair. Crying, she bathed
in the shallows, rubbing the sea water into her nostrils softly,
and then into the philtrum, the soft cleft between her nose and
mouth.

Then she panicked because if he was still here, hiding
somewhere, watching, he could drown her in here, hold her
under. She thrashed around as her legs rose up with the flow of
the waves and she lost her footing. The heaviness of her clothes
dragged her back out and exhausted, she fought her way back
onto the beach. She crossed the main strip. Was he watching
her? Should she go to the police? Should she go and find Dave
and Belinda? She had left them kissing in a bar. She needed to
inspect herself, make sure she was intact.

The bathroom light was forensic blue. She had never noticed
its severity before. It hummed. Her nose was the same shape but

swollen. There was a tiny patch of dried blood. Numbness had set in. She had been drunk.

Her top was covered with a V-shape of red, which ran tie-dyed into the white cotton. She took it off, careful of mouth and nose. Did she need stitches? She wasn't sure. She ran a bath. The steam filled the small room. She went to the front door and checked the lock. She went to the kitchenette and checked the balcony door was locked. She went back to the front door and checked it again.

She went into the bedroom and opened every wardrobe and looked inside. She looked under the bed and turned on every main light and every lamp. It was silent, just the hum of hotel electric. She lit a cigarette and inhaled. The heat of the cigarette near the cut scared her, but she still smoked gently from the other side.

She eased herself into the bath. There was already a huge bruise across her wrist and lower forearm where he had kicked her. She put her head back and tears came. She let herself cry only for a few seconds, before she breathed deep and willed her shaking hands to stop.

CHAPTER TWENTY-FOUR

Leytonstone, London. Belinda had snuck in so easily. Her words became like silk and anchored themselves to Karen Phillips' soul and then Belinda reeled her in. She promised Karen money. Money for her story, and Karen, lank of hair and so very tired, had said yes silently via her exhausted, deep-set eyes.

Karen's children buzzed around her like flies in Paw Patrol pyjamas. She had no milk for tea and so Belinda had immediately gone back out to the shop and returned several long, silent minutes later with a bag containing not only milk but assorted crisps and chocolate, bold wrappers crackling.

Belinda tipped the bag on the floor and the children piled in on top. Karen lit another cigarette. The boy, Ben, at whom Kay could not stop staring, popped open a bag of Quavers and shoved three into his mouth. His belly, which peered out from over the waistband of his pyjama bottoms reminded her of Simon Bell, but the curl of hair stuck to his forehead was all Benedict, because this boy, Ben, was technically the biological offspring of both; the son of Benedict and the nephew of Simon.

In Belinda's desperate mission to make amends and solve, well, what were they actually solving? Belinda had persuaded Kay that the most likely person to send that video would be Benedict's ex-wife, and so they found themselves on her sofa.

Kay knew this Leytonstone street well. It was less than two hundred yards from Dave and Ariana's flat. Kay had been here many times, to this street, to the same corner shop where Belinda had bought the milk.

Belinda went into the kitchen to make the tea. Kay felt like it was part of Belinda's routine to make feel people comfortable by pushing back the boundaries.

"They are still off school," said Karen, "not that I don't want this Christmas over. I'll be glad to get it over and done with, get them back to school, get back into a routine, try and move on from all of this. At least he dropped off their Christmas presents before he died." A brand new un-cycled bicycle leaned against the television. "We took the tree down when we found out, seemed like the right thing to do at the time."

Belinda came back in with three cups of tea in pink floral mugs and a packet of digestive biscuits.

"I wasn't with him," said Karen. "We were divorced so I don't know anything. I certainly don't know what he was up to socially. I've told the police that, several times. But now my brother's lost his job and it was nothing to do with him. His wife has walked out. It's a mess." Kay shuffled in her seat. The guilt she carried had transcended the mundane, like spending time with her father; it was the guilt of getting innocent people into serious trouble. Poor Simon, and then just as quickly as she felt bad, she felt angry again. Fuck Simon.

Belinda sat next to Karen in brazen view. If Karen had sent that video then she would recognise Belinda. Belinda was willing the recognition; she leaned in, but Karen's face remained completely blank.

"I've told all of this to the police, everything I know, and I don't want the kids in this piece. I'll do it, but leave them out of it," Karen said.

"What about the French girl? The nurse? Valérie? Have you heard anything about her?" asked Belinda. Kay was starting to like Karen, much better than she liked Simon. It wasn't her fault that she got pregnant as a teenager; she had done well to keep her kids and try to do the right thing. Imagine being surrounded by all those men, all those fucking arseholes trying to dominate you. She was condemned to always being someone's little woman.

"I've seen her face on the news," said Karen. "Pretty girl, nurses do a great job and get no thanks. She was too good for him."

Then a small voice interrupted.

"I saw her," the boy, Ben said. He was stood inside the kitchen doorway. And now looking at him properly Kay could see that his eyes looked absent and sad. They carried an extra crevasse that underlined the lower lid. He was grieving. The beast whose demise Kay had rejoiced in was this boy's father.

"It's OK," said Kay. "This is just between us, come here and sit down with us." He made his way back to the sofa and squeezed himself up against his mother and she put her arm around his back.

"You can tell them, love," Karen reassured him. She was open and interested and certainly not frightened. "You're not in any trouble."

"I won't print this. OK? This is just between us for now," Belinda said, and he nodded and Karen nodded to give him the go-ahead to say more. "When did you see her?" asked Belinda.

"On Christmas Eve," he said.

"Where?" asked Belinda. He fell silent.

"Was she with Dad?" asked Karen gently, to coax it from him.

"Yes," he said. "Dad came to give us our presents and she was with him."

"Here? At your house?" asked Belinda. He nodded.

"He didn't come in, I don't allow that," Karen said to Kay and Belinda.

"They took me to the pub and I had a burger and chips. My present was too big so my dad gave it to me when we got back here."

"Do you know where they were going afterwards?" Belinda asked.

"They changed their minds," said the boy. "They were going back to her house to leave out carrots for Rudolph, but then they met her friend."

"Her friend?" asked Belinda, leaning in so close Kay could see the pores on her skin.

"I don't know if it was her friend, but it was another lady," said the boy.

"A lady?"

He nodded.

"Did you meet her in the pub?" asked Belinda,

"No," said the boy. "Outside here, around the corner." He pointed to the street.

"Here, outside your house?" asked Belinda. The boy nodded. Karen rubbed his back.

"Don't be scared, you're not in any trouble," said Karen.

"She lives around the corner," said the boy, lip curling down, starting to cry.

"That's enough now," said Karen.

"What does she look like?" asked Belinda,

"Belinda that's enough," said Kay.

"Taller than you lot, taller than my dad," said the boy.

"What colour hair?" asked Belinda.

"Blonde," said the boy. "She was walking along the road, she said she had to go to work, she had to do something last minute that she'd forgot to do and she didn't want to get into trouble with her boss." Kay flinched.

"Did she say what?" asked Belinda.

"Something about a computer. She didn't want to get in the car, but my dad got out and said something to her and then she did. She just got in the back next to us. We had to squeeze up." Kay scrolled through her phone and pulled up a picture of Dave and Ariana's wedding. She held it up to the boy.

"Is this her?" asked Kay.

"Yes," he said, "that's her."

CHAPTER TWENTY-FIVE

It was such a police woman's car. Vauxhall Astra. Meant to slip into the background to seamlessly blend with its surroundings. It was grey. Even though it was blue, it was grey. In her mind's eye she had seen Polly in a vintage Daimler. Imagined her driving with an arm resting out of the window. Her hair being swept by the wind.

The car was leaning back, parked on the upward slope of an aggressive road bump. Sleeping policemen they called them. Kay was on a stakeout. Lacey to Polly Harvey's Cagney. She felt like she was going into an exam, sat in a car, clock ticking, doing nothing. Polly's outline flickered in her right eye. She tried not to look. She was taking her all in. Slowly. Every centimetre.

"Surely you would want to know?" asked Polly.

"No, I don't think I would. Some things are better just left alone. Everything doesn't need to come out," Kay said, wondering whether she should tell Polly about what Karen's boy had told her. If she did tell her, then how would she explain that she knew? She wiped away the images for the moment.

Kay was excited that she was sat in Polly's car. She had been eating with Julia, thinking about Polly. When she had been sacked by her client, she had been thinking about Polly. She had been watching Dave get married, thinking about Polly. When she was being held in a police cell, she had been praying that Polly didn't appear to witness her fall.

"The truth always comes out in the end," Polly said, though Kay was scared stiff to think what that truth might be. Who sent the videos to Kay and Belinda? Where was Valérie now and how was she involved and how was Ariana involved?

"I saw Valérie Lagarde's parents on the television," said Kay. "They looked desperate."

"She's an adult Kay, not a little girl. She could be anywhere. She could be back in France. You can't tell what else might have been going on," Polly said.

"The mother looked distraught."

"We missed the window to find Valérie at the start. We didn't even know that she was missing for over a week," Polly said. "The bloody hospital didn't report her missing. Can you believe that? Some jumped up senior nurse told me it wasn't her job to babysit young girls. She didn't turn up on shift and it just fell through the cracks. Her parents were angry with her for not calling, but they thought she was having a good time. She might be in the river, she might be on the run."

From the image that Kay had seen of Valérie, it was clear to see that she was too good for Benedict. She guessed you never really knew who you were getting involved with on these dating apps.

"There's one thing that doesn't sit well with me. I would have expected that a nurse would have made more of a clinical slice," Polly said. "The ear was hacked off. It wasn't a tidy job."

Kay checked her phone; she had tried Ariana a few times but hadn't heard from her. Why didn't Ariana tell Kay she knew Benedict? Maybe it was nothing. Polly's hands rested on the steering wheel. Kay had been looking at them for over an hour. Polly traced a finger along the black rubber of the wheel. Was she doing it on purpose? Her hands. It was worse when she was driving. Polly's hands were sending Kay mad. Kay couldn't stop looking at them.

The houses were built in London stock brick, white with flecks of browns and shades of black, like a tabby coated cat. All were different. Most were flats she guessed from the buzzers and bells lined up like parked cars along the doorframes. Kay didn't know how Polly kept finding the time to help her, but she did.

Polly's coat was on the back seat. She wore a black jumper. It was tight and Kay could see the outline of her tits. Sporty, svelte and bigger on the bottom half, curved like a tuppence. She watched so intently that she could see the rise and fall of Polly's breath. Polly's bottom lip was rounder than the top; it gathered, puckered. Polly flexed a leg and shifted in her seat, extending her neck where a tendon cast a long delicate cleft. Was she tensing? She smelled of perfume, yes of course she did, but there was another smell. Butterscotch, cherry, warm fuzzy indigo. She was unctuous. Kay couldn't explain. She was dessert. Delicious.

"Can you stop looking at me please?" asked Polly.

"Yes of course. I'm actually looking at the house," Kay said.

"Are you? I thought you'd been staring at me for ages," said Polly.

"No. You're just in the way. In my eyeline," Kay said, indicating her eyeline with her flat palm.

"You do know that the house is over there," Polly said, and she pointed in the other direction to Kay's left.

"Oh yes," said Kay. "I'm rusty. I haven't been on stakeout for ages." Polly sat up and then dropped down deep into the seat.

"There. Look. It's him," she said.

A woman, Kay's age, probably older, was carrying a baby. Not a newborn. It was wearing a puffed up all-in-one coat. It looked like a tasty plum. Cheeks, bum, round hands poking out. Kay could see its rosy cheeks from across the road. The baby rested on her hip. She kissed Kenneth Spiers. A hasty old-fashioned peck. Kay imagined the rough scratch of his beard. He touched the baby's cheek, kissed it. Talked into the baby's face, under its hood. The baby looked out into the street, towards Polly Harvey's car.

Kenneth Spiers had toffee coloured curtains and a row of micro fir trees cut tight with concentration. This was retirement before dementia. A hacienda of satisfaction and regret. Trimming the hedges at the edge of the abyss. He would enjoy watching that child grow. When that baby learned to eat, he would give it sweets. The baby would call Kenneth Spiers Grandpa or Papa or Pops. He would smell of peppermint and wood.

The woman belted the baby into a seat in the rear. He stood watching; his austere gait was familiar. One hand in a pocket. The other hand, that in 1994 held a cigarette with arrogant intent, was empty now. He was void of vices. Probably a dodgy ticker or breathless episode had warned him off. Now through nagging and fear he only dreamt of rolling his own down the end of the garden in the shed amidst the smell of winter garden floor. The woman shut the baby in nice and tight and walked around the back of the car to the driver's side, offering an unobstructed view of her face. She shouted loud, even from across the street they heard it:

"Bye Dad, see you next week," she said.

A bus bisected the scene. Cutting the invisible spider's web of connection. A trail of red, people's heads, a new film comedy laughing from the side of the bus. Polly reached for her seat belt and started the engine.

"She looks like you Kay," said Polly. "She looks just like you."

Ridiculous. Ludicrous. What was Kay even doing there? She

was exactly like her mum. Everyone said she was. They would catch the light on her in a certain way and then they would say, 'you've got your Mam's mouth,' or, 'your Mam's eyes,' or, 'your Mam's nose.' Once, in front of Dave she crossed her arms and rested them flatly under her breasts. Up high. Her boobs resting on her folded forearms. Dave laughed.

"You look just like your mum standing like that," he had said.

At the funeral, so many faces pushed into Kay's. Kay felt like a celebrity coming out of the church, and they appeared, all those faces from the past, touching, holding, speaking words.

"You're your mum all over."

Never Jim. No one ever said Jim.

CHAPTER TWENTY-SIX

Polly's flat was in an ex-local authority block in the heart of Hoxton. Polly had told Kay that she thought about selling it to a trustafarian hipster, but it had been her Nana's. It had been the council flat that her father had grown up in before he passed all his exams, got a place at grammar school, worked his way up to be an inspector in the metropolitan police and moved down to Kent with a nice girl for fresh air, golf and babies.

The entrance was via a curved stairwell which was open to the street. It was a classic London design for Victorian tenement buildings. It caught the light and funnelled it through to the lowest recesses. The light illuminated fossilised tiny bumps of blistering paint where there was once damp. Kay smelled the earthy, nutty scent of geraniums, red flowers tumbling down the sharp stairs. Kay minded her footing; the stairs were sharp and there was a bend in the middle where thousands of shoes had traipsed.

Polly's calf muscles tightened and released as she went up each step. Kay could see their outline as her skin tight jeans clung to the muscles as if afraid to fall. Kay stumbled. Polly turned around and gave Kay her hand.

"Careful," Polly said. A dog barked behind a door. "Shh, don't let Reggie hear us. He'll go mad if he knows I'm here."

"Do you want to collect him?" asked Kay.

"In a minute. He's at number six with Maureen eating digestive biscuits," said Polly.

Polly's hand opened the lock. She had a red front door. Inside, a window stretched along the entire front wall. Kay could see the busy street below, could feel the tension of the city, the rub of taxi and bus. Kay's skin prickled; she could feel her clothes standing out on her own body. She folded her arms. Unfolded them again. She was getting that electricity, excited energy feeling. She hadn't had it for years. She used to get it with Julia.

Polly's desk. A photograph of Morrissey in a silver frame. Postcards from the TATE gallery. A leaflet about Frida Kahlo. She must have been to see the exhibition. Condé Nast Traveller and Wallpaper magazine. Kay's pulse started up, somewhere in her neck, she was aware; her heart was speeding up but time was slowing down. Polly had a life. Polly was interested in things. She was plugged into London, free to enjoy and learn and young enough to have hopes about the future, instead of just regrets about the past. Oh God, Kay wanted her.

At the far end of the room was an open plan kitchen. Polly filled the kettle. Kay leaned against the desk. Say something. The quiet was ear-splitting. Pin drop. Kay focused on the water gushing out of the tap. It was thunderous.

"This is an amazing flat," blurted Kay.

"My sister's husband is a builder," said Polly.

"I really like it," said Kay.

"We modernised the entire place. It was really old-fashioned before," said Polly. "Are you hungry?" Food? Was she kidding? Kay couldn't eat. Hadn't eaten for a while. Kay's stomach was spinning.

Kay wanted to close the gap between her and Polly Harvey. Forget tea. She wanted to run her hands over Polly's naked stomach. Kay wanted to lick Polly's side where it dipped in at the waist. Put her hands there. Pull up her jumper.

This is where Polly sat. This is where Polly lived. She wasn't the police woman anymore; she was made of flesh and she was coming towards Kay. Walking. Kettle starting to boil and rock over, then steam flying up behind Polly as she walked over to Kay. Kay was here in her front room. Alone with her. She wanted to make the gap between her and Polly Harvey smaller.

Lightheaded. Look away. Kay traced a hand over the desk, touching a pen. Picking it up. Kay put it back. Kay knocked the magazines onto the floor. The gap between them got smaller.

"I asked if you were you hungry?" said Polly.

"No. Thank you," said Kay, shaking her head.

"Are you alright? You look a bit stunned. It's a lot to think about," said Polly.

"I'm not thinking about this morning," said Kay.

"What are you thinking about then?" asked Polly. Polly walked right up to Kay and put her hands on Kay's waist. Kay sucked in a breath like jumping into a freezing cold plunge pool. Inches away. Blue eyes. That bottom, those lips.

"What's this from?" asked Polly, as she lifted a finger and put it on Kay's scar. She traced the outline of Kay's lips with her finger. Kay couldn't breathe right. Let out a noise. Touched Polly's finger with her tongue. Kay might just snap. Polly bent her head and brought it where her finger was and she touched Kay's mouth and kissed there. Polly was leaning up. Kay was taller and curved her head, leaning in to kiss Polly more.

"I'm going to fuck you all day," said Polly. It was 11.45am.

Polly moved her hands to Kay's belt, undid the metal spoke and yanked the buckle free. Kay shook. One electric bolt cold through her body as Kay's belt came undone. Jesus Christ. Alone in Polly's flat. Kay had thought that she might never feel like this again. Polly opened the button of Kay's jeans and bit down on her full bottom lip.

"I want you to remember every detail of everything I do to you," said Polly.

A warm aching reaction underneath Kay's abdomen, stretching to her legs. Polly pushed her hand into Kay's knickers. Kay glistened. "I've been wanting to do that since the first moment I saw you," Polly said. When was that? At the Excel, the Sunday, the press conference and Kay had wanted it too, desperately staring trying to get Polly's attention. Kay's head tumbled back, and then forward. Her mouth hung open, riding Polly's hand. Polly locked onto Kay's eyes; she wouldn't drop their stare for a moment. Kay could tell that Polly liked watching what she was doing. She liked to watch herself touching Kay to bring her off.

Intense, dizzying, pure pleasure. Everything else fell away. Polly Harvey all over her. Polly slipped her hand around Kay's buttocks and loosened her jeans further. Kay felt Polly's hand slipping up inside, pushing. Relief. Deep yearning escalating to a hot intense sensation. Kay started to moan. Be quiet Kay. But she couldn't stop herself; she wanted to unzip Polly Harvey from head to foot and climb inside. Polly liked it. Liked making Kay gasp. It was making Polly aroused, making her work faster.

Kay parked her tongue in Polly's mouth and they bounced up and down. Polly smiled and braced herself between Kay's legs, pushing her own feet to stand inside and pushing Kay up against the desk so that her bottom was resting there and Kay put one hand behind and Polly fucked her. Oh my God. Her whole body wanted to give way.

"I want to get into you," said Polly, and she pulled Kay's jeans down around her knees so that she could get her face into Kay. She dropped down and nuzzled her face into her and started sucking, licking between her lips. Polly moaned herself and sprang into action, uncontrollably going at Kay.

"Oh, don't," Kay said, and she looked down because she was pinned against the desk, unable to move. She could just see Polly working at her. Then it all started to roll down Kay's body; she was coming in Polly Harvey's mouth, and as she did Polly moved her hand inside and pumped.

Kay shouted 'don't stop, don't stop.' One deep droplet in a pool, radiating circle upon circle upon circle. Again and again, Kay screamed.

She didn't think of anything else. She just wanted Polly Harvey. Everything else had simply ceased to exist.

CHAPTER TWENTY-SEVEN

They were lying in bed in Polly's flat in Hoxton. They hadn't eaten any dinner. "If and when the time comes," said Kay.

"Let me take a strand of your hair," said Polly, ignoring her and tugged at Kay's scalp. Kay swiped her hand away from her head. "We've got a new fast track service, it'll be done in twenty-four hours. Actually, I can just get it off a brush," Polly said. "We've got a sample from Jim already, so if that's not a match we'll look to Kenneth Spiers."

"Listen. If and when the time comes, are you...interested in me?" Kay asked, but Polly had already walked over to her long white dressing table which housed a tubular hair brush in black plastic and metal; six bottles of perfume; a Metropolitan police warrant card and police paraphernalia; Metropolitan police regulation handcuffs; and an orange rubber sex toy. She held the hairbrush up to the light, pulling off thick strands of hair with her fingers.

"I really like you," Kay said, and seeing Polly holding up a dark brown strand of hair, "that hair could be yours, not mine."

"It's yours alright. Right length. Right shade. Your DNA is all over this room."

"Polly, can you hear what I'm asking you?" Kay asked, but Polly had already dropped the brush into a clear bag with a plastic seal. She pushed it into her coat pocket which hung on the back of the door on a row of pegs made out of pool balls. She was going to do the test whether Kay wanted her to or not.

"You're very sweet, Kay, but I've only known you a week."

"Is it only a week?" Kay asked, and as if it made a difference she added, "more like ten days surely? And I don't want to know about the DNA Polly. I'm thinking about other more important things and I don't think it would be a good idea to worry about that."

"It's your right to know, Kay. You said before that you had a feeling and it is your right to know the truth. What can be more important that the truth?" Polly asked.

"I don't want to know the truth. I don't see how knowing the truth will make my life any better; it'll only make it worse. Seriously, Polly I don't think it's a good idea, a DNA test. I think we should leave it alone," Kay said.

"I think you would feel much more secure when you can confirm that Jim is your dad," Polly said, not mentioning the sample in a plastic bag in a coat on the back of the door.

"He is my dad," Kay said.

"Biologically?" Polly said.

"You just can't stop yourself."

"No, I don't seem able to stop myself, do I?" asked Polly, and she knelt upright back on the bed and Kay put her head between Polly's breasts. Polly sighed, looked down at Kay's head moving slowly up and down. They were beginning to be stuck together like glue. They were always being pulled together. Kay looked up.

"Do you want to go away with me somewhere?" asked Kay.

"Don't leave Julia for me. You can't put that on me. If you want to then you should do it for yourself. Your decision, your life, Kay. I've got to go to work," Polly said, annoyed that Kay was able to captivate her.

"Have you found Valérie yet?" Kay asked.

"The DI is stepping things up. One last push before we have

to hand it over. He's embarrassed. There's talk of a new DI being brought in or even handing it over to MI5 because of who owns Excel," Polly said, but Kay pulled Polly's head down and kissed her. She was able to forget about serious responsibilities very quickly when she was with Polly.

"I don't mean go away with me right now. I mean plan a holiday or something. We could go to Italy?" Kay asked.

"You and me?" Polly said, moving her right leg over Kay's body so she was straddling her. Kay's hands moving around her sides onto her bottom.

"Yes, just you and me," Kay said.

CHAPTER TWENTY-EIGHT

Kay was at her desk in the offices of Christie Dean PR in Paddington allowing her mind to wander into dreams. She was still floaty, there in front of Ariana, she could still feel Polly's hands all over her. The future was full of possibility. In spite of everything, she had something new and exciting with Polly. A real connection.

Then something dawned on Kay, just enough to chink her armour. She had forgotten all about Jacquie. In fact, Jacquie had not called Kay for over a week. It was enough to flatten Kay, to make her fall back to the earth with a bump and all her troubles landed right down on top of her in a heap. Her heartbeat quickened and she wanted a drink.

Kay's mind was flickering. Memories were popping up on top of each other showing their faces like a stack of playing cards:

Jacquie fainting over Benedict's severed ear;

Simon Bell eating meat;

Polly;

Julia in a tan trench coat and glasses;

Dave smoking pot in his Dad's underground garage;

Ariana's sister Rhea asking 'what kind of man does that?';

The trembling in Kay's mother's clavicle;

Lying on a pile of dirt in Cyprus, while Benedict Phillips stood over her, pissing onto her face.

Kay pulled her chair up under her desk. Ariana rested a boney buttock on the far end of the desk. Kay wanted to point a long acquisitory stick into Ariana and ask her what she knew. You knew Benedict, Ariana, you've known him all along. Kay knew what she had done and was piecing it together with Belinda. They had agreed to wait it out a little longer. Karen Phillips was happy to keep quiet and to keep her boy out of the limelight. £250 from Belinda had seen to that.

There had been a new computer. Kay had bought it for the press room and Ariana had sworn weeks before Christmas that it was installed and ready to go. But it couldn't have been. That's why Ariana must have been heading there on Christmas Eve. But what did Ariana know about Valérie Lagarde? Could she be here hovering around the office making chit-chat if she knew that something bad had happened to her?

"Julia's called the office looking for you; she told me not to tell you that she'd rung," Ariana said. Kay had enough of her voice and of the way her mouth moved when she spoke.

"What did you say to her?" asked Kay.

"Nothing," said Ariana. "I said you were in a meeting."

"And Jacquie. What did Jacquie sound like?" Kay asked and through the glass partition she searched for Jacquie but saw only an empty desk.

"She sounded normal," Ariana said. "Kind of boring."

"And where is Jacquie?" mumbled Kay.

"She's doing the team update meeting in the boardroom. Why is Julia looking for you?" Ariana asked. "Did you have a late night again, Kay?" Ariana handed Kay a copy of the Daily Mail.

"What's this?" asked Kay, and Ariana leaned in too closely over Kay's shoulder and she could smell her tacky perfume. She resisted the urge to hit her away with the back of her hand.

The article read: 'Being with a woman takes me to deep emotional highs; Julia Rothman and partner Kay Christie.' Half the page was dedicated to a photograph. Julia was sat on the sofa looking omniscient. Cleopatra? Kay leaned in behind her. It was a good angle. A good photograph of Kay taken the morning of Dave and Ariana's wedding. At least she looked slim. Was the building moving? Kay swore she could feel it sway. The whole piece made her feel sick.

"Oh, Jesus Christ," Kay said.

Kay wanted to reach for a small jar of tablets and take one tiny pill, urgently shaking, fingers kerfuffling over the jar as in an emergency, as they do in films. Then everything would be fine.

Ariana's coffee was strong. Kay had wanted to buy a coffee machine for the office, but Ariana said it was another thing for her to do. You know keeping it clean, buying a stock of pods or whatever it required. Kay's body wanted a real drink. Craved the numbness. But she wasn't drinking; since the driving incident she was starting over. Polly didn't know that Kay liked to drink. Kay wasn't going to tell her. It was Kay's fresh start. They would live in that cool flat in Hoxton. Kay and Polly and Reggie. And maybe a girl dog too, Kay's puppy. What was she going to call her again? Jill Gascoine? No. Not Jill, Vera. That was it. Vera Wang.

Jacquie knocked on the door and came in. She pressed her palms together and pushed the praying hands up to her heavily oiled lips. She always got chapped lips at this time of year. Brittle swollen appendages which she swathed in Vaseline. She opened the hands to either side of her face.

"Kay," Jacquie said, slow and formal. She had chosen the chair by the door, which was only there for Kay to put her handbag on. An escape hatch. The walls of Kay's office were made of glass and the team's faces peered in.

"Yes?" Kay said.

"There's no easy way to say this," Jacquie said. Oh no. No. Kay didn't think she could do it anymore without Jacquie. Who would do the work? Who would organise everything? Who would motivate the team? "I love working here and I respect you a lot. So much, Kay. I respect you so much."

"Yes?" The anticipation was the worst thing.

"But, I've been offered another job," Jacquie said. "I'm going to be getting a twelve thousand pound salary increase. I know you can't afford to match that and well, it's a lot of money. Plus health insurance and a new business bonus. The money will come in handy with the wedding."

Kay thought she might just offer it. It would be imaginary money of course as there were going to be no clients left to pay it. Kay had a new business bonus in place except no one brought in any fucking new business except for Kay. These thankless bastards. She was on her own in every respect in life.

"Who?" Kay asked. It was like being cheated on. Kay felt like Jacquie had been unfaithful to her.

"I think you might know him," Jacquie said.

"Who?" asked Kay.

"VAPOUR PR. The MD is Mitchell Kramer," Jacquie said, and Kay felt like she had been crushed between a truck and a wall. Pinned. Naked. Humiliated. She did know him and he was an awful, small, competitive bastard. They would all be laughing at her. Mitchell Kramer would take Jacquie for a few drinks, get the lowdown on Kay, she imagined in a whiny voice: 'What's Kay like to work for? Is she really a lesbian? What's Julia Rothman like?'

"Sorry, Kay," Jacquie said, full of remorse but mainly feeling sorry for Kay. Kay didn't want her fucking pity and her stupid handbag and her boring steadfast hair and her bloody rules and the stupid time she passed out like a drip just because of a missing ear. Who does that at work? She was shite anyway. She wasn't very good. Traitor. There's loads of people who could do her job.

"I know," Kay said, "I know what you did with Simon. Just so we're clear, I know everything." Jacquie gulped for air, took a big mouthful in.

"Please, don't tell anyone," Jacquie said. She didn't deny it for one second.

"How could you?" Kay asked. "Get out!"

"I'm sorry, Kay."

"At least I don't fuck my clients!" Kay shouted for all to hear as the door rattled on its hinge, as Jacquie uncharacteristically slammed it shut.

It seemed like hours, but only a few minutes had passed when Ariana opened the door and ushered Polly inside. Kay was still seething, her adrenaline still pulsing bull-like around her body. Ariana gave no warning, just opened the door like the incompetent assistant she was.

"Hi," Kay said, "what are you doing here? Come in, come in." Ariana's face was frozen with intrigue. Kay had to prise her back out the door. "Thank you, Ariana."

"I'm sorry for just turning up like this but something's happened," Polly said.

"What?" Kay asked, coming round to lean against the front of her desk. Ariana stared in with an open mouth. The rest of the team swivelled around to look from their desk chairs.

"You won't believe what's happened, Kay. I ran your DNA and it just pinged with a hit straight away," Polly said.

"My DNA got a hit?" Kay asked.

"I had to log the sample to get it tested. I couldn't send it anonymously."

"You did what?" Kay was reddening. She could see small crystallic stars trembling in her peripheral vision. The team, petrified, sensing wrath, wrath pretended to turn back to their computer screens.

"Your sample was a match to material we found on Benedict Phillips," Polly said.

"Me?"

"Your hair fibre was on the blanket the victim was wrapped in," Polly said. This is it. Fucking should've said something now. Should have said ages ago that she knew Benedict. Polly took a step further into Kay's space; she stopped short of touching her, but her face but was right in front of Kay as if examining her for any trace of recognition. Seeing only anger on Kay's face, Polly took it to mean innocence? Kay moved very little because she was frozen in rage. If she did move, it was possible that she could unravel entirely right there on the floor of her office in front of everybody.

"My hair?" Kay managed.

"A Boat Show branded blanket was wrapped around Benedict Phillips' head. It places him inside the Excel. I'm thinking specifically your press room, S17, the blanket must have come from there, right? Was it locked?" Polly asked. Think, Kay think. What should she say? Help. Could the team hear this through that glass?

Perhaps if Kay offered up the information from the boy she could get herself off the hook? She could throw Ariana under the bus so to speak. She could open the door and point out Ariana and say 'she's the one you should be speaking to – she's the one that was with them both on Christmas Eve', yet she says not a word. Ariana just stares in at me all day like a perfectly manicured dummy. She's the one you need to speak to, not me!

"What did you even have my hair for? I don't understand, Polly? What DNA are you talking about?" Kay asked.

"I was testing it. Remember? I was going to cross reference with your dad and then with Kenneth Spiers if your dad came back negative," Polly said.

"What the fuck? Polly? No," Kay said, shaking her head.

"That will have to wait now. Benedict must have been snooping around for information in the quiet of Christmas. Thinking he wouldn't be noticed. Did you keep it locked? Your room. S17?" Polly asked. She bent her head to look up into Kay's eyes again. Kay held her gaze, aghast. Polly shook her. "Was it left open Kay?" she asked. Think fast.

"Yes. Yes, we had passes for the main doors. But for some reason I think we left S17 open, because there was something wrong with the lock. We hadn't reported it. It needed to be fixed," Kay lied irrationally. Don't say anything else. Don't make anything else up. They could check and see there was nothing wrong with the lock. "Look to be honest we only had one key between us. We were only issued with one key and so we used to keep our door propped open with a box of paper. We shouldn't have, but we did. I obviously didn't think it was in any way relevant or I would have said before now."

"OK, OK, that's good, that's good," Polly said, relieved that Kay had answers.

"Who else have you told about my DNA?" Kay asked.

"No one, yet. I just got the information and I wanted to tell you first," Polly said. They were going to pull that room apart, S17. "We're assuming it must have come from there; you'll be questioned fully but don't worry, it's just to establish that you owned that blanket or that it was in your possession," Polly said.

"Questioned?" Kay asked.

"Yes, it's a major development, you'll be brought in."

"But I've got nothing to do with this," Kay said. Polly turned around to look out through the glass; the team shuffled their heads back to their screens. Ariana remained staring.

"Why didn't you tell me that you got done for drink driving?"

"I don't know. I was ashamed," Kay said.

"But I can't understand why you wouldn't tell me?"

"I didn't want you not to like me," Kay said.

"When I said that you should leave Julia for yourself, and not because of me, I should have been clearer. I really like you, Kay. I should have just told you that I like you but I didn't want to scare you off," Polly said, moving in close against Kay, her hip pressing into Kay's thigh. "But I can't let my bosses know about us, so you shouldn't say when you're questioned."

"Of course. We can't let anyone know," Kay said, taking a step away.

Kay had thought at one time that she could tell Polly about Cyprus, but thank God she hadn't. She trusted Polly enough to think that she could say, one day. That she could tell her about her biggest secret and greatest shame. It was a heavy burden to carry on your own. Once you knew something like that about another person you could never let it go.

"Did you have an unsecured computer in there that Benedict could access?" Polly asked. Kay didn't even know Polly. She was a stranger and strangers were dangerous.

"I don't know, maybe, we had computers," Kay said.

"Phillips might have seen it as a way to hack into their system," Polly said.

"You think Benedict Phillips might have wiped the CCTV himself?" asked Kay.

"He might. We have him in the concourse. We have a print, almost the entire hand, but I didn't know what he did when he got in there; now I think we do. Do you remember when you last saw that blanket?" Polly asked.

"No. Not for a long time. There were loads of them. We have so much stuff like that coming through the office," Kay said, but she was worried because she did have a favourite blanket and it was from that show. She kept it on her chair at the Excel. They were really soft and expensive; they never had them made as nice again. Should she say? She shouldn't say anything without advice.

If Kay opened her mouth now, where would it end?

"And you had never seen Benedict Phillips before?" Polly asked. Kay was sure Polly had asked her that before and the only reason she would ask again was if she didn't trust Kay. Surely? Why would she ask again? Keep calm. If Kay had said she didn't know him then why was she asking again?

"No," Kay said but she saw him all the time. Every day. Whenever her confidence wobbled, she saw him. In the dark she saw him lurking in corners where brick met shadow. She was sleeping better knowing that his lungs were filled with water. That she would never pass him in the street by accident.

CHAPTER TWENTY-NINE

Kay needed to go home. But where? She needed to curl up in bed. After her mother died, she slept all day. Just fell asleep on the sofa, body powering down. Kay had stalled, frozen; there was no point remaining in this same vein of consciousness. Alarmingly, she was calm. The memories had stopped. She had gone to crisis mode, for real.

There was only one memory left. A shuddering, violent memory that came to her in times of trouble. A lonesome, bothersome memory which reminded her that underneath it all, she really was shit. She was on the floor, in Cyprus, dirt up her skirt and under her fingernails. In the clarity of her new frame of mind she only had questions.

Why was Benedict at the Excel? What had he been doing there with Ariana? Was that nurse Valérie with them in Excel? Belinda was right. It was not a coincidence.

At home in Hampstead, Julia's son, Henry, was eating a pizza and watching TV. It was a cheap frozen pizza that he had bought at the corner shop; Kay could see the box sticking up out of the bin. Julia would not like that. Not only was it sticking out, but it was in the normal bin, not the recycling bin, and Julia was rigorous about recycling.

"A box came for you," said Henry. "I think it's from the Excel."

"What is it?" asked Kay, trying to move the box. It was huge.

"It's a computer," said Henry. "It says so on the side." It was the new Mac that they had installed in S17. The computer that Ariana had installed ready for the opening of the boat show.

"Thanks," said Kay.

"She's been going mad you know," said Henry.

"Who?" asked Kay.

"Mum. You must have done something bad," Henry said.

If she just had that bottle of tiny little pills. Her fucking dad. Jim. If it wasn't for him then none of this would have ever happened. None of it. Kay's movements became slow. Staggered. Arrested. She paused. Take a deep breath. Can't run away. She would like to run away.

Julia knew. Kay went up the stairs. Julia knew.

One at a time at first, then running; the second flight she flew up, falling, coat flapping, catching the steps to tumble like she was wearing a clown's over-sized shoes and that spinning thing that happens when you are really drunk and you know you are going to be sick. Oh. Oh. She ran to the toilet and vomited. The two pints she had at the North Star, plus Ariana's coffee deposited with a tart twist.

Then into their bedroom. Julia was sitting on the edge of the bed. She must have heard Kay come in. Heard her go up the stairs. Heard her be sick and confirm everything in that bodily expulsion. Her face was red. Tears. Angry, teeth showing, snarling like a dog. But her eyes were soft, injured, wide, disbelieving.

"Say it's not true," Julia said, but Kay could see that Julia already knew it was true. Then slowly a new tear descended and her right eye blinked slowly on its own, blinked in slow-motion. "Say it isn't true."

Kay lifted a hand to her hair and held her head at the back. Silent. Mind blank. Erased. No spin. No. Kay shook her head.

Small movement. Moved the hand over her mouth. No. No. What have I done? Sorry. So sorry. Kay's eyes filled with tears. Julia looked away. She looked out of the window. A big gesture. A blank. A disgust. You are nothing to me. You have hurt me. Away. Then she moaned, like a feral animal sound. She let all the air go out of her body and she jerked, like a giant hiccup when the air went back in. Kay shook, not from shock, she actually shook with fright because she had never hurt someone else so badly in all her life.

"You were seen Kay. You were seen in Primrose Hill carrying on with some other woman. It's around the corner for God's sake," said Julia.

"I'm sorry," said Kay.

"So it is true then?" snapped Julia and she span around.

Silence.

"Go," Julia said.

"I'm sorry," Kay said.

"Go." Julia said.

Kay walked towards her and put out her hand to touch Julia on the shoulder, a featherlight touch, because Kay wanted to help her. Kay cared about her. No, she loved her. It was Julia for God's sake. Julia turned and stood up and slapped Kay hard across the face. It stung until the following day. It felt so fucking good that at last someone had the balls to just hit her.

"Get out of my house," said Julia, and then it was Kay who was crying, because in that instant she knew she had lost her. Lost everything. On the way out, Henry called out after her to ask if she was OK. But Kay didn't know if he meant her or Julia, and stunned, Kay just kept saying;

"I'll see you later, I'll see you later."

"What the fuck is going on?" said Henry, exasperated.

CHAPTER THIRTY

Instinctively, Kay got in her car. Pending a ban. She was yet to be disqualified from driving and wasn't sure about the consequences, but cared not for rules and void insurances and, if she was caught, potentially a short custodial sentence. Drive. Run. Get away. Get home, wherever that is.

What had she done?

Kay drove east; the car was driving itself. It was unlocking all of those previous times visiting. All those times in recent years to save her mother. To do her duty. Memories were stacking up on top of each other. One time Kay's mother had fallen out of the bath. Jim had dropped her and her poor leg with her dry scaly skin was cut deep. Kay's mother used to fuss over Kay's cuts and bruises when she was a child. She would clean the wound and dress it. Kay hadn't even bothered to look at that deep cut on her mother. She winced with the pain of regret.

They're not your precious babies, are they? Your mothers. But you are theirs.

"You ain't taking my baby from me," Kay's mother had shouted at the hairdresser, spittle coming out of her mouth over and over again. "You ain't taking my baby from me." And all these people; carers, the hairdresser, helpful neighbours – all texting, updating, reporting.

"She's getting worse. The disease is progressing. She's done this. She's done that," They all said.

"I know. I fucking know!" Kay screamed alone in her car on the A406 north circular road. Kay pushed the accelerator to the floor. Gripped the wheel in both hands.

What time was it? She was losing time. Her neck was itchy again, under the chin, creeping up into her cheeks. She stopped in a retail park. There was a giant pet shop and she went in. She picked a brown leather collar, with orange trim and a matching lead. She would buy it for Polly's dog Reggie. Would she buy it for Reggie? Yes, yes she would. She bought it for Reggie. And a pig's ear. A leathery pig's ear.

She sat in her car smoking. Three cigarettes in a row. She drank Lucozade. She watched drops of rain scatter on her windscreen and she inspected the way that they took the red brake lights and filtered them and made them their own shape. New. Distorted.

The Golden Lion reflected radiant in the car park puddles, like New York reflects in the Hudson River at night. Out loud Kay said to herself in a baby's voice, 'The Golden Lion'. And she put her middle finger up at the pub as she drove past on the other side of the dual carriageway. The thought of sleeping the night in her old room was horrifying but a horror that she must endure. Her penance. She was being pulled home. A spirit guide was bringing her back here.

Kay wanted to get her mother's rosary beads from the drawer next to the bed, get on her knees and pray. Up the path she searched for a key in her bag. Her dad wouldn't be expecting her. Kay didn't care. They would have a passive argument, a dazzle of friction then they would settle down in front of the telly for the night.

As usual the curtains were open. It was dark and you could see the room lit inside. She caught a glimpse at first. Jim was sat in his chair. But there was someone else. A woman. Her blonde head was in his lap. Kay was spoiling for a fight. In her mother's house. It was not right. Something was askew. She pushed opened the door, a fraction. Jim stroked the head. The woman was kneeling on the floor, but to the side. At first Kay thought, well, she thought… But the angle wasn't right for that and the woman was crying and Jim was soothing her. Like she was his baby.

"There now. It's over now," said Jim, Kay's dad.

"Oh, Jim, oh," said Ariana. That stupid accent. That voice. Kay knew the voice. Ariana. But before she could hear what she was saying, Kay was slowly pushing the door open a fraction more and they could see her. Startled, Ariana jumped.

"Kay. What are you doing here?" asked Ariana.

"What's going on?" asked Kay and Ariana unfolded her long body which had been curled up at Jim's feet. She was like an ancient dragon opening up her huge sinewy limbs. The taller she got, the more Kay recoiled. Something wild rose in Kay; she felt like she would lunge at Ariana and rip the eyes from her head, bringing her head down crashing to the floor and shattering her brains. The vibration was palpable. Kay was trembling. Her fists were clenched.

In this house was something secret. A shattering secret. What is it?

"Why are you here Ariana?" asked Kay.

"Now Kay, calm down love. Let's all have a sit down. Let's talk about it," said Jim.

"Talk about what?" asked Kay. Ariana started to shake violently. She brought her hands up in front of her body and then heaved. She cried, the tears flushing down her face, and then she dropped suddenly back onto the floor. She hit the floor hard. Jim leant forward in the chair and started patting Ariana like a dog.

"I am always here. I'm always here with Jim. Aren't I, Jim?" said Ariana. Kay strained to hear.

"I think you know love," said Jim. Kay did not know.

"I don't know anything," said Kay, "I don't know what is going on here. What she is doing here? What are you doing to her?"

"It could've been you," Jim said.

"Dave is coming now. He will sort this all out," said Ariana, sitting herself up.

"What are you talking about?" asked Kay. Jim scratched his head. Cleared his throat. Shifted in his seat.

"It could have been you, you know. Or your mother, or another girl," he said. "I would do the same again. I'd do it all over again."

"What on earth are you talking about? Dad?" asked Kay.

"Shhh Jim," said Ariana. "Don't speak. Shhh. Dave will sort it out."

Ariana clawed at Jim's hand. Her head moved in jumps. Like she was possessed by a spirit. None of her movements were smooth; she had lost her fidelity. The spinning top had come off.

"What have you done?" Kay asked. Something terrible. Jim, or they, had done something terrible.

"He'd been following her," said Jim.

"He would pull up in his car, say 'get in', or he'd make things up about me to tell Dave," echoed Ariana, nodding, terrified.

"Who?" Kay asked.

"Benedict Phillips of course," said Jim.

"I told you Kay. I told you," Ariana said.

"He'd been making a nuisance. Stalking or whatever you call it," said Jim.

"His ex-wife moved into our street, and then this girl was

with him. I had to set up that stupid computer before the Christmas holidays, and I left it to the last minute. I forgot to do it, and you would have gone mad –" Ariana said, but Jim quickly interrupted.

"I saw them walk into Excel together. I watched Ariana and Benedict on my screen and I came down to your press room to check she was alright because I didn't know who he was," said Jim.

"The ex-wife lives around the corner. I still see her. He was there every weekend. Watching us. Walking past. Knocking on the door. Dave warned him to stay away. Dave saw him at an army meet up and he threatened him," Ariana said, and she panted on short-circuited breaths. Her eyes darted. Jim put his hand flat on her head.

"The bastard had got hold of her. In your press room," Jim said.

Jim needed new bulbs in the front room. The light wasn't right. It was too brown. Like warm blood and thick as sugar water. It looked like it was running down the walls.

"I hit him. Only once mind, but it was hard," said Jim.

"You punched him?" asked Kay. He couldn't punch anyone. He was weak. A weak man. He couldn't overpower a trained soldier.

"No, I properly hit him with the present you got me last Christmas," Jim said. Two years ago Kay had bought him a short-handled camping axe.

"An axe?" repeated Kay.

"It was a small one. Yes. But only with the flat end. It must have caught him on the temple," said Jim. Kay had searched camping shops for that axe, trying them out in her hands, feeling the weight, wanting to please him with a gift that he would love. She had paid on her credit card and she assumed that was probably traceable if police ever found the axe. She knew he took it to work and that he held it as a weapon in his security shed, his version of the baseball bat.

"Where is it?" asked Kay. The question fell out of Kay's mouth, in lieu of anything else to say. She wasn't still quite sure what she was being told.

"Gone. Burned. It nearly ricocheted out of my hand and flew across the room," Jim said, satisfied.

"Did he get up?" asked Kay.

Ariana shook her head and looked at the floor. She kept doing it over and over and saying, "No, no, no..."

"No. Christ no. There was a crack. A big noise. The flat end, as I say, must have got him sweet, right on the, I don't know. So no. No, he didn't get up again," said Jim.

"Jesus Christ. What have you done?" asked Kay.

"He was on her Kay. Do I have to spell it out? He was raping her. He didn't even see me. Just for a moment, just before it landed, he knew I was there and then he was out of it," Jim said. Kay stood in the doorway. Ariana wiped her face with her hands. Breathed.

"You went to install the computer?" asked Kay.

"He kept following me, Kay. He said he would give me five hundred pounds. I wouldn't have sex with him. He got in my car with me. I just thought I'd get rid of him before Dave saw him and went crazy. I didn't think he would do anything," said Ariana, trailing off into a whimper.

"Does Dave know?" asked Kay.

"I thought you could see the bruise on my face Kay. I thought you could see it. You could see it, couldn't you?" pleaded Ariana. Kay shrugged. She didn't know what she was being asked. She was hearing what she was being told but was not understanding.

"Does Dave know?" asked Kay again.

"I thought you could see that I was in pain, Kay." Ariana said, pleading. Kay felt her shifting blame onto her.

"No. I thought you were pregnant," Kay said, and Ariana roared with crying. She clutched her stomach. Jim leaned forward and stroked her head again. He had never touched Kay in thirty-eight years. The closest she had ever got to him was sitting on the cross-bar of his bicycle.

Jim. It was Jim. It was Jim all along.

"Why didn't you tell the police?" Kay asked. "I don't understand why you wouldn't just telephone the police? If it was self-defence? Why wouldn't you just call the police?"

"No police," Ariana said.

"Well we should have but we didn't, did we? Then it was too late," Jim said.

"No police," Ariana said again, and she started to laugh. In between sobs and laughs she snorted words, but it was hard to understand her.

"We didn't want to get you into trouble, at work. A scandal. We thought it was the only way to keep you out of it," said Jim.

"Me?" Kay said. "It's got fuck all to do with me." But of course it did have. Why hadn't Kay gone to the police in 2006, because if she had, none of this would have ever happened.

"You think it's the end of the world when your client sacks you, Kay, but you don't have a clue. When my clients were unhappy, they beat me or they raped me!" Ariana screamed.

Kay steadied herself against the wall. Two feet on the ground. She would have felt better in trainers. More able to run. She didn't know where to. She was running out of places.

She opened her mouth to speak. Nothing came out. Her mother swirled slowly around the living room with Kenneth Spiers, exactly where Ariana sat buckled, a malformed version of herself, facial features melted away; although clothed she was as naked as the day she was born. She reminded Kay of a foal who won't walk after birth. Something wrong with it. Something for the farmers to tend to, to discuss putting her down. Do the decent thing. Put her out of her misery.

"It was a life. Was it better than the life I lead now? No, of course not. I'm not going back. My life is with Dave. We want to have a family. I'm not going back, I'm never going back. No police," said Ariana.

"We didn't want to drop you in it. We wanted it to go away quietly," said Jim.

The pile of the living room carpet was flattened with the burden of this house. It was compacted with the weight of miscommunication. Remnants of human excrement and piss knotted the threads together.

Kay still didn't know. She had never asked Ariana, had never wanted to know where Dave had met her. On the internet? Tick. I believe you Dave. That's all I need to know. Ariana had a job. Everyone's happy. No questions asked. All fixed.

Kay turned to try and get air. Breathe. Must breathe. Need to get out. "Must get out," Kay said. But she had left the door open and Dave was standing there behind her. He clenched his fist so that his car keys made a clustered jingling sound. He filled the doorway, blocking the beam of light from the street lamp.

CHAPTER THIRTY-ONE

Dave took Kay by the hand and led her outside, away from Jim and Ariana. They sat in his car. Kay wanted to leave, but Dave was insistent that he wanted her to stay with him for a while. To talk things through. Dave sat in the driver's seat, Kay in the passenger seat. They were quiet for some time. All around was silent, London at three or four in the morning. It was like the times Kay used to creep in late at night, like a restless tom cat.

Jim's stolen bicycle was propped up in front of the blue gate – for all to see. He would get into serious trouble for riding a stolen bicycle. She expected a night street cleaner to come by, or something to mark out the time. She had lost track. She didn't know how long she had been where. The clock flashed in the car with the time; she still could not see it in front of her.

Kay was sane.

Kay was in her right mind.

Everyone else around her was mad.

Everyone.

The engine was idling. People could hear a car engine at night. They might look out from behind net curtains like Kay's mother used to. Dave trained a cursory breath of warm air from a vent aimed at Kay. It dried Kay's eyes to the bone. She rubbed them. Dave massaged his brow between the eyes with his index finger. He was thinking.

"I took his ear off," Dave said. "He came round while I was doing it. The sensation must have woken him. The pain. So I had to slice it quickly. I had the knife there, but I'd already bound him. Legs and wrists. He started making a right noise, so I grabbed the blanket. Didn't think. Had to work fast. It was the only thing I hadn't thought about. Well I didn't know he was going to wake up, did I? I thought your old man had finished him off, but I should've known better. Anyway, I shoved it in his mouth, a good portion of blanket. That shut him up. And before I pulled the rest around I said to him, 'oh good, you're awake'. You should have seen his face!" Dave started laughing and his chin disappeared into his neck. "He looked so frightened, Kay. I had my knee on his chest, my full weight."

Kay remembered training with Dave. The way he leaned on her. Used his weight to stretch her muscles. If he wanted, he could have smothered her.

"So I wrapped his head in that blanket," Dave continued, "I thought about it after, but too late then. It would have made too much mess and noise to start again. I didn't know when anyone might turn up. Your dad was catatonic. They were holding each other. Ariana had blood all over her face. Her skirt and blouse were ripped. He'd really knocked her about. I can't believe you didn't notice the bruises, Kay? Sometimes, for a bright person, you are so unobservant."

Dave was usually so quiet. For their entire lives he had never said more than a few words at a time. Now he couldn't shut up.

Kay looked out the passenger window and imagined her mum travelling backwards in time up the front path. She held her hand up to the car door glass. Kay could see her Mum's homemade shopping bag. The sweet gap in her front teeth which was meant to mean she would be rich one day, but she never was.

"I'll never see her see again," said Kay, as a thick tear ran down her cheek. Kay's face was wet. Her breath steamed the glass. She smeared it clear. Sniffed a nose-full of mucus. Rubbed her snotty nose upwards on the fleshy mound of her thumb.

"I did it for you," Dave said.

"Shut up. Shut up, Dave. No you did not," Kay said, furious. But the fury made her weak and exhausted.

"I wondered. I thought that he'd done something to you. But by the time we got back from Cyprus he was promoted. He was out of my reach. He went mental in Pristina with the girls. Shocking, the things he got up to. I mean he really had it coming Kay. No one's missed him. Not one person. Everyone's better off without him. Even his kids are better off without him. Some people shouldn't be allowed to have children," Dave said.

Please stop talking. Kay shut her mouth. Tight.

"I need you to understand," Dave grabbed Kay's arm. His grip was too tight. He wanted to talk. Kay's body was flaccid, broken.

"Benedict got into the business end with the girls. Got into dealings with local organisers arranging for girls to come into the camp. Ariana, or Lucy as she was called then, when I first met her, came in a few times," said Dave.

Kay nodded.

"I really liked her. I just clicked with her. The sex was incredible," said Dave, as he released Kay's arm and stared out into the road ahead. Kay nodded. Dave was unravelling, unburdening his soul. He turned to look at Kay. "I told you. I told you years ago that I'd had the best sex of my life with a prostitute in Pristina," he smiled at the thought, "then I found her. She was in these rooms," said Dave, "with another girl and an older woman who took care of business. It seemed like a nice place, not what you'd expect at all. I tried to take her out. But you couldn't really go on a date. She was still working. She was better off than a lot of them. She wanted to come to England."

"I bet she did," Kay said off the cuff.

"She wanted to live a normal life. No war, no soldiers. To be safe. To not have to worry about violence. The sort of life you take for granted, Kay, having your own business, freedom. After a year I got sent on." He welled up, his eyes ringing with tears and his Adam's apple plunged. "I told her I loved her," he said.

Jim was on his own so much. Kay had neglected him. Hadn't she? Kind of on purpose, drawn away after her mother's death. She had cut the apron strings. No wonder he took to Ariana, stroking her head like that. His grainy yellowing fingers in her peroxide hair, like kernels of corn in a field of yellow flowers. Ariana had no parents of her own that Kay knew about. Perhaps she had been disowned. At least Kay knew what her sister, Rhea, had been talking about. Dave said she had told her family that she was doing humanitarian work in Pristina. But she serviced soldiers, from all sides, all day and all night. She mustn't have believed her luck with Dave. The one who wanted to stay and talk, and not just screw until his hour was up.

"I came back to Colchester for three months. Remember?"

"I remember," said Kay.

"Then I went to Afghanistan and all that time I thought about her every day. I tried calling the rooms where she lived. She'd moved on. When I got back to England the last time before I came out of the army, I was in a bad way. I couldn't get her out of my mind. Then she emailed out of the blue. Her name was Ariana. She'd gone to her sister's in Germany. I flew straight there. We've been together ever since. Hardly a night apart. I won't be parted from her."

"Dave, why did you not just call the police straight away?" asked Kay.

"He wasn't dead was he? I had to finish him off. I'd already cut his ear off before I realised he was still alive," said Dave, resigned. "I was trying to make it look gang related. Couldn't call the police after that."

Dave leaned into Kay. For a hateful second her stomach dropped as she thought he was going to kiss her. She braced herself. She knew that to run would be the wrong thing to do. Let him talk. Talk herself. Try and get some normality back, try and redefine the boundaries of their world. Let night become day.

But instead of kissing her, he reached across the hard plastic molding of the dashboard and unclicked the glove box. He took out a small metal tin. The kind that holds soft sugary biscuits or fudge that you buy in gift shops in Devon and Cornwall. It was gold and white with old-fashioned drawings depicting beach scenes, families crabbing, beachcombing, and a boy with a fishing line.

"I kept it for you," said Dave, and he handed Kay the tin. She let it sit in her lap for a moment and then opened it. The lid sprang open and back on its hinges. Dave smiled.

"Go on. Open it," he said, like it was a birthday present. Inside, there was a piece of white cotton. Kay tugged at it gently looking to the side at Dave. She chanced a smile herself and she could see that he liked that. With both hands she gently moved the cotton apart and at first could not make it out. Something big. The same length as her index finger, but round, oval, a hole in the middle and a brown zigzag laceration up the right hand side. It was the same colour as Kay's finger for it was flesh. The blood had dried black. An ear. Benedict's ear.

CHAPTER THIRTY-TWO

Kay's vision shut down to a horizontal white buzzing line. A terrible pain came over her left side and she saw swirling dots of black and white spinning. She couldn't stop looking at it. It was like a child's joke toy, the bloody ear in a tobacco tin. It looked like it was made of wax. There were thick black hairs in three places and a tiny pin prick in the baggy lobe where he must have had it pierced. It looked like a tiny fetus, a miscarriage held in Kay's hands.

Kay thought she might have been hit over the head but she wasn't. Dave was right there, arm around her. He pushed his fingertips into her neck muscles. At the front. They massaged the area where her Adam's apple would have been, had she been a man. She could feel their pressure. She could feel the ends of the four fingers and a thumb dipping into her skin, pressing on her oesophagus.

"We need to keep this to ourselves, Kay. Don't we?" said Dave. Kay nodded; his fingers remained still against the movement of her head up and down.

"Good. I knew you'd understand. It is very important that no one else finds out," said Dave.

"Yes," said Kay. He released her throat.

"He's gone. Forever," Dave smiled. "Keep that," he said, gesturing to the tin open in Kay's lap. So tired of the action, Kay remembered that she had wanted to sleep hours before. Her eyes were vibrating in their sockets. Then Kay's phone buzzed with a message. Dave grabbed her phone and read the message. 'I can't wait to see you again.' It was from Polly Harvey.

"I can't believe you would do this to Julia," Dave said.

"I didn't plan it," said Kay.

"It's the worst crime that you don't get locked up for. What's your password?" asked Dave. Kay gave him the number. She did not resist. He smiled when he realised it was her parent's old telephone number. He typed it into Kay's phone.

"I really like her. Polly, I like her," Kay said.

"What have you told her?" asked Dave, turning off Kay's phone and putting it into his pocket.

"Polly?" asked Kay.

"Yes, the policewoman, what exactly have you told her?" Dave asked.

"Nothing. Absolutely nothing. I don't know anything to tell her. Jesus Christ."

"Have you told her you knew Benedict?"

"No, Dave, I haven't I swear. It was so long ago I didn't say at first and then I thought it would be weird to say after a while, and now I can't say because I'll look like a liar," Kay said.

"You are a liar, Kay."

"None of this has anything to do with me, Dave."

"You're lying to her already. How can you be in a relationship where you lie? Fucking liar, Kay. Come on, Kay, sort it out. I'd never lie to Ariana. Truth. That's what we do. Truth. No matter how hard it is," Dave said.

"Please Dave. Leave her out of this. It's nothing to do with her. I won't see her again. She's nothing to do with this."

"She's obviously bright. It's all swirling round isn't it, not going to take her much to put it all together. Then we're fucked." Dave punched the ceiling of the car. Left a mark. Nearly put his hand through the roof. He didn't flinch.

"No. She doesn't know anything. They think it's to do with

Russians and Arabs, people Benedict was working for. Polly's been given another case, a hit and run. She would never guess this. Honestly, Dave, come on," Kay said.

"She's phoned me, Kay. Today," said Dave.

"What?" asked Kay, "No."

"She's left a message," Dave said.

"Why?" asked Kay.

"Why do you think? She's checking all known contacts. I served with him," said Dave.

"I swear she does not know a single thing, Dave please. Don't think like this because there's no need to escalate this. It's just routine. She doesn't know a thing," said Kay, wondering what exactly did Polly know? Had Kay left her phone out? Did she know she was lying about knowing Benedict? Did she know that Kay knew Dave?

"What about that other one? The stiff one with the square haircut at your office?" asked Dave.

"Jacquie? She's doesn't know a thing. So please don't even bring her into this," said Kay. "Dave, no way, leave her alone, it's nothing to do with her, honestly."

"Ariana said she was all over it, down there at the beginning," said Dave.

"She was just taking notes," said Kay, "Jacquie's nothing to do with this."

"We'll have to go away for a while. No rush. Nothing hasty," said Dave.

"Me? No, Dave, no," said Kay.

"Not you. Me and Ariana. Just quietly, like as if we've planned to for a long time. An extended honeymoon," Dave said. "The passports are all sorted now. Had to spend two grand on a new computer. Your dad knocked the fuck out of the other one with a small axe. The one Ariana was setting up. That's why she was there Kay. For you. You should have seen her trembling when she went back with the replacement. I couldn't be seen, but she went in there and put it back in that bloody room. What a woman she is." He pleaded for Kay to come back inside the house. Kay shook her head and looked down at Benedict's dismembered ear sitting in her lap.

"Come back to mine," he said. No fucking way. It grew like a small seed. A paranoid drip. He might cut off her ear. She might know too much. Don't let him see. Why hasn't he finished off Jim too? That would be an easy shut up for drunken big mouth Golden Lion Jim. Where had Dave been in all these years since they were kids? In brothels and bunkers and chopping people up. "I'll put you to bed. You're in shock. I've seen shock before, Kay. I need to keep an eye on you."

"I'm fine. I just need to process," Kay said. Don't let him see. Don't let him. The line between them stretched across the void of gear stick and radio. The space between them was dark matter. Solid. Impenetrable. Kay felt as though she were pressed up against the passenger side window but at the same time his face was just two feet away from hers. She could see his pores. One dilated, open, cavernous.

"I'll drive you home then." Dave said.

"I can't go home. Julia's angry with me. That's why I came here," Kay said.

"I'll take you to Belinda's. You are not to say a word. Neither of us would want Belinda mixed up in all of this now would we? I'll message her, see if she's up. Say you've fought with Julia. Say that's why you are upset."

Kay nodded.

"I'll keep hold of your phone for now," Dave said, "I need to just keep an eye on you for a while until you settle down. You are very upset. I better keep this for now, you can have it back later."

He tucked the ear back inside the cotton handkerchief and closed the tin but left it in Kay's lap. He drove to Belinda's boat. It didn't take long. Fifteen minutes of silence. He texted as he drove, pretending to be Kay, having a whole conversation. Belinda came out to the gate in her dressing gown. There was a frost. The temperature plummeted. Kay slid on the pontoon and Belinda held her fast. Dave pretended to drive away but Kay looked back to see him turn off his engine and sit waiting in the car park.

CHAPTER THIRTY-THREE

He's out there.

Belinda put Kay into the spare room and she drifted in and out of sleep. A mass of words softly spoken came out of Belinda's mouth.

In her head Kay made a list of all the people that he had punched. When he snapped. When he got angry. Rarely. Very rare to see him lose his cool, oh, but when he did! Polly. Belinda. Everyone was in danger now. Was he there? Was he out there? Rain was pelting the roof of the boat. It sounded like a fire crackling on fast forward.

Dave swirling in the water.

Dave climbing onto the boat in the middle of the night.

The bruises on Ariana? The black eye? The sickness. No. That was Benedict who had done that. Still, Dave climbing onto the boat in the middle of the night. A knife in his hand, or in his belt, or in his teeth. No one could hear him. He could do that. He had killed before. In the army. He would creep in, in the night, and slit their throats. Cut off their ears. Cut out their eyes. Stuff material into their mouths.

She shouldn't have come here. Shouldn't have put Belinda in danger.

Kay looked out of the porthole. She couldn't see the car park. Her line of vision was swaying with the motion of the boat. She should not have brought Belinda into it. Keep her out of it.

Benedict's body had been in this same water. Dissolved. Maybe minute, microscopic fibres or DNA were all around Kay.

Kay got up, swaying. Into the corridor. She vomited into

the sink in the bathroom. She pushed open the door of Belinda's bedroom. Belinda jumped. She turned over quickly, her body outlined under the duvet, white-blue in the darkness hit up by the neon of Canary Wharf.

"What are you doing?" Belinda asked.

"I'm frightened. Can I get in with you?" asked Kay.

"Are you alright, Kay? You're scaring me. Get in," Belinda said and she moved to the right hand side of the bed to make more space for Kay. The cotton sheets were warm and comforting and then Kay felt instantly repulsed at who might have been in these sheets before. Then it hit her.

"He sent us the video, Belinda."

"Who?"

"Dave. He sent it to us both. He doesn't want us to be friends," Kay said, and they curled up together trembling like little girls with no mummies to comfort them. They pushed the wardrobe up against the door, but still they felt like sitting ducks bobbing about in the basin waiting for the hunter to split the reeds.

The dead came back that night. With her eyes closed Kay saw a hessian cloth being stitched into a semicircle from the inside. She became convinced it was someone telling her from beyond this earth about when they were stitched into cloth inside their coffin. She wasn't sure if they even did that. Put you inside a cloth, inside your coffin? But what else could it be? Why would she think it? Did they stitch her mother inside a hessian cloth? She saw her mother's face suffocated under cloth.

Kay started to fade into sleep but saw a face. The girl. Valérie. Where was she? Kay sat up in bed. The girl. The little girl. Dave had her. Dave had the girl somewhere.

"Where's the girl? Benedict's girlfriend? Where is she?" Kay asked. Belinda sat up in the bed too. She wouldn't stop talking, pleading with Kay to stay inside. But Kay knew what she had to do. Belinda remonstrated with Kay and followed her through the kitchen while Kay climbed the ladder out into the night.

The pontoon rocked softly under Kay's bare feet. It was so cold they stuck to the metal. She crossed the car park to Dave's car, knowing that he would still be there. It was frosting up with ice but she heard the hum of his electric window and then she saw his face.

"Where's the girl? Where is Valérie?" Kay asked.

"Oh she's fine," Dave said, "she's just taking a break."

PART III:

SUFFOCATE

CHAPTER THIRTY-FOUR

3rd July 2010

The TV was on full blast at Kay's parent's house. It was always too loud but today especially as it was the Wimbledon final. The TV amplified the echo of the bounce of ball. 'Forty love' boomed. Long ago, Kay's mother dreamed of Kay playing there. Kay's mother was wearing a green dress with white flowers. Buttons up the front. It was hard to get it on over her head. She was particular now about what she wore, favouring jumpers with pink stripes. Childish. That's what she liked and she put up a fight if you tried to put her in anything else. The stripy tops were thinning threadbare at the elbows and stained with tea and beans from missing her mouth.

Dave wanted Kay's mother to come. He called her Mrs Christie half out of cheek and half out of respect. He was very fond of her. It was old people and babies during the day for drinks in the garden of the pub and then later that night they would move on to the Hurricane Rooms. It was his thirtieth birthday. He had called Kay and invited everyone. She hadn't spoken to him for a while. He had a new girlfriend he wanted to introduce to Kay. He was buzzing. According to his own messages and emails he was in great form. The black dog had lifted.

Jim raced in from the back door, his trouser legs ballooning where he had kept his bicycle clips on. He wore two. You only needed one. He seized the remote control and changed channel to horse racing. Clare Balding launched her microphone at a boysy horse owner in a red tie. He had won. Working class lad done good. He was clenching both fists in victory, eyes glassy with tears, chest inflated, and veins in his neck straining.

"Missed it. What's the price? What's the price?" Jim asked, as he flicked the channel again to teletext and punched in numbers. He was doing it wrong. Flustered. It was 665 but he had just put in 65. Kay snatched the remote control from Jim and pressed the correct number in for him.

"Hello Jim," Julia said. Kay's mother was pretending to dust an imaginary sideboard. Moving around the room rotating her hand in a circular motion saying, 'there now. So.' Jim laughed and nodded at Julia but didn't take his eyes off the TV.

"What's she doing? Silly bugger," Jim said.

"She's tidying. Leave her alone," Julia said in a quiet fury. A solitary fly was bombing around. The shiny neon bluebottle buzzed desperately for freedom amidst the fabric of the net curtains. Jim caught it between his thumb and forefinger. He squeezed it. It popped and perished in his fingers.

"Dad," Kay shouted, "for God's sake, that's disgusting. This is a madhouse." He pushed out the front window and flicked its body off his finger into the front garden.

"Seven to one. Seven to one!" Jim said, and he jigged side to side and giggled, immediately turning the TV back to the tennis where they were interviewing Martina Navratilova in the commentary box. He gave the remote control to Julia and winked. "They're bloody taking over!"

The doorbell rang. Mrs Christie looked confused. Belinda Salas shouted, 'hello' through the open window. She had come straight from the hairdresser. She looked immaculate. A tiny doll with soppy eyes wanting to be loved.

"Who is that now?" Mrs Christie asked, angry that someone had knocked at the door.

"Mum, it's Belinda!" Kay said, opening the door.

"Hello Mrs Christie. Lovely to see you. I haven't seen you for ages," Belinda said and she scrunched herself up and smiled big, embracing Kay's mother, whose face beamed with delight and recognition.

"Belinda, of course! It's lovely to see you!" Mrs Christie said. Jim squeezed out through the front door. He smelled of cut grass and lemon and the mild sweat of gardening on a summer's day. He wasn't coming with them. He couldn't be taken anywhere.

"I've got to collect my winnings," he said. Belinda held Kay's mother's arms.

"You remember Belinda, don't you Mum? From when we went to Cirque du Soleil," Kay said.

"Yes. Yes. You work with Kay don't you?" Mrs Christie asked. Belinda didn't work with Kay, but they all nodded and said 'yes' anyway. "How are your mum and dad?" This was a stock question that she always asked everyone. To make Kay feel better people often said, 'Your mum's fine, she was asking after my mum and dad, there's nothing wrong with her.' But she asked everybody the same question.

"Let's go and have a few drinks shall we Mrs Christie?" Belinda said.

"Me?" asked Kay's mother, like a little girl. "Am I allowed?"

Julia drove. Belinda sat in Julia's son Henry's booster seat in the back that made her the perfect height to see out of the window. It was smeared with the white residue of an ice cream; its corners were full of crumbs.

"What's Ariana like?" Belinda asked. She was trying to hold

Mrs Christie's hand in the back, but Mrs Christie was looking at her like she was mad while humming 'Ave Maria'.

"Whose is this? I never knew my car was this big in the back. All these years and I've never sat in the back. You'd never think it, would you?" Mrs Christie said.

"It's not your car Mum, it's Julia's car. Julia is driving. Look. It's her car. We left your car at home so you could have a drink," Kay said, but she had hidden the keys. Jim had been letting her drive. He had been sitting next to her telling her when to stop and when to go. He had done this on the motorway and at roundabouts. It was reckless and dangerous. The feckless idiot.

"You mean Ariana, Dave's new girlfriend? He met her on the internet. Just so you are prepared Belinda, he's really into her," Kay said.

"Really?" Belinda said, her eyes wide in disbelief or grimace. She gripped Mrs Christie's hand tighter. "I'm going to speak to Dave today and, I'm going to tell him how I feel about him and, if…" Belinda shook her head and looked down at the floor, clearing her throat, "and if he's not interested then I'm going to marry Bobby." Christ. On Dave's birthday. Kay hoped there wasn't going to be a scene.

"Bravo. That's the spirit Belinda. You need to get on with your life. Get on with Bobby. You can't be waiting around for him, letting him mess you around," Julia said. Belinda had the odour of desperation that seemed to make men screw her and run. Even Kay could smell it.

"Who's messing you around?" Mrs Christie shouted.

"Dave," Belinda said, "I think he does really like me Mrs Christie, he just can't show it." Kay's mother screwed up her eyes and her fists.

"That good for nothing," Mrs Christie shouted.

"Mum, it's fine. We're just having a joke, aren't we girls? We're OK. See?" Kay said.

"Bastard! That fucking bastard Ken. Took it from me," Mrs Christie shouted, spitting onto the window; flecks of white spittle peppered the glass like snow. Belinda leaned away, increasing the space between her and Mrs Christie.

"Mum! That's enough please," Kay said, undoing her seat belt to turn fully and lean around into the back seat. Julia and Kay had sex in that car many times.

"Dave. It's Dave, not Ken," Belinda said with her eye for detail.

"I know that." Mrs Christie said. "Dave is Kay's boyfriend since they were teenagers."

"I'm sorry about this," Kay said to Julia.

"What on earth is she talking about?" Julia asked.

"I don't know, she's being silly," said Kay. "Are you alright Mum?" Mrs Christie had her head held down chin to chest, in a mood, bottom lip stuck out like an impertinent child. "Don't cry now. Hmm? It's fine Mum. Julia's going to sing. Come on Julia, give us a song."

"He's got the whole world –" Julia sang.

"That's it Julia," Kay said. Her mum recognised the song immediately and looked up.

"In his hands!" They all sang, even Mrs Christie.

Julia pulled into the car park of the Alford Arms. White washed walls and wooden beams, an old coaching house turned urban country boozer off the A417. All the spaces at the front were taken, so she drove around the side to the bigger car park and that's when Kay saw Benedict getting out of a red Audi TT. She squashed down in her seat.

The outline of the shoulders into the stout neck up into the hairline told Kay that it was definitely him. She didn't have to see more but she turned to look and saw his face full on and it was him. Oh Jesus. It was him. The first time since. Why was he here? Why had Dave invited him? It was a big do. She didn't know. She never imagined that he would be here. She steeled herself. A wave of panic contracted up her arms to her temples where it raged vice-like. It felt like her eyes had fallen back into their sockets.

"What's the matter?" Julia instinctively asked. Thank God Mrs Christie was too distracted to notice, her empathy dimmed, switched to off. She wouldn't be able to understand Kay's fear.

"It's him," Kay said.

"Who babe? Who?" Julia asked, holding Kay's wrist and looking around frantically.

"Him."

Julia stopped in her tracks. Belinda was reapplying make-up. She had missed Benedict as they drove into the car park. Now, she started twisting and turning to see who or what on earth they were talking about.

"Oh, him from Cyprus. Gross. Sod him Kay, we'll ignore him, we don't have to speak to him. There's plenty of people to speak to," Belinda said lightly, not understanding the gravity for Kay. Not sensing Kay was petrified and on the verge of flight.

Heat. Rough palm. Mouth. Spit. She couldn't go in. Nothing worked. Legs. Hands that could not punch. Feet that could not run. You loser Kay.

"Bastard! Bastard!" Mrs Christie shouted with globules of saliva rattling around her lips. She soaked in bad energy like a sponge. She took it upon herself. Kay could see her mum's emotions were heightened, not diminished, as if that was all that was left once you took reason away was love and hate. Julia put her hands on Kay's shoulders.

"You're not going in," Julia said. "I'll go. Belinda and I will go. We'll make your excuses. It's too much for your mum anyway. Take the car and drive home. We'll get a taxi in an hour. Understood?"

"Yes," Kay said, and undid her seat belt. Julia was up and outside the driver's door looking back. Her shoes crunched over sand and gravel. A small fog of dry earth dust flicked up off the surface of the floor.

"Which one is he?" Julia asked.

"Over there. Going in. Blue shirt," Kay said.

"That one there?" Julia asked quietly to Kay alone. Kay nodded and climbed over the gear stick into the driver's seat. They were the same height, but Kay had longer legs so she put the seat back a couple of inches.

"What's going on?" Belinda asked.

"It's too much for Mrs Christie. Kay's going to take her home. It's not fair to let her cause a scene. Come on Belinda," Julia said and she tapped the roof of the car. Once Belinda saw Dave she would forget this interlude. Kay turned and circled and came back to pass them. "I love you," Julia said. Run. Go. Stay safe. Kay drove out passing the red Audi TT. Hung up on its rear view mirror, swinging steadily, were a pair of cherry boxing gloves.

CHAPTER THIRTY-FIVE

Kay had spent two days on board Belinda's boat. Against her wishes, Belinda had telephoned Julia and invited her to come around to speak with Kay. Kay roused herself to climb up and stand on the kitchen island to allow an obscured view through the upper portholes of Julia and Belinda conferring on the pontoon. Kay saw Julia. Oh, Julia. She was wearing a white mohair poncho and one hand rose up from underneath and Kay saw the burning ember of a cigarette. Oh Julia. The other hand was on her hip. Julia.

Kay went into the bathroom and when she emerged she knew that Belinda had gone and that Julia was there in the room. There was utter silence. Kay inched herself into the room. It was different. Re-owned. Julia's rage simmered on the stove. The boat rocked.

Julia must have heard Kay, but she didn't look up. First she reached forward to the coffee table and picked up a cigarette and lit it. The packet sounded satisfyingly full as she dropped it back onto the table. A swirling puff of smoke enveloped her face. Julia's eyes were red and swam in a thin skein of tears. Her tears didn't seem to roll. They didn't issue from her eyes, they sat there, two watery pools and now and again she put up a finger to usher them away.

"She's pretty. Young. Where did you meet her?" Julia asked.

"At work," Kay said.

"At the Excel? The body? How predictable. A police lady. It's your teen fantasy, no?" Julia said.

"No. Yes, during the Excel investigation," Kay said. Julia

pulled on the cigarette and placed two fingers and a thumb between her eyes and pinched there. Her hand was shaking. She shook her head.

"She's not got very far with that has she?" Julia said.

"Well..." began Kay. Julia looked swamped in her oversized coat. She was washed out of all colour. Thin. Her wrists knocked about like sticks in the gaping arm holes of the coat.

The day that Kay had got together with Julia she had worn an expensive looking raincoat. She had the collar up like it had been raining, but it wasn't raining. It was tan with a belt and double lapels over the shoulder, with a flap at the back. Kay could remember the rub of the material, the tension of the fabric.

Kay stood rooted to the spot. Shocked. You've done this to her. You've ruined her. You've soiled her. Killed her lifeblood. Silenced the most vibrant person you've ever known.

"I can see the attraction. I deserve it. It's what I did to Arthur after all. I deserve it. They say that don't they? Relationships that come out of an affair don't last, that they are somehow doomed," Julia said. She trembled and stubbed the cigarette out in a little white dish. She picked up the packet and lit another one. "I was so stupid about this fucking book. Caught up. Ego. I made a mistake, I admit it. I should have given you more sex. I made a mistake," she said. She looked up at Kay. Her eyes seemed to tremble too, looking from left to right, searching Kay's face for hope. Any sign of a chance. "Are you going to go off with her?"

"No. No, I'm not," Kay said.

"Aren't you even going to ask who told me? You're not so clever after all, are you? Dave told me, your supposed best mate Dave," Julia said.

"Dave told you?" Kay repeated in shock. Why would he do that? Why would he do lots of things? Was he trying to ruin Kay? Was he trying to set her up?

"You were on a bar stool in that pub in Primrose Hill, The Engineer, and your legs were entwined with hers. That's how he knew. Your legs tangled together," said Julia. She'd said this before. It must have stuck in Julia's mind. Cemented. Lay there. Poor Julia.

"You wouldn't have noticed," Kay said in a small voice.

"I could tell by your eyes, Kay. You've been a wreck, stressed, moody, depressed," said Julia.

"I'm not depressed. I'm grieving," Kay said.

"Then all of a sudden, you're dressing up, you're busy, you've got new clothes. Happy. Laughing. It was lovely to see you like that. I remember you being like that about me," said Julia. But Kay was thinking about the first time that she went for a meal with Polly Harvey. Polly wore a skirt! A skirt! With a plunging shirt. Kay could see everything. And they sat in a booth and Kay's hand wandered up Polly's leg. In the end they had to leave, early, unfinished food, because they were so desperate to get into each other.

"Julia, I'm sorry," said Kay. It felt as though a hood of shame was being placed on and around her head. How could you?

"I'm not even angry with you. I'm just numb with it all. I hate her. I hate her so much," Julia said.

"I'm so sorry," Kay said, and she was.

"I don't know if I can ever forgive you," Julia said. They were both quiet for quite some time. There was a soft knocking noise when the boat rose and fell and a red float came together with the wood of the stern.

Kay knelt down on the floor next to Julia's legs. She put her head on Julia's knees. After a while, Julia put her hand on Kay's head. Kay had to look up to see closely into Julia's face. Did she now feel how Kay had felt? Alone? Superfluous?

Enough.

"Do you still feel anything for me?" asked Julia, wiping her eyes on her designer sleeve. Kay put her head back onto Julia's lap and Julia stroked her hair.

Enough. Kay needed Julia.

After she cried, Julia's eyelashes stuck together in long black points, fused together by tears. Kay wanted to kiss them. Close Julia's eyes and kiss there. If she did she might be stabbed. Murdered here on the boat. She reached up anyway and touched Julia's face. She wasn't killed.

Hours later they went up the harsh metal steps that led to Canary Wharf to buy food and bring it back to the boat. Though it was dark, Julia still wore sunglasses. Kay was aware of eyes on her? Or not? She wasn't sure where Dave might be now.

When Julia was in conversational free flow, her nostrils widened and caught the breeze. It was lovely.

"We can get a dog. I don't care about the mess, or picking up poo. We can get a dog, if that's what you want," said Julia. She had not eaten. It had hollowed her cheeks, made her age a couple of years in a couple of days. Julia did not say 'if you stay', but Kay thought that was what she meant. "If you get a poodle cross they don't shed hair." Julia had already looked online.

Kay ate a burger but Julia just picked at the chips.

"That house isn't really your house and I realise that now. How hard it must be for you with Arthur around. It's the kids' house really and they are grown up now and I want to be with you, so we could get our own place together?" asked Julia.

"You can't do that. Who would look after Henry?" said Kay.

"He'll be at university soon, by the time we get things sorted. And also I was thinking that if you wanted to have a baby," said Julia.

"I don't want a baby," said Kay, but she desperately did want a baby.

"You say that now but you might, most women do. You don't have to decide now, you don't even have to think about it, but what I am saying is that I would support you. I would help you if that is what you wanted," said Julia, setting out her stall. Kay chewed her burger.

"When you have children Kay, everything is different because as long as they are okay, then you are. Things that would have killed me before, don't. I always thought that with the age difference this might happen. You know someone your own age. Are you the same age as her?" asked Julia.

"More or less,"

"You are an idiot Kay,"

"I know I am," said Kay, but it was Julia's eyes that ringed with tears again.

"Because of the way we met, and Arthur, I think it's my karma. But I'm not naive. I'm not a fool. I'm not proud. People might think I am. You might even think I am, Kay, but I'm not. I am who I say I am, there's nothing else, there's nothing you don't know," said Julia.

Then they sat there on Belinda's sofa. When she felt enough time had passed, Julia made her offer.

"If you promise never to see her again," said Julia.

"You should hate me after what I've done," said Kay.

"I wish I could," said Julia.

"Well you should," said Kay.

"I don't hate you, I love you. I would forgive you anything," said Julia.

Then Kay waited. Should she say? Who should she trust? Really and truly, she knew there was only one person that she could trust:

"Julia, I'm in a lot of trouble," said Kay.

CHAPTER THIRTY-SIX

Julia stooped over the cardboard box and dropped inside a lit match. She pulled her head back so it wouldn't burn her face. Under her arm was a plastic bottle of clear flammable liquid which she uncorked and sprayed into the flames, causing them to erupt up into the air.

They were sure to be seen now. In the dark with that fire, someone might call the police. They needed to be quick.

Kay could not rest. Her eyes were glancing from fire to river and back again. She held up one shaky hand, index finger extended, pointing into the river. They had already hulked another bulkier item into the water and it seemed for those ancient, meandering seconds that it wasn't going to sink at all, that it was going to float.

As the large cardboard box itself caught alight, Julia kicked it into the river. Messy, unsteady, hacking at the box with her foot until the whole burning thing dissolved into fire and water and the black river gulped it down. It hissed as it went out, a last breath trying to whisper its dying declaration. It was impressive work. Julia was unexpected.

The bulky item was still afloat. It cruised slowly away from the bank towards the centre of the river which was moving, a strong current luring them all out to sea. Kay was jerking with nerves and she moved as if she was going to leave the river's beach and go into the freezing water fully clothed. One foot squelched in sand, mud and sharp stones. Julia grabbed her arm and pulled her around to face her.

"We had no choice," she said, and as if her words broke the

viscosity of the water, the floating mass seemed to rupture. A smaller section unravelled and started to float away. Kay made a fearful noise, cat-like, and put a foot forward again, as if to go in. Julia had to hold her back with force by both arms, fingernails piercing her bare forearms. She had no coat in this cold, at this time of night. They looked like skinny drunks about to fight.

"It's going to float. Look!" said Kay.

"Let it be," said Julia as if she knew, as if she had done this all before. The floating lump tilted dramatically with one shiny wet end rising up out of the water and then swooping down, devoured. Kay didn't even think they needed to burn all this stuff, but Julia was adamant and Kay would do exactly as she was told. The computer, a load of receipts Julia had said to get rid of 'just in case', and the cushion, a lilac cushion of her mother's. The water sucked it in, changing its colour to a deeper, darker purple, and moved it away, out of their control.

The water sucked it in, changing its colour to a deeper, darker purple, and moved it away, out of their control.

It dropped beneath the surface. Slipped away. Gone.

CHAPTER THIRTY-SEVEN

Kay had been drunk the last time she was in a police station, so she hadn't registered just how bright it was. How much it smelled of lunch, of mashed potato and gravy, and something else. Vinegar?

She walked like she was headed to the confessional box. She argued with herself about how she should look, how she should hold her head, and this started up the redness about her chest. She had worn a shirt with a collar buttoned to the top for this purpose.

Kay couldn't look in Polly's eyes. Looked down at the floor instead. They were carpet tiles. Industrial brown. The DI sat next to Polly. Face scrubbed. He didn't seem vexed for a man with no progress made thus far. Or was he relaxed because he now believed they were on to something?

He thanked Kay for coming in. Polly kept dipping her head trying to catch Kay's eye.

"This is a bit heavy-handed Kay, isn't it?" said the DI.

"Just to clarify," Rachael Massey, Arthur Rothman's girlfriend said, "Kay has not employed me in any capacity to offer legal counsel. She has not engaged me as her lawyer. In fact this is not my legal area. I am here just to offer support as a friend, owing to the serious nature of the incident that these questions relate to."

"Thank you, Ms Massey. How's your dad, Kay?" asked the DI.

"Well, he's –" Kay began.

"Don't answer," Rachael said to Kay, and then to the DI,

"this is not relevant to the information Kay is here to provide you with."

"Kay. You are familiar with the murder of Benedict Phillips. His body was found at the Excel Conference and Exhibition Centre," the DI said. Rachael nodded at Kay, indicating that she should answer.

"Yes," Kay said.

"About Benedict Phillips's person. Namely about his head and shoulders was a blanket. On forensic analysis we found a number of hairs. The majority of which were identified as belonging to the victim, Benedict Phillips. Separately and subsequent to your arrest for an alleged drink driving offence, a profile was established for you on the PNC, the police national computer. Do you follow?" asked the DI.

"Yes," said Kay.

"You subsequently provided a voluntary DNA sample. Do you follow?" asked the DI.

"Yes," Kay said.

"This was a hair sample. Subsequently, this sample was matched with a hair fibre on the aforementioned blanket. So in other words Kay, your hair was on the blanket around Benedict Phillips's head. Do you follow?" asked the DI.

"Yes," Kay said.

"At this point," said Rachael, "Kay would like to point out that this is factually incorrect. Kay did not provide a voluntary sample. She did not volunteer DNA and was unaware that a DNA sample had been taken. She did not consent to DNA testing or the holding thereof of her DNA on the PNC."

"But you did," Polly said. The carpet tiles were hairy, like

Kay imagined an aged Orangutan would look close up. Kay perspired. It would all be over soon. Stiff. Upper.

"You have a consent form then? A record of consent that you can produce?" asked Rachael.

"She verbally consented! We were talking about it for ages," Polly said.

Rachael continued, "and while Kay seeks to be of every assistance possible in this matter —"

"You can just give retrospective consent! And sign a document!" Polly said.

"The sample was illicitly collected during a sexual liaison with DS Harvey," Rachael said.

"Kay? What are you doing?" Polly asked.

"DS Harvey had taken it upon herself to test Kay's paternity using unauthorised police resources," Rachael said.

"Don't do this, Kay," Polly said, but the DI put his hand on Polly's arm. Polly went still. Julia had been very clear.

"DS Harvey step outside please," the DI said.

"Sir, this is bullshit," said Polly, pleading in shock, and dazed as if clonked on the head.

"Thank you DS Harvey. Could you wait outside please?" the DI said.

"I think it is very clear that this has gone off the rails Detective Inspector," Rachael said.

"Kay? Seriously? You fucking bitch!" Polly shouted, and threw her arms up at the ceiling.

"You, DS Harvey! Outside. Now!" the DI shouted.

Polly got up trembling with rage and left the table. She left her jacket on the back of her empty chair. Don't think. Just do. Kay was split in two with shame. She wore it like a scarlet coat. Rachael opened up a red folder.

"Under S45 and Schedule 4 of the Human Tissue Act, it clearly sets out the provisions regarding DNA samples."

"Well I see your point Ms Massey, but can I remind you that we are not bound by those provisions because we are using the information for detection of a crime and potentially the conduct of a prosecution," the DI said.

"In addition, Kay's DNA has been used for a purpose other than the issue discussed here, namely Kay's paternity testing, which Kay had not expressly given permission for. It is illegal in this country to carry out paternity testing without consent."

Silence.

Rachael continued, "Kay is keen to stress that she wishes to help in any way she can and has collated the following documents to assist you. Here is the original invoice for the item in question." She produced a piece of pressed white paper with two holes puncturing its sides. "You can keep all of these documents and please check with the issuer to confirm, but to summarise, one hundred and fifty blankets, five colour embroidery."

It was hard to do, five colour embroidery, made the logo really thick. They had never done it again. Never made them as nice again. That's why Kay had hung onto hers.

"£6.99 per unit. Made by Mango Merchandise in Lewes, East Sussex. One hundred and fifty blankets were received in plastic sealed packages containing twenty-five blankets per packet. Inside these containers the blankets were folded once in half," Rachael said.

The DI looked looked mad as hell. He tapped the end of his pen on the table and stared at Rachael. It was too much. Kay didn't know. She was doing what she had been told to do. Julia had been insistent that not only did she never see Polly again but that they drew 'clear boundaries' for the future. Rachael was doing all the talking.

"Each blanket was then removed from the packaging and refolded into a gift box and distributed to journalists. Please see the diary entry," she said.

She produced a printout from the Christie Dean PR office calendar.

"On this occasion this was done at Kay's house. Kay?" asked Rachael, indicating that Kay should now speak the rehearsed monologue that they had prepared.

"Yes," Kay spluttered, "the team, um, were very busy with the media sell-in, yes, and as I recall we were concerned about lack of media interest and I wanted to relieve pressure on them so I packed the boxes for them. It took nearly a whole day. I can remember doing it, because I never did it again, knowing what a ball ache it was."

"This next document is the invoice from Addison Lee," said Rachael, "the courier company, dated December 12th 2012, and it specifies where the packages are collected from in a small van and hand delivered to each of the journalists. Pick up is from Kay's house in Stoke Newington; it was Kay's address at the time. There was often more than one journalist at each location. But here, item three, is the full list of journalists that received the blankets. Twenty-five blankets were also sent to Excel executives on site as a gift. So, what we are saying Detective Inspector –"

"Yes, I get it thank you, Ms Massey, that Kay handled all of those blankets, and that they were stored at her home," the DI said, sitting back folding his arms.

"In all likelihood, Kay's DNA should be on all of those blankets," Rachael said.

"Thank you," the DI said.

"No, thank you," Rachael said.

"Ms Massey, does Kay wish to pursue a complaint in relation to DNA collection by DS Harvey?" asked the DI.

"Not at this present time," Rachael said, collating her things into her black button down briefcase.

As Kay zigzagged through the exit doors, on her own, without Rachael, the DI appeared behind her. He touched Kay gently on the arm.

"Just one last thing," said the DI, "as that lead has come to an abrupt end, Ms Christie, in all likelihood this will go up the chain. By that, I mean the security services, namely MI5, because of the possible international implications. I know they'll want to go back over old ground. I'm sure they'll start with your dad, Jim, and his CCTV deletion. Probably they'll give him a good going over. Perhaps get him on the wagon, Kay. He'll need all his faculties intact."

Kay left the building and left her love behind. Smashed and broke the future that could have been, for the past that already was.

CHAPTER THIRTY-EIGHT

Dave came to Belinda's boat. Kay had telephoned him and he hadn't answered. Only minutes later he was at the boat. Trembling, filling any anxious gap with words, Belinda flew up the stairs when she saw his trainered feet approaching. Kay caught a glimpse of his feet in one porthole, and the next. He was wearing shorts; his calf muscles were lithe and hairless. Panting, moving like a cat, Belinda stalked him from inside the boat. The Klasina wobbled a fraction with his coming on board. He banged on the wheelhouse door.

"Shhh," Kay said, putting her finger to her lips. You love a monster. He's not our friend. He's a monster. Belinda put one foot on the ladder and pirouetted upward to let him in.

"He knows we're here," Belinda said. "What would you rather I do?" She turned and went up the ladder; Kay grabbed her hand to pull her back.

"Just be careful, don't pry, don't ask him any questions, you don't know anything, right?"

"I'm not fucking stupid, Kay, it'll look stranger if I hide in my bedroom, just chill the fuck out," she said and she shot up the ladder. An expert flirt, her voice raised an octave and slowed down a beat.

Dave didn't want to come in. He stooped to look inside. His face said that he was frightened of the soft light, the glow of the warm fire, and the smell of Belinda, her hair and her cooking. It was as if it might stop him from taking flight.

Kay's fear lay on her skin like a layer of dust after a wall had had collapsed.

Shock.

Fright.

Ghostly. She didn't want to let him on the boat but was too scared to say 'no'. Better to play along and leave on good terms. She was scared of his harsh jaw and steely eyes. She couldn't stop thinking about all those times in her life when he had physically loomed over her. As kids. Alone. Drunk. It was like having a caged beast in your bed the whole time, but at the same time he was her friend. Just Dave.

Before, she had been impressed by his discipline. Now his muscles were sinew, like ropes ready to tie you down. His bones straining through would cut you. Thank God he had not stayed with Belinda. His strength. His temper. Kay didn't know anymore. He had never been relaxed. He wasn't laid back. He was waiting to pounce. Biding his time. He had been doped down in their teenage years by smoking so much pot, like a soldier sipping bromide in his tea.

"Do you want to come in?" Belinda asked.

"I haven't got time," Dave said. "I just wanted to say goodbye."

"Kay told me you're going to the Cayman Islands?" asked Belinda.

"Yes. My old Army Captain owns a hotel in Grand Cayman. I'm going to be a personal trainer in his hotel," Dave said.

"We'll have to come out and visit," Belinda said. "It'll be like when we were in Cyprus."

Dave forced a smile and Belinda hugged him. Held on for too long, then climbed down the stairs. Kay heard her feet run to the end of the boat where she went into her room, tears streaming down her cheeks.

He was dressed in his usual sports gear. Blue lycra running

top with white chevrons down the sleeve. His headphones were loose around his neck, but Kay could hear the drone of an American motivational speaker. Tony Robbins was telling Dave to visualise.

"It'll be nice being on here in the spring," Dave said, as if nothing had happened. He looked around, acknowledging a couple of sitting ducks on the water.

"I don't think it's for me – boats," Kay said, shaking her head. She drew on all her skills as a fake and phony to make him feel like she wasn't petrified.

"There's a place for everything on a boat," Dave said, and Kay thought about the little shelf where she had left Benedict's ear. "Shall we pop out?" He cocked his head for Kay to follow him.

He watched Kay skip across the water onto the pontoon and they walked slowly, silently side by side. It reminded Kay of when she was about to sack someone and that awkward walk with them to the boardroom before she laid it on them. Both careful not to say anything incriminating. A dagger drew across Kay's stomach. She needed the toilet. Her mouth was dry.

Dave kept looking up, mapping out the corners of the buildings. Looking for what exactly? Cameras? Of course he was the ace cameraman, or ace cameraman disabler. He walked ahead and looked back over his shoulder at Kay. He was careful not to make eye contact because if he did, he might just become regular Dave again. Non-threatening Dave, at least the part that Kay had never seen but always known was there.

Kay was dizzy with nerves. She had sea legs, wobbling on the secure concrete of Canary Wharf. Her body, her heart and mind screamed at her, 'Get back on that boat! Now! Get away from him as fast as you can.'

But she was moored to Dave. He was her anchor. Valérie Lagarde was Kay. Kay was Valérie. Kay couldn't leave. Should not and would not, and so instead of running away she walked with Dave to his car.

"Get in," he said, his voice like tar. He was teasing her, threatening her, but she had to see things through.

"Where's the girl, Dave?" Kay asked.

"I know you spoke to the police yesterday," Dave said. "What did you tell them?"

"Nothing," Kay said, and is if she had nothing to lose, she spat it out at him. "Nothing yet. Where is she?"

"Get in the fucking car," said Dave. Kay froze rigid. Had he killed Valérie too?

"You are avoiding it Dave, not telling me anything about Valérie, but I swear if you don't tell me I will go to the police, and I don't care what happens, I'll tell them everything and we can all go to prison together."

"Get in the fucking car, Kay, now." His eyes were flicking up to a black CCTV camera lodged on the side of the apartments.

"Canary Wharf is full of them, Dave. You can't dodge them all you know?" Kay jumped up and down in a star shape, her tongue sticking out and shouting 'La-la-la-la-la.'

"Stop it," he said.

"I know," said Kay. "I've got a witness who can put Benedict and Valérie with Ariana together on Christmas Eve."

"Who?" Dave asked.

"If anything happens to me then Julia will go to the police. Information will be sent to DS Harvey, and her boss, and to the newspapers. I've arranged the dissemination of this information in detail. You know that I'm organised, Dave, so you have to trust me that I have done this. Benedict was one thing, but Valérie is another."

"She's alive," Dave said.

Dave frisked Kay before she got into his car. Bent her frontwards over the bonnet and spread her legs open and ran his hands harshly down each leg, up into her crotch, into the crease of her breast, his palm flat up against the mound of her vagina. You piece of shit, Dave.

Kay let him drive her, God knows where. She was beyond fear. Her nervous shivers had become so fast that they were negligible. She was shot through with adrenaline, cortisone. She resisted the urge to take flight. She was staying put to fight. Put one hand on me and I will rip your eye open with my claw. He was a soldier, but this was Kay's battle to win.

"We are where we are," said Dave indicating, the car making a soothing clicking sound. It was his car again. Kay wanted out of cars, and boats, she just wanted to sit still, to be still.

"Where is she, Dave?"

"She was there, you know. With Benedict. She says she didn't know him really, that she'd only met him a few weeks before, but she was there, watching, when Benedict tried to rape Ariana."

"That sounds very hard to believe, Dave." He put his foot down in anger and Kay had to hold onto the dashboard to steady herself.

"She was there, he wanted both of them. Ariana said no and he attacked her; the girl tried to stop him, and he knocked her out. Not me. She was out cold on the floor when I arrived. She's lucky to be alive. She came round when I was sorting out Benedict, started screaming blue murder, so I had to shut her up again."

"Jesus," Kay said. He had probably threatened her too. She must have been scared stiff. The poor girl thought she was going on a Christmas Eve drink with her new boyfriend and ended up part of a sexual assault and a witness to murder.

"She was lucky she didn't go into the water with Benedict, what was I supposed to do? I mean I didn't know that she wasn't in on it with Benedict."

"No woman is going to be in on the rape of another woman," Kay said.

"She wanted to go to the police," Dave said.

"Of course she did. That's what you should have done," Kay said, noticing familiar streets. They were back in Walthamstow; there was the Golden Lion, the shining beacon of shite. She had no fear. Everything good was gone. There was one hope, and in that one hope lay the hope of everything; the whole entire world of Kay's life lay in saving Valérie.

There was the block of flats, derelict now, condemned to demolition, where Dave's father had once lived. Splashing through puddles and mud they stopped at a chainmail fence. Dave got out and unlocked the gate. He drove through, pulling up underneath the brutalist monolith. Kay remembered these flats full of footballs and kids with choppers. Tracey Grubb lived here, the terror of Tracey Grubb and the sanctuary that knowing Dave afforded her.

Dave re-locked the gate, and drove them round and down, underneath the abandoned block.

Underneath were the garages where they used to smoke pot as teenagers, in one half way along on the left. Dave's headlights came on. It was pitch black. The tunnel of garages was 100 feet long, narrow, and pitted with puddles of water. Once this had been busy with kids and cars and an old Italian man who painted terracotta pots. All long since gone. Dave's dad's garage was half way down on the left.

"I never planned this," said Dave, getting out, "but I need you to see. I need you to understand what'll happen if I find out you've talked. I can't have anything getting in the way of me and Ariana. Not now."

The door slammed and echoed down the tunnel chamber sending a shiver up Kay's back. She should run. But she couldn't get away now. It was too late. She was too far gone.

CHAPTER THIRTY- NINE

As soon as Dave put the key in the garage door there was an overwhelming stench of piss and shit.

"Urgh," Dave said, pulling his sports top up around his mouth. Kay noticed that he left his keys hanging in the door. "That's disgusting. Need to change that shit bucket for you." There was a scuttling sound from the back of the garage. Kay could see the pale green of her filthy nurse's uniform, her black stained face. Valérie. She was alive.

Dave moved towards her the way you approach a dog with a history of violence. No muzzle. No mouth gag.

"No one comes down here anymore, not even the junkies. This building's marked for demolition. We've had some good times here. And some bad." Dave bent down and removed the bicycle lock and chain around her neck. "See," he said, "she's fine. For now."

Kay stared in disbelief. Water dripped down the wall. The patch of oil she remembered from her teenage years was there, but just a shadow across the filthy floor. Valérie Lagarde panted. Her tiny movements were sketchy like a cat. She was so frightened. Kay could feel it as though an electric wire was tied between them, sending Kay tiny shock waves.

"Need to empty this," Dave said, "it stinks. And we can't have all these remnants of you in here can we?" He pulled a pair of black leather gloves out of his pocket and picked up the swishing bucket of shit and piss and balanced it in both hands. What were the black leather gloves for? For Christ's sake. Kay's breathing increased. Black gloves.

Kay looked at Valérie, then saw Dave's car keys hanging in the door, and Kay tried to focus, tried to think 'how many steps to the car?', and then 'where is the ignition?'. Kay's hands were up in front, moving to act out the movements she was imagining. She needed a weapon.

Kay took one foot back and through the crack of the door; she saw Dave, his shoulders swaying, hulking the big bucket of faeces and urine to the end of the tunnel. How far would he go? What would happen when he got back? What were the gloves for? No one could hear them. Absolutely no one. It was the one place in London that you didn't exist. A deserted inner tunnel running underneath an abandoned building. No one would come down here until the men came with carefully prepared sticks of dynamite to blow the whole thing up.

Kay's mind raced, but her feet were frozen in place. She missed her opportunity. Dave stepped back in and placed the bucket down. Kay was sweating, her heart pounding, she could feel her heart in her ears. Such a coward, Kay. You should have done something while you had the chance.

"I believe you, Kay," he said, "that you didn't turn me in. But I need to be sure you won't say anything once we leave here." He stepped towards Valérie. "And the only way to do that is to make you guilty too."

He bent toward Valérie and she cowered in fear. "No, no, no," she cried, as he grabbed her by the hair, pulled her to her feet, and wrapped his hands around her throat.

"Dave! Stop," shouted Kay, still frozen in place. "Stop, this isn't you."

"I told you, nothing is getting in the way of me and Aria –"

The long arm of a car jack cracked the back of Dave's head. Kay felt something split under her hands. He groaned and fell to his knees, releasing Valérie from his grip. Blood oozed from the wound. Kay dropped the car jack, shaking.

"Come on," Kay said, holding out her hand. Valérie locked eyes with Kay. She didn't know whether to believe her. Kay shook her hand up and down. "Now!" she said, "you have to trust me, you have to."

Valérie got up stumbling, bare red knees, the stiff white piping of her nurses uniform dirty grey. Dave stirred on the floor – he was down but not out. Valérie was shielding her eyes from the slip of light coming through the door.

"Now!" Kay said. Valérie could move alright. Three weeks of solitude hadn't capped her athleticism and she wound out her spindly limbs and moved not like a cat, more like a leopard, all gangly shoulders and downward gaze.

Kay swiped the keys out of the door. They came out slick, no sticking, too easy.

"Come on," she said, and Valérie followed her out of the garage door into the tunnel.

Kay ran around the front of the car, pointing crazily directing Valérie to the passenger door. "You go that side. That fucking side. Quick!"

"Oi!" shouted Dave. He was on his feet, stumbling, holding his head. They had only made it 50 yards down the tunnel. Kay fumbled with the keyring. Which was it, which fucking key? Maybe she should just run, but there was a fence once you got outside and he was too strong, too fast to outrun. He's a killer. He's...

Kay found the fob and the doors clicked open; blinking orange lights lit up the tunnel like a burst of sunshine. Kay bundled in. She could hear Dave's footsteps. He was so close already.

"Kay!" he shouted.

"Fucking get in!" Kay said to Valérie, who slipped into the passenger seat and slammed her door shut. Valérie was straight in, lithe across the seat, panting and smelling of sweat and piss and something else, metallic, fear or blood Kay assumed. Dave was running now, sprinting, furious. She looked up, saw him closing in, his eyes wide, pumping fists, angry spittle all over his face. She felt along the door for a lock button, stabbed it quickly with a shaky finger. The car doors were locked.

Dave was at the door, pulling the door handle, his face at Kay's driver side window.

"Come on, Kay, don't be silly," he said, repeatedly pulling at the door handle. "I can't let her leave, she knows too much." Kay put the key into the ignition. Please start.

"I'm not going to hurt you, Kay," he said. "I just want her." Valérie made a little panicked mewing noise.

"Please hurry," she said, "please come on, please, he's going to kill us both." The engine roared up. It roared through the tunnel. The radio dial glowed orange and music started up.

"Fuck!" shouted Dave and he banged on Kay's window with both hands. "Fuck you Kay, you ungrateful cunt!" Kay put the car into first gear. Don't stall. Don't stall.

The car moved off. Dave ran alongside, banging, shouting, cursing her. Could she get out at the end? You used to be able to years ago, it was a drive-through tunnel, a one way system straight through.

Dave was still running by the side until she picked up enough speed into the darkness, headlights on, and he could not keep up. The seatbelt warning noise repeated over and over. Valérie reared up in the seat to look behind as a brick hit the back windscreen, shattering it. Jesus Christ! Valérie put her hands over her head and screamed. Kay reared around the corner and up the ramp that led to the exit and then braked immediately. It had been bricked up! Only a tank could get through this. Fuck. Fuck. Fuck.

The car sat in semi-darkness, fumes clouding from the exhaust and red brake lights illuminated. What shall I do? We can't go forward. Turn around, turn around quick. Where is he? Where is he? A crashing boom and more breaking glass. In her rear view mirror Kay could see Dave was closing in on the back window.

Kay put her foot to the floor to reverse. She whipped the steering wheel around too fast and the car smacked into the back wall. She felt metal concertina. Don't stop. Can't stop. She changed gear and he was there, smashing the bonnet with what looked like the same long arm of the car jack that Kay had hit him with. He was laughing, fucking laughing, going berserk with the long metal rod. All around was blackness.

"Just drive, just fucking drive!" Valérie shouted. Dave jumped onto the bonnet. He was frenzied. Bizarre. He was smiling, his bald head spattered in oil and blood.

"I'm going to fucking kill you, Kay!"

Kay put her foot down to the floor and drove at full tilt along the tunnel. He smashed at the windshield, his face inches away from her. She slammed the brakes and he flew off the bonnet, cartwheeling over and over, until he stopped twenty yards away. He looked like a pile of rags in the headlights.

"Don't stop! Please," Valérie said.

Kay hesitated; she thought she had killed him, but he was already moving, sitting upright like the Terminator. His left arm was bent at the wrong angle and the front of his shirt was ripped open. Dave smiled at them and got up to onto his feet. Valérie screamed.

"Drive!" Valérie wailed. "Drive!" But Kay was suddenly feeling calm. She put the car in gear. She revved the engine. His frenzied run ate up the ground between them. He was an angry bull, sweating and panting.

"Put your seatbelt on," Kay said, and Valérie turned and clipped herself in, grasping for the latch and fumbling to get it into the slot. "You in?" asked Kay, clipping in her own seat belt.

Kay moved forward slowly in the car as he threw himself onto the bonnet. She put her foot down again. There would be no stopping this time. She picked up speed, not much tunnel left. His fingers grasped the groove where the windscreen wipers attached, but he was slipping, despite gravity, off the front, and as the ramp lifted them up and out of the darkness of the tunnel she saw a wide cement pillar. She must be sure. She must do the job properly. She looked him in the eyes, his snarling, mad eyes and –

Bang.

Smash.

Airbags exploded.

A whirring siren of the car alarm.

The radio played.

Kay reached over to Valérie. Let her be alright, please God, after all of this let her be alright. She moved. A trickle of blood ran down her face from her hairline.

"Are you OK?" asked Kay, and Valérie nodded.

"What about him?" she asked.

Kay pushed away the airbags until she could see Dave pinned between the cement pillar and the car. The back of his bald head was cracked and flattened and matted with blood. His head must have bounced off the pillar and back down onto the bonnet. He wasn't moving. From the waist down he was pinned firmly in place, his body broken between car and concrete.

Kay opened the door. His eyes were open. Blood came out of his mouth. Valérie felt for a pulse.

"He's dead," she said. Oh friend. Oh my God. Sweet boy. Oh relief. Kay let out a long low scream and dropped to her knees.

"What have I done?" Kay said, trembling, and Valérie took her wrists.

"You saved me," she said. "Now you have to go."

"Go?" asked Kay.

"Too many questions. I'll say I was on my own, and then we're even. I never saw you." Valérie, her nose bloodied and bruised, helped Kay to her feet. Kay walked out into the light with Valérie. She searched every building top for a camera, and seeing none, Kay ran. She didn't look back.

A car is like a loaded gun.

CHAPTER FORTY

Julia rammed the car up onto the pavement in a clear violation of the Highway Code. A black taxi blew his horn as he fired by, almost taking off the rear bumper. Julia was oblivious to anyone else on the road. She drove like an axe splitting timber. Wonderful but sometimes costly; a wing mirror here, an argument in the supermarket car park there. She pulled up outside Sloane Square tube station. Kay looked up for CCTV cameras.

Julia had bought Jim trousers made of tent material, with zips at the knees where the bottom leg comes off to wear them as shorts. She wouldn't be seen dead in them herself, but they were appropriate kit for Jim's trip. They were khaki. He had always liked green. Spinach tie, peppermint shirt, khaki slacks. One of the last coherent sentences Kay's mother had ever said to Jim was: "You look like a Brussel sprout." Now, he looked like a prematurely aged teenage backpacker setting off on a gap year. A bit like someone from the Marigold Hotel but mossy green and smelling of tobacco.

Julia had sent Henry to the camping shop. A random choice at the junction of Chancery Lane and High Holborn. He struggled with the right sizing. Jim was a mixture of short leg and rotund stomach, more a square than a rectangle. She had bought a range of T-shirts from a cheap high street shop; they had argued about ties and eventually she had relented and let him pack two ties and a sports jacket.

Julia asked Kay to book a car and two adults on the ferry from Fishguard Harbour. The six o'clock morning sailing.

She thought it more Jim. It was booked in Jim's name and paid for with Jim's credit card. Discreetly and with various agreements and financials in place, Mirasol, Julia's loyal Filipino housekeeper, drove Kay's mother's Ford Fiesta, the same one that Kay had learnt to drive in, all the way to Ireland. It had lain quiet for years, around the back of Jim's house on pale cream cement made slick with oil leaks. Out of London, along the entire length of the M4, through Wales to Fishguard, and then boarding the ferry and weaving through the quiet roads and lanes of Wexford, which in some ways reminded her of home. Mirasol found her way to Cork.

Now it lay quiet again. In a car park in Clonakilty. Mirasol was remarkable. She had even left tea in the oven for Henry before she hit the M4. She didn't require a hotel. She slept in the car, in the queue stacked up at Fishguard harbour. No one asked for her passport as she drove up the ramp and into the boat. And after she drove six hours at the other side, she ditched the Fiesta back where Kay's mother and Jim were born. She flew back on the business flight from Cork City that night.

If anyone bothered to look then they might find something of Mirasol but if they didn't, they would just see a passage booked on a boat and eventually his car, plastered with parking tickets, would pop up on some police officer's screen. The question would be whether he was still alive and if he was, what was the point in using police resources to find an old man? But Julia was particular and wanted him away just in case. Polly had her killer now anyway. Poor Dave delivered on another mortuary slab.

Kay had wanted to take him all the way to Heathrow, to terminal 4, to ask him if he had everything and wave him off teary at the security gates. Julia had said: "No. Under no circumstances is he to be accompanied at all." Even if they found out that he had flown, and not driven to Ireland, then Kay was not to be seen waving him off. She looked at Kay as if she was crazy. Julia wanted to get him off and away before he was taken into custody again and this time, quite possibly, examined under more scrutiny. The name MI5 had filled Julia with dread. She imagined herself taken into custody, enveloped in a scandal and whatever else might come up, because she knew that people were like sponges; they could only absorb so much before it all came trickling out.

"I know what I'm doing," Julia had said, "I will take care of this." And she was taking care of this. Jim was booked on a flight to Paris, then a change to Frankfurt and then a third change of flight to Manila.

Manila. The Philippines. Excessive of Julia. Perhaps she had become too excited by all the drama but Manila it was. He had been to Spain many times, obviously, and Tenerife.

"He won't survive. He'll die," said Kay.

"He'll be fine," said Julia.

"I'll never see him again."

"You might," then threading her fingers through Kay's, "you will."

Ariana had fled to Germany. Her picture had been in the newspaper, but she wasn't suspected of any wrongdoing. Perhaps police thought she had fled with a broken heart. Kay could never speak to her again knowing that Ariana must be devastated at the loss of Dave. Kay tried not to think about her.

Julia knew that any investigation into Ariana would lead to Kay as her employer, and to Dave as Kay's friend and then to who knew what. Julia thought that if the police caught hold of

Ariana or Jim in light of what had happened then it wouldn't be good for Kay, and so she sent him away.

The radio news cackled to life. Julia moved to turn it off but Kay stopped her.

'Missing NHS nurse Valérie Lagarde has flown back to France today accompanied by her mother. Lagarde, the girlfriend of murdered soldier Benedict Phillips, escaped from an underground garage where she been held captive for twenty-six days. In what police are describing as an unprecedented act of bravery, Valérie overpowered her captor to break free.' Julia switched from radio to CD and Patti Smith began to play.

"Mirasol's sister will pick him up. They live in a family compound. He'll be fed and watered. He'll be better off," Julia said.

"I think they're very poor Julia. It'll be rough at his age," Kay said.

"Better than prison?" Julia said.

"A hole in the floor for a toilet?" Kay said.

"He could never piss into a toilet anyway – it always ended up on the floor," Julia said. But Mirasol's family wouldn't be poor anymore. Julia had seen to that. And she had arranged with her ex-husband Arthur for Mirasol's eldest son to start work at his firm. Best for everyone.

Jim came back to the window shaking his head. He had left his bag at the station entrance. He couldn't work out how to buy a ticket from the machine. Useless. He would never survive. Julia unclipped her seat belt and stepped out. Jim looked like an old man next to her. Julia had taken to carrying large amounts of cash in her pocket 'just in case'. She was seconds at the ticket machine before she turned and she pointed out the barrier; she held Jim by the elbow, pointing things out to him. He knew all of this of course.

He couldn't have lived in London all these years without knowing the basics, but he wanted to be looked after. Jim gave Julia something small into her hand and they stood face to face. They embraced by holding each other's elbows and talking into each other's open faces. Nodding. Smiling.

Julia got back into the car. She had left the engine running. Outside was cold; Kay could see the exhaust fumes flare up in the rear view mirror as Julia's foot grazed the accelerator. He stood there like a little boy. A little evacuee. No mum.

"Go on Kay. Say goodbye. Don't linger. You'll make it worse," said Julia. The cold snap had left the pavement frozen solid. She felt that if she fell over on it she would shatter like a glass on hard tile into a million tiny glass fragments. There was nothing to say. She didn't have words.

"I don't know why we're not dropping you at Heathrow. It's ridiculous really, but Julia's paranoid about being picked up on camera or something. You know the flight number don't you? Air France first. Try not to drink too much on the flight. Oh, and please don't be drinking before you board the plane. Because they won't let you on and they'll call the police to escort you out and then who knows what –" said Kay.

"Kay –" said Jim.

"You get the Piccadilly line, you know that right?" asked Kay.

"Kay, I'm fine," said Jim.

"Mirasol's sister is going to pick you up from the airport at the other end," said Kay.

"I know," said Jim.

"She'll let us know that you got there safely. She'll telephone," said Kay.

"Well you look after yourself Kay. There's more to life than work," he said. Kay wanted to say 'shut up you stupid old fool, now look at the mess you've got me into'.

"There's lots of things I still wanted to do here," said Jim.

"Well you'll be back," said Kay.

"Important things."

"Sometime," said Kay.

"Kay, if you want to do something, you should just go for it," said Jim. A mound of clasping hands drew Kay's neck tight, swarming, choking on words unsaid, stuck in her throat.

"There's an Irish pub," Kay said instead.

"Oh good," he said.

"You better go," said Kay.

"I'll be seeing you," he said, and Kay kissed him on his ruddy, scratchy cheek. His skin was red like Irish potato. He had a shaving cut, like a boy who couldn't shave. He looked like a turtle in his rucksack. He turned back to wave. The woman let him through the barriers and then he disappeared down the stairs. Kay thought of her mum's last breath. Her last gasping, gruff, noisy breath. Tears filled her eyes, but there were no sobs, just noiseless, pointless tears flowing across her face, dripping like rain drops onto cold hard cement.

CHAPTER FORTY-ONE

It was a cold morning and the clouds were knotted together like the noduled digits of old men's fingers. There had been lots of rain overnight and in Queen's Park the earth was puckered with muddy puddles of cloudy water.

"Come in," said Kenneth Spiers when he opened the door. He was wearing a cardigan zipped up to the neck and a shirt and tie underneath. He was older than Jim, a good ten years older or more. A tight knit of grey and brown. He was of the generation that wore a tie to do the garden or do an oil change. Kay was shocked. His eyes had a blue milky character, diluted, the colour leaving before the soul. Why did she always leave everything so late?

Kay had rung ahead to make the appointment, but in her anxious state she was early and had to kill time. She waited in the park, burning her mouth on volcanic coffee. As she sat there nursing her tongue, she realised that she did know the park. She remembered the swings on the right hand side, the old fashioned bandstand, even the little farm with chickens tucked away at the side nearest his house. She had been there with her mum. More than once. She must have been very young.

Kenneth went out the back to make tea and left Kay alone in the front room. There were pictures of his daughter, a man, boy and girl, a baby. Kay was trying to see herself somewhere there amongst all these things.

"That was in Singapore," said Kenneth. Kay turned and apologised while Kenneth paused in the middle of the room with a small tea tray, two pink flowery cups and saucers and a packet of digestives. "Could you pull that out for me dear?"

"This?" asked Kay, pawing a small wooden side table.

"Yes, that's it. Thank you. I worked out there for five years. In a car factory. Fantastic life, but my wife wanted to come back to London. Her mother was getting on. Well, you'd know about that. So, we came back here. Would you like a biscuit? I like a plain digestive but I know what girls are like now, don't eat anything, always too worried about what they're eating," said Kenneth.

He settled himself into what must have been his armchair. It didn't match the sofa and was higher for aged hips Kay guessed. Kay sat on the sofa. Kay took a biscuit and bit it in half, gobbling it into her mouth to silence herself.

"So, Kay," he said. Kay chewed the biscuit. Looked at the sideboard. He was looking at her. She could feel his pale eyes on her, like a breeze. "I suppose I was expecting you, but I didn't know for sure that you would come."

"Have we met before?" asked Kay. He shuffled in his chair. His eyes flickered as if he rolled back the memories in his mind like an old rolodex.

"Oh yes, when you were quite small, a few times," he said. She couldn't pin anything of hers on him, or rather his on her. She studied his hands. They were small for his height. They were skeletal now, where the fat had disappeared, as it tends to do on older people. They reminded her of fossilised flippers that she had seen at the Natural History Museum. Kay's hands were not like that. They were succulent. Like her mum's. Her mum used to flatten her hand and look for mounds of flesh on the back between the knuckles and say, 'That's when you know you're fat, when you've got rolls of fat between your knuckles.'

Kay searched his ears, pale eyes, neck, gait, foot, length of elbow to wrist. Wrist. Voice? Perhaps voice? Brain?

"Is that your wife?" asked Kay.

"Yes, that's Patricia. Been gone now, well a long time, sadly, eleven years," said Kenneth.

"Eleven years?" asked Kay, repeating.

"Yes. Can't quite believe it. I still think she's going to walk through the door," he said. They both sipped their tea. "Time flies. When you get to my age you look back and wonder what you did with all the time you had." His accent was pure London.

"I thought you were Irish?" asked Kay.

"Me? No. Honorary perhaps. Patricia was Irish. From Dublin. So many around here, brilliant fun it was in the sixties with all the Irish," he said and offered Kay another biscuit. When she declined, he put the packet down and gestured to the wall. "That's my daughter. Sarah. She's a doctor." At last. In her high cheekbones, in the colours of the face and hair and eye, Kay saw something of herself. A look, a glint, something of when she turned her face a certain way, not always, but yes, when she put her lipstick on and looked straight at herself with mouth puckered and intense stare, perhaps in there she saw something of herself.

"I thought that she looks a bit like me, Sarah," said Kay, and Kenneth nodded.

"So, you and Mum," said Kay. He stopped abruptly and frowned.

"No," said Kenneth.

"But —" said Kay, confused.

"No. Absolutely not," said Kenneth.

"I just thought, well I read a letter and I was piecing things together," said Kay.

"I loved my Patricia," he said.

"I think there's a lot I don't know and I'm trying to find out about my mum's life, when she left Ireland, and what are you to me?" Kay asked.

He paused. Kay's teacup was still in the saucer.

"Why do you think sixteen-year-old girls left Ireland suddenly in those days?" asked Kenneth.

Kenneth went out to the kitchen and made more tea. It was strong. The tannin made her lip curl back in shock. Kay sat very still. He was nothing to her. Kenneth Spiers. All those hours spent imagining him and the life she could have had when he was nothing to her. Jim. Poor Jim.

Yet Kenneth was the link somehow to something else, to someone else, and back to a new piece of her mother that she had never known. Kay was laughing then wiping her eyes. Hand shaking, cup rattling in the saucer, the tea like a jacuzzi.

"Here," he said because of course he had a cotton handkerchief. Pale blue, a silvery pattern in the run of the fabric. He leaned into her. He had a mouth like a little bird, all puckered, ready to tell the truth; it hovered in front of his face. "Got themselves in trouble as they did. She wouldn't tell on him. Wouldn't tell the family who he was, so she got sent over here to an aunt. The plan was that the aunt would pass off the baby as her own, but there was a falling out. Your mum went into a convent just off Ladbroke Grove."

Kay still did not know exactly what it meant. She knew that Kenneth Spiers was sitting very close to her on the sofa, holding her hand sternly and rubbing its back with the warm underside of his palm, like rubber.

"Patricia and I tried for twenty years to have a baby. We couldn't, so we applied for an adoption through the church, and what with her being Irish Catholic, we got a little girl, Sarah," said Kenneth. "We went to Singapore in the seventies and when we got back I took a job at Ford in Dagenham, and your mum recognised me. She'd seen me when we'd come to pick the baby up. Wasn't supposed to see, but she did."

"Sarah?" asked Kay.

"This is Sarah, and this is her husband, and this is her baby girl, bit of an accident that little one. She's got two big boys," said Kenneth, proud. Kay observed their round faces, brown eyes, boys in sports kit and a little baby girl, the one that she and Polly had seen that day. "Your mother didn't want to give her up see? But she had to. Later she said they should have just run away, it was 1971, the summer, but she would not dare. Anyway, a couple of years later Jim followed her over here and they got married, but it was too late to get the baby back by then. And then they had you."

"Me," said Kay, the apple of her mother's eye.

"She was a right pest your mum. Turning up. I could see her watching us. I had to tell her several times to leave us alone. But after Patricia died we became friends, and we talked about it for years — telling you and Sarah. With you girls being grown up there was no reason not to. But then she got ill. I don't know if in the end she forgot. I didn't know what to do."

Kay looked at the picture, at her sister. Her mother hadn't gone at all. She was right here all the time. Cloned in Sarah Spiers.

CHAPTER FORTY-TWO

23rd February 2017

Kay took the pillow away from her mother's face. A lilac cushion. Her mother's favourite colour. She could see the necklace twisting on her mother's skin. There was no resistance. The rasping noise that echoed through her mother's body ceased. Kay put the pillow back on the chair. She looked at the door. The hackles on her neck stood on end. She tried to close her mother's mouth but it was fixed, gaping open where her mother had been struggling to breathe. Kay pushed her chin but it was surprisingly hard to move as she was already starting to lock.

Seven years of struggle. Fighting. Finished. Her mother had laboured into the night. Her body was strong. Built for working in the fields. She would not go. Kay told her over and over that it was alright to go, but she would not.

Kay could not let her suffer anymore. Her mother's legs had trembled upward, shaking from the feet through the knees into the body. Kay thought of a washing machine on spin cycle. Vigorous. Contained.

Then, stillness.

"Kay?" said Julia, a cup of coffee in each hand. Jim by her side. Had they seen?

Kay caught Julia's eye. Fully locked on. It was like Julia could see right inside Kay's head. Julia dropped one cup. It slipped through her fingers and crashed silently. The liquid chased itself away across the floor like mercury.

"You didn't?" said Julia quickly, panicked. Kay raised her

voice, as if to silence Julia. To continue as she always did. Doing her duty. Her voice was cracking.

"She's gone, Dad. She's gone."

EPILOGUE

1st July 2018

Inside Belinda's boat was boiling hot and unstable, moving more than usual, like being in a rocket propelling through the atmosphere.

"You pay extra and you get one to drive and one to pleasure the eye," Belinda said.

"How old do you think he is?" asked Kay, knowing that she would never drive again. Not anything, not a boat, not even a fairground bumper car.

"Twenty? Old enough. He looks like a boy but look at him."

"I suppose he is very beautiful to look at," said Kay. The boy bent in front of them; there was a sheet of glass between them. He did something with a rope. He was wearing white shorts. He had taken his top off. It was the hottest day of the year. At least 80 degrees. His torso was tanned and defined. Belinda climbed up into the wheelhouse and leaned against the glass; when he turned around he saw her and she winked, and he laughed.

"I think it is actually wrong, Belinda, isn't it?" Kay asked.

"No, I don't think so, Kay," said Belinda, shaking her head.

"Strikes me as a bit pervy."

"Just a bit of sport. A woman can say it about a man – it's the only double standard we have going for us. Anyway, Kay, he might be the man of my dreams," Belinda said. The spray of the river was welcome relief against the heat on Kay's face.

"More like the boy of your dreams," Kay said.

"Perhaps," said Belinda. The glass and concrete monoliths of

Canary Wharf moved in the background, at first getting smaller and then reappearing as if they were moving towards them. They joined the main current of the river. In the distance Kay glimpsed the iceberged outline of The Lusciousness. She poked her head out. Kay felt her salute. Kay tipped her hat back.

It was one of those rare British days when everything looked like it was melting, and as they pulled away from Canary Wharf, the towers began to look like they might liquefy and slip into the river like ice lollies. It was as if they were setting sail for America, or to discover a new continent. Kay was hiccupping with excitement. Seeing London like this on a hot sunny day from the water. Breathe it in. The rotten air was hot in her nostrils. She loved the smell of tar and creosote and the muddy freshness of the tidal river. Spray hit the side of the glass again.

"We'll have lunch in Richmond. Soak up all the sights en-route with a few aperitifs," Belinda said.

"Do you have to move out?" Kay asked.

"Yes I do. I can sleep on board tonight, then I'm going to a hotel. I have to batten down the hatches. Literally. They're going to lift The Klasina up. They take her out of the water. Put her in a dry dock. Then they scrape the barnacles off her bottom," Belinda said.

"Lucky girl, I wish someone would scrape the barnacles off my bottom," said Kay.

"Oh, me too," said Belinda, laughing.

"How long does it take?" asked Kay.

"A week. They smooth her down. Paint her. The bits you cannot see which take all the tension of the water. The stressed and fractured bits underneath. They fix her up. She'll be as good as new," said Belinda, before disappearing down the ladder into the kitchen.

"And you chose a wonderful day for it, Captain Belinda," Kay said.

"I'll pass you up the tray," Belinda said, but it was difficult because the boat was heaving from side to side, like a proper boat does. Instead of treading water in the safety of the basin, it was doing what it was born to do. There were fumes smoking out of its chimney stack. Excess water gushed around the sidings and through holes back into the river. The Klasina was fulfilling its birthright just as a cat stalks a mouse. Below deck, on a high shelf at the back, a little tin sat undisturbed. Kay must remember to get rid of that, sometime.

"I like her. Always have," Belinda said.

"Do you really?" asked Kay

"Yes I do. You made the right decision."

"I must have been out of my mind," Kay said, and she looked up to the front of the boat and saw Julia in her white bikini. Julia had bought it in the Nicole Farhi sale and had toyed with not buying it. She was worried about a bikini on a woman of her age. She matched it with oversized Chanel sunglasses that she'd for donkey's years. She bent over, picked up her sun hat and tiptoed around to the other side of her sunbed. She had brought a book and two thick magazines as if she had just come down from her hotel room.

"At last! Refreshments!" Julia said, and she picked up a menthol cigarette from a sparkly green packet and lit it with Jim's lighter; he had given it to her as a present when he left. She was blaming Kay that she was smoking again, and so she should. She stood inhaling for a moment, watching Kay struggle around the slim sideboards with a tray of Pimm's, a tightrope above the river. The boy was on hand with sea legs and he took the tray, carrying it easily over to the seats crying 'careful ladies'.

Muffled music began to play. Nineties house. The hull of the boat acted as a giant bass speaker. For a moment it looked like Julia might start dancing, one hand went up, a finger pointing upwards, a leg bent at the knee, the hips shifting one way and then the other. But she didn't. Instead she carried on chatting away as she had been all morning, non-stop, and passed a glass to the doctor, Sarah Spiers. They were similar in age. Had been to the same discos in the late 1980s. They were both regulars at the Wag Club although they had never met before.

Sarah was a clone. She had the same eyes but not quite the same. A doppelganger, not of Kay, but of their mother.

"I think your sister would make a great teacher, don't you Sarah?" Julia asked.

"I'm sure Kay can do anything – she's brilliant," Sarah said.

ACKNOWLEDGEMENTS

Most grateful appreciation for all their help, inspiration and knowledge to Matthew Smith, Dan Dalton and Richard Skinner.

Huge thanks and love to my wonderful talented friends at Faber Academy Kelly Allen, Alice Feeney, Alison Marlow, Daniel Grant, Giles Fraser and Trisha Sakhlecha, and our writing group Anjola Adedayo, Sybil Baleanu, Kate Vick, Adele Lawson and Maria Ghibu.

Thanks to my early readers; Sue Saunders, Suzanne Holland, Lucy Flynn and Julia Silk.

Thanks to Patty Dismore (always Mrs Cohen to us) for the books, plays and inspiration.

Thank you to the Cassons who won't look at their boat, The Klasina, in the same way again.

To those who are no longer here but have been with me throughout the writing of this story; my mother Eileen Trevorrow and my friend Rachael Scholes (nee Dean). I see you everywhere but most of all I hear you in familiar words spoken by strangers.

Thank you to my wonderful girls, Vicky and Ruby for all your love and support and all of our adventures.

Helen Trevorrow is a graduate of the 2016 Faber Academy creative writing programme. She studied at Leeds University and has worked in marketing and public relations in London. She is a specialist food and drink PR.

Helen's debut novel *IN THE WAKE* is a feminist crime thriller about family, unrealised trauma and alcoholism. Helen has ghost-written many articles for newspapers, magazines and websites. She lives in Brighton, Sussex with her wife and child.

Urbane
PUBLICATIONS

Urbane Publications is dedicated to developing new author voices, and publishing fiction and non-fiction that challenges, thrills and fascinates.
From page-turning novels to innovative reference books, our goal is to publish what YOU want to read.

Find out more at
urbanepublications.com